Jim Henson's™

SHADOWS
OF THE
DARK CRYSTAL

Special fala vam to Claire; to Kate and Kathryn;

to my mom for raising me as an artist and a

dreamer; to my dad for making me watch a scary

puppet movie at an impressionable age—J. M. Lee

For K. G.—Cory Godbey

PENGUIN WORKSHOP
An Imprint of Penguin Random House LLC, New York

TM and © 2016 The Jim Henson Company. JIM HENSON's
mark and logo, THE DARK CRYSTAL mark and logo, characters,
and elements are trademarks of The Jim Henson Company. All rights
reserved. First published in hardcover in 2016 by Grosset & Dunlap.
This paperback edition published in 2019 by Penguin Workshop,
an imprint of Penguin Random House LLC, New York.
PENGUIN and PENGUIN WORKSHOP are trademarks of
Penguin Books Ltd, and the W colophon is a registered trademark of
Penguin Random House LLC.
Printed in the USA.

Visit us online at www.penguinrandomhouse.com.

Library of Congress Control Number: 2016946598

ISBN 9781524790974   10 9 8 7 6 5 4 3

Jim Henson's

SHADOWS
OF THE
DARK CRYSTAL

BY J. M. LEE

ILLUSTRATED BY
CORY GODBEY

COVER ILLUSTRATED BY
BRIAN FROUD

Penguin Workshop

Silver Sea

Ha'rar.

The Black River

Stone-in-
the-Wood

Caves of Grot

The Black River

ni
ket

At first, there was silence . . .
and then the song began.
The Dark Crystal: Creation Myths

CHAPTER 1

The visitor appeared in the early morning, before the Great Sun had reached its summit in the pale blue sky.

Naia watched from the cooler canopy of the great tangled apeknot trees. At first, she put her hand to her rock-and-rope *bola*, but paused when the visitor hesitated to shed her cloak, which was heavy with mud and algae. Beneath the hood, Naia saw a stern-faced Gelfling woman with long silver hair. What was a Vapra doing so deep in the Swamp of Sog? It was peculiar—maybe even suspicious—yet Naia felt no fearful quickening of her heart, and her hand dropped away from her *bola*. All around, the Swamp of Sog stretched and yawned for morning, the droning of buzzers and chirruping of climbers *crik-crik*ing in harmony with the great song of the world. Watching the visitor, Naia took a sour alfen fruit from her waist-pouch and munched on it in thought.

"She must have come a long way," Naia murmured. Her companion, Neech, coiled in her vine-like hair, gave only a quiet burble in response, burying his head further in her locs. As the visitor resumed her journey, Naia balanced the alfen fruit's smooth knuckle-size pit between two ridges of apeknot bark. A quick flick of her finger sent the pit tumbling down through the spirals and twists of the tree's bark, disappearing into the depths of the gnarled trees. Then she followed, another flicker within the kaleidoscope of canopy shadows.

The stranger spent the afternoon traveling toward the heart of the swamp. Once or twice, Naia thought about running ahead to alert her village, but she worried she might lose the visitor to quicksand or any number of hungry swamp creatures. An alternative would be to make herself known and offer help, but strangers were called *strange* for a reason. Confronting an outsider in the depths of the swamp might be just as dangerous to Naia as a swamp creature might be to the Vapra.

What would have taken Naia a few hours on her own became an all-day trek. Just as the sky began to dim, the dense apeknots gave way to a circular clearing where the trees were huge and ancient, lovingly maintained by Gelfling hands. They'd reached the home of the Drenchen clan. Naia looked from the system of boardwalks that floated on the swamp floor between the apeknots to her village above. Lattice walkways and walking-ropes connected buildings carved into the crooks of the enormous trees to those hanging from thick pendulums. A whole world suspended above the swamp.

While the visitor, shining with sweat and bruises and buzzer bites, paused to catch her breath at the Glenfoot, Naia made haste toward the heart of the village. She leaped from a branch to the closest walking-rope, gripping with her bare toes as she dashed along it. At the center of the glen loomed Great Smerth, the oldest tree in the swamp, in which her family had lived for generations. Winding walkways circled its enormous trunk, studded by circle-shaped entryways and windows decorated with lush flowers and thick, dangling vines.

She took a flying leap, clearing half a dozen paces and landing with a calculated *ka-thump!* on the outer landing balcony. The wingless landing made her sound like a boy, but it was unavoidable. She didn't have time for grace, anyway. As she shouldered through the doorway, her footsteps echoed against the golden heartwood of the rounded hall within. Friendly faces met her on the way, but she had no time to return their greetings now.

"Mother!"

Neech gave a tiny chirp of relief and fluffed the fur around his neck into place as Naia entered, breathless, into her family's chamber. Her mother, swathed in an embroidered cloth of deep turquoise and gold, was seated on a small stool, while Naia's two younger sisters wound beads and colored string into her thick locs. Maudra Laesid looked every bit the *maudra* of the Drenchen clan, her kind face patient with wisdom and young with laughter. The spots that dappled her clay-colored skin reflected the spring green in the light, and her wings shimmered like a beautiful cloak of indigo and turquoise. In her hands rested a fledgling muski, only half the size of Neech. It was ailing from a small cut that broke its slick black skin.

"Ah, Naia, good evening!" said Laesid. "You missed lunch, though I suppose you're in time for supper."

"An outsider," Naia said. She plucked a damp cloth from the basin near where her sisters were tending to their mother, swabbing swamp mist off her cheeks with it. Her sisters gave her a tilted look, and she realized she hadn't begun at the beginning. "This morning, on my watch. I saw an outsider enter the swamp. She's here now, at the Glenfoot. She seems a Vapra—a Silverling, fair of hair and face. Mother, did you call for the All-Maudra?"

"No," Laesid said. She had not looked up from the baby eel where she held it gently in one hand, waving the other above it in a slow, circular motion. Her fingers shone with a gentle blue gathering light as if it were a palmful of crystal water. By the time the *maudra* withdrew her hand, the cut had closed and the puffiness had receded, leaving the eel to chirp in thanks before flitting away out the window.

Eliona, the *maudra*'s middling daughter, stood and perked her ears up with any excitement their mother failed to express. "An outsider!" she exclaimed. "From the Ha'rar? Has she brought gifts from the All-Maudra?"

"If she has, they're heavy with mud by now." Naia snorted. "She took the low way. It took all day, Mother! Haven't Silverlings any sense in the swamp?"

"No, they don't have swamps on the Vapran coast," Laesid replied wryly. "You could have helped her, you know. It would have helped you, too."

Naia pressed her lips together, crossing her arms and choosing not to respond to the light scolding. Her mother always seemed to have a better solution on the tip of her tongue, no matter how much thought Naia put into her decisions. That was what being the *maudra* was all about, after all—and Naia wasn't *maudra* yet.

"Anyway, what shall we do?"

"If she was in fact sent by the All-Maudra, we had better greet her, and sooner better than later. Meet her at the Glenfoot. Pemma, summon your father, have him join Naia and our visitor. I'll see her in my chamber if she calls for it."

As Pemma, the youngest, scampered out to fetch their father, Laesid reached to the floor and grasped her crutch, leaning on it to pull herself up. Naia dried her face with her sleeve. She was unsure about greeting the visitor alone, and although she was too old for a child minder, she was secretly glad that her father would be there. There was something about the Vapra's arrival that was causing a worming feeling in Naia's gut.

"Mother," she said, quieting her voice. "Could this be about Gurjin?"

Maudra Laesid shrugged, raising an open hand with no answers in it.

"Not everything is about your brother, my dear," she replied, but her voice sounded uneasy, and the salt in it fed the worm in Naia's stomach.

"The last time a Silverling came—" she began.

"And not every messenger from the All-Maudra is here to take your family away," Laesid finished. "Now go on, don't keep our visitor waiting. Show me your skill with formalities. Invite her to sup, and we'll see what all this huff-puff is about."

Naia kept her mouth shut, unsure how to explain what she was truly feeling. When Gurjin had first been sworn into service at the Castle of the Crystal, Naia had been filled with resentment and envy. Though she and her brother were precisely the same age, same in skill and will, their fates were different. His was to respond to the summons while she remained in Sog to apprentice to her mother. It was the duty of the eldest daughter, after all. That was the way it had always been. Naia had since come to accept it, but it didn't stop her from hoping that one day a soldier would arrive to summon her to leave the swamp as well. Her mother, however, seemed to know better.

Swallowing her pride, Naia took the Stone's Way: a long, twisting tunnel down to the foot of Great Smerth. She ignored the careful glances and smiles from the men and children in the winding passage as she hurried by. She worried about what they might be thinking; even Eliona's wings had bloomed, and she was one trine younger . . . Naia pushed the self-conscious thoughts out of mind. It was only a matter of time, her mother had told her: *Coming of age is a journey, not a destination.*

The Great Sun had long been at full height, its red brother peeking just along the border of the visible sky and warming the glen and shining on the pensive faces of the Drenchen scattered across the walkways and rope bridges. Above and around, Naia's clanfolk whispered, gray and green and brown faces peering out their carved windows at the exhausted traveler resting against the knees of a nearby root. Naia approached and took the closer look she hadn't been afforded earlier in the day. Unlike the sturdy Drenchen, the visitor was as skinny as a stick, with a narrow face and high, soft cheekbones. Where Naia's thick locs were bound in twists and ropes of black and green, the Silverling woman's hair hung in sad sheets of pale lavender, and though she had a proud, even brow and the posture of an adult, it would be easy to lift her with a hand and toss her back into the swamp through which she'd come.

"Hello," Naia called as she approached. Startled by her voice, the visitor's ears flicked toward her like delicate white cup-flowers.

"Hello," she replied. She spoke with an accent, shaping the word a bit sharper and shorter. Despite her weariness, she stood and did a quick, formal bow, holding the carved, unamoth-shaped brooch at the neck of her cloak.

"Perhaps you can assist me. I am Tavra of Ha'rar. I'm hoping I might ask the inconvenience of your clan's hospitality—if I could speak with your *maudra* . . ."

When Tavra trailed off, Naia realized she was done speaking, even if she hadn't finished her sentence, letting Naia guess the rest instead of saying it out loud. Naia tongued her teeth and took on a relaxed posture while still holding her chin up, a pose that was well practiced.

"The *maudra* is my mother, and I am her eldest daughter. You may speak with me in her place."

A look of relief passed over Tavra's long face, though her eyes still watched Naia the way she might look at a wild Nebrie, wondering whether it was dangerous or not. Was that what outsiders thought of the Drenchen? The look, and whatever words Tavra was about to utter, flitted away when Naia's father joined them. Bellanji was stout and heavy, with the locs of his great beard wound with string and beads, a spear held loosely in his hand as a formality that might befit the role of husband to the *maudra*.

"Hello there!" Bellanji said in his big voice. "Naia! I thought I asked you to clean your catches before bringing them to the supper table!" Then he let out a big laugh, mostly at Tavra's expense, and Naia felt a little smile prick the corners of her mouth.

"Father, this is Tavra," she said. "Of Ha'rar."

Bellanji raised one thick black brow.

"Ha'rar, eh?" he said. "Did the All-Maudra send you? Or maybe you're one of her daughters! How many of them are there now? No fewer than sixty-four, I'm sure."

Tavra's cheeks were so pale that they turned pink, and she raised a hand.

"I am merely a traveler who happens to hail from the home of the Gelfling All-Maudra," she said. "I have long since heard of the sights and . . . smells . . . of the Swamp of Sog. I was hoping I might ask the inconvenience of your hospitality, that I might witness all you have here for myself."

Bellanji waited, allowing his daughter to do the decision making, though she was not *maudra* yet. Naia let the talk fall quiet, sensing something riding below Tavra's words. There was much the Vapra wasn't saying, but so far as Naia's instinct could tell, it was nothing more dangerous than the Drenchen clan could take care of, should trouble arise. Resolved, at least for now, she gave her father a decisive nod. His smile returned, and he stomped the butt of his spear on the boardwalk before striding away.

"Well then, we'll all witness something either way, won't we?" he said over his shoulder. "Naia, find Tavra of Ha'rar a place from which she might enjoy our hospitality. She may stay as long as she likes—and tonight at sup, she can enjoy the sights and smells she's so longed for!"

Though Tavra's request had been granted, the look on her face was hardly enthusiastic.

CHAPTER 2

That night, Tavra sat to Naia's left at the head table in the Feast Hall, deep in the belly of Great Smerth. After a bath and some rest, the Vapran visitor looked more noble than weary. Naia imagined their guest standing in the white stone halls of Vapra Ha'rar, the home of the All-Maudra. From her seat, Naia had a closer view of the woman's face and the nervous expressions she was stifling as the servers pushed carts of traditional Drenchen fare before them. On each cart were tiered trays stacked with wide wood-and-leaf bowls filled past the brim with squirming delicacies: fuchsia wort beetles and fermented Nebrie-milk dumplings, mushroom wing-fronds, and Naia's favorite, blindfish plucked from the very bottom of the swamp floor. Naia took her helpings by the handful as the carts passed, piling them on the wide leaf in front of her as the drum singers played and sang from the balcony overlooking the bustling hall.

"Where are—" Tavra began, glancing up and down the long table before rethinking her question and trying again. "Do you use eating utensils?"

"Skewers," Naia said. She gestured at the reed cup holding a dozen pointed eating skewers at the end of the table, near Gurjin's usual place and the only empty chair. Tavra shook her head, looking paler than usual as Naia slurped a wriggling white blindfish whisker. After a few carts had passed, hunger finally got the better of her, and she reached for one of the leafier dishes as it passed, only to find it was seasoned with crawling, furry algae. In the beginning, Naia struggled to contain her amusement at Tavra's dilemma, but she soon felt a drop of pity in her heart for the poor woman and pushed her chair back.

"Come on, Neech. Let's find something that our guest can catch."

Neech stirred from his coil around her neck, his slippery skin sliding until he balanced over her shoulder and stretched his webbed wings. He gave a little chirp and darted out to catch a leaf hopper that had hopped too far from the table, munching on it lazily while Naia wove between the cart servers and the gregarious group of feasting Gelfling. Between bites, some of the Drenchen pounded on their tables along with the music of the drums, the tumultuous rhythm resounding off Great Smerth's interior like a heartbeat. All sorts of creatures from the swamp heard the music, and even now were creeping in through the carved windows and between the feet of the chairs and tables, hoping to catch a delicious bite that had fallen to the floor.

Naia gathered a platter of greens and a blindfish that she carefully cut into bite-size fillets. She returned with it and set it before Tavra with a glass of Nebrie milk. Beads of sweat dotted the Silverling's forehead like a tiara, as if the feast were more stressful of an ordeal than her journey to the glen.

"Thank you," she said, though she still looked faint. Concerned

about their guest, Naia forced a grin to set the other Gelfling at ease. Eventually, a warmer smile crawled across Naia's face. Although she'd been doing it for Tavra, Naia found the gesture unexpectedly comforting.

"Sorry we don't have . . . utensils," Naia said, taking her seat again. "We believe that feeling your food is part of the experience. Smell, taste, sight, *and* touch."

She showed Tavra how to wrap the greens and fish in the crisp leaves, and she took a bite. The Vapra's squinted eyes widened from apprehensive to surprised, and she remarked, after swallowing, "This is quite good!"

Naia laughed and took a bite of her own meal, rolling a tendril of leafy algae between her fingers before tasting its salty, musty flavor. She watched Tavra eat with rising enthusiasm and smiled to herself. From down the table, she saw her parents watching, and they were smiling, too.

"How do you like Sog, now that you're not waist-deep in it?" Maudra Laesid asked.

"I have seen many places in my travels," Tavra replied after clearing most of her plate, "but this is certainly the place I would call most different from where I come from, near the ocean."

"I can imagine," Bellanji said with a chuckle.

"I've never seen the ocean," Naia said.

"There is a profound difference between the swamp and the sea. When you stand near the swamp, the water and the earth are one. At the ocean, you can stand on the earth where the water begins, and then it goes toward the horizon as far as the eye can see."

Naia tried to imagine such a thing, but it was difficult. In Sog, there were always things to see nearby, and far away, in all directions. Even looking into the night sky, there were countless stars and the three glowing white faces of the Sister Moons. Imagining that any one thing might go on farther than she could see sounded boring—or maybe, she realized with a shiver, overwhelming.

"Who is that around your neck?" Tavra asked.

Naia looked down at Neech, who was lazily looped across her shoulders like a scarf.

"His name is Neech. Muskis are trained for hunting—once you hit your target, you never know where it will fall, and losing your quarry or *bola* is a big waste." She scratched Neech under the chin, and he let out a content purr. "He's just a baby now, but he'll get to be bigger as he gets older. My mother's eel was nearly big enough for both me and my brother to ride on when we were young."

Tavra reached out to pet Neech, but he puffed out the fur and quills near his head and spread his wings to look bigger. Tavra jerked her hand back and apologized. Naia shushed him, smoothing down his spines.

"Your brother . . . ," Tavra said aloud, though it was quiet enough that she might have been talking to herself. She tilted her head toward the empty chair, past the scrabbling of Naia's sisters' hands as they reached for passing trays of dumplings. "Gurjin?"

Naia nodded. "He is sworn to service at the Castle of the Crystal," she said, though mention of him formed an uncomfortable bubble of silence around them amid the drumming and clamoring and feasting. "Two trine ago. He used to visit, but it's quite a journey between here and the castle, and I suppose with how magnificent and grand everything is there, with the lords and all, visiting us back in the swamp doesn't get his gills in a giggle."

Naia tried to sound proud of her brother, as she should, but it came out flat. When Gurjin last *had* made time to visit, all he had done was talk about the castle and the world beyond Sog. It was always about him, and the elaborate celebrations and the visitors from all corners of Thra. As much as Naia loved blindfish, Gurjin had once said the lords' feasts were second to none—not even those of the Drenchen. She longed to see the banquet hall he'd described, with its tall vaulted ceiling encrusted with jewels and shining metals—to taste the rich broths and sweet-cakes and crawlies, piled high in opulent mounds across dozens of cloth-covered tables. Was he feasting at one now, while she was here in Sog, spending every day wandering the same old swamp and suffering her mother's strict *maudra* training? Probably.

"Sibling rivalry can be difficult," Tavra said. She was trying to be consoling after Naia's rigid tone, but her attempt only brought an outburst from Naia's mouth. What did this traveler know about rivalry?

"Rivalry, ha! Gurjin and I have the same skills, the same interests. We're even exactly the same age—twins! But I'm the eldest daughter, so I have to become *maudra*, and he was sworn to the castle. If it hadn't been so, we would both have gone."

Tavra shut her mouth with an audible click, held her breath, and then uttered a quiet "oh," and that was the last either of them spoke of it. Naia let the old soreness fade before brushing it aside completely.

Something barreled into them from behind. Naia let out an *ooph* as she tumbled into Tavra, knocking them both out of their seats and to the ground. Naia leaped to her feet, shouting after the two roughhousing Drenchen boys as they darted from behind to upon the table, upsetting wicker platters and bowls and drinking pods before racing through the hall, laughing the whole way.

"Sorry!" Naia exclaimed. She stooped and offered her hand to Tavra, who was lying on her back, the breast of her recently cleaned robes now soiled with the food that had previously been contained by her plate. Tavra reached for Naia's hand, and when they touched, Naia gasped at the sudden images rushing before her mind's eye: a beautiful Vapran Gelfling with a gleaming circlet, bedecked in flowing silver robes, her white hair braided and coiled in intricate swirls and knots. Her otherwise gentle face held a hint of hardness: the burden of guiding the Gelfling people.

A voice rang in her mind's ears. The voice of Mayrin, the Gelfling All-Maudra . . .

Find Rian. Find Gurjin.

Her brother's name brought forth memories that slipped into the dreamfast before she could stop them: saying good-bye to Gurjin the day he left with the other soldiers. The fights with her mother when she was denied permission to go along as well . . . and the day Naia gave up, hiding her anger in a little black ball. Accepting her duties to become *maudra*, and learning healing *vliyaya*, history, and how to settle disputes among the people of their clan.

The All-Maudra's voice surfaced from Tavra's memories again, this time harder and more harsh:

Find them. Find any of their allies—

The command dissolved into air when Naia finally pulled her hand back, letting Tavra fall again to the floor. When the touch was broken, the visions ended.

"I'm—I'm sorry," Naia said. "I didn't mean to— Here."

Focusing on restraining her mind, she reached again. When Tavra grasped her palm this time, there was no dreamfast—no sharing of memories. With warm cheeks, Naia helped Tavra douse her ruined garment with some water. Tavra said nothing the whole time, though Naia was sure she was thinking about what had happened. Inadvertent dreamfasting was an intrusion of privacy, and certainly something a Gelfling of Naia's age should be able to control.

"I'm sorry," Naia said again.

"I ought to be turning in," Tavra said instead of acknowledging the apology. "It's been a long day for me, and I fear I won't be able to keep my eyes open much longer anyhow."

Naia stood by, wringing her hands, as Tavra made her hurried thank-yous and final exit. When she was gone, Laesid beckoned. Chagrined, Naia stood near her mother and rubbed her forehead with the back of her hand.

"That was a hasty exit," Laesid remarked, absentmindedly stroking Naia's locs. "What's happened?"

"I accidentally dreamfasted with her," she muttered, half hoping her words would melt away before her mother heard them. She gently pushed her mother's hands from her locs, wanting anything but to feel like a child just then. "I'm so embarrassed."

"So long as no harm came of it, I'm sure you'll both survive," Laesid said, folding her hands in her lap. Bellanji, apparently having overheard, leaned in.

"Did you see anything important?" he asked.

Naia thought at first he was teasing, but his eyes weren't smiling at all. She had already been trying to forget the private memories she'd seen in Tavra's mind, but when her father asked, the images of the beautiful Gelfling All-Maudra came to mind too easily, as did the ominous words:

Find Rian. Find Gurjin.

Who was Rian, and what did he have to do with Naia's brother—and more importantly, what did Tavra want with either of them? Naia told what she'd seen, and after her telling, Bellanji and Laesid leaned away, looking to each other and exchanging the silent conversation they sometimes had—the kind that required neither words nor dreamfasting. They nodded to each other in agreement.

"Naia," Laesid said in an even but stern voice. "In light of this, I believe the time has come for us to clear up our guest's less-than-satisfactory pretense. Finish your supper for now, but after, meet us promptly in my chamber. We are overdue for some hard-talk with Tavra of Ha'rar."

CHAPTER 3

Naia did as her mother suggested, though enjoying the rest of her supper was difficult when her gut was tying itself in knots anticipating the confrontation planned for later. It was a relief when the carts stopped coming out of the kitchen and the clanfolk left for the evening, saying their post-meal thanks and prayers with a slap of hands over their heads and a deep bow before ambling away to their dwellings within Great Smerth and the surrounding apeknots.

While Eliona went to give thanks to the night's musicians and servers, Naia helped clear the head table and stack dishes in the wicker cradles hanging off the balconies near the kitchen. When the nightly rain came, the dishes would be washed clean, any scraps or sauce leavings brought to the swamp floor, a midnight snack for the creatures dwelling there. After her chores were done, Naia climbed the rope walkways to the upper arms of Smerth, headed down a twisting hall, left and right, and entered the tunnel entrance to her mother's chamber, the greatest in Great Smerth, near the very center of the tree.

It would have been dark within, so deep inside Smerth and so late at night, but the rounded walls of the circular chamber were lined with glowing cave moss that gave the room a gentle blue-green glow. Tapestries strung with beads, feathers, scales, and carved ivory decorated the otherwise bare walls, painted and dyed with protective figures and incantations. In some places, mostly over the doorway and her mother's medicine box, wooden talismans dangled, engraved with etchings done long ago when a dream etcher had been *maudra* of their clan. The words were dark, as if burned, in rich black and red that had not faded no matter the time that passed. Dream-etching was a rare skill indeed, and the talismans were held in particularly high regard. Overhead, a single wide chute was bored through the wood to the outside. When the Blue Moon—the largest of the Sisters—was full and passed directly over the tunnel, it marked the beginning of a new unum.

Maudra Laesid was reclining in a hammock chair, swinging herself gently with her single foot while her husband filled and lit a pipe made of a hollowed Nebrie tusk. Seated on a floor cushion, back straight, was Tavra, hands formally resting on her pointed knees while she suffered the inescapable gaze of the Drenchen wise woman. Naia kept quiet on careful feet, circling the room to sit on a stool near her mother's hammock. The atmosphere of the room was tense, though Naia was grateful to be on her mother's side. She had many times been the subject of such a stare, and she did not envy Tavra one bit.

"Now that we're all here," Laesid began, "Tavra of Ha'rar. Although we offered our hearth and home to you, it seems now there's more to your story than you've said."

"My apologies, *maudra*," Tavra said. "I only—"

Laesid cut her short with a swift hand wave. "I could go on

and on and draw it out from you bit by bit in the soft-speak the All-Maudra and all you Silverfolk from the north prefer, but here in Sog, we Drenchen have little time for it." Laesid's voice grew powerfully serious. "Tell us why you're here, and in particular what it has to do with my son, Gurjin."

Naia expected Tavra's voice to grow reedy as it had during the banquet. Instead, though, the woman drew a calm breath, closed her eyes, and exhaled before meeting Laesid's gaze with a steady, practiced eye.

"I am a soldier, sent by All-Maudra Mayrin," she said. She glanced at Naia, not so much with accusation but only with knowing. "Your daughter must have told you that much by now. Her dreamfasting is stronger than most her age."

"She did, and it is. But I prefer water fresh from the spring," Laesid said. "On what errand did the All-Maudra send you?"

"Though I would have preferred this to have come to light in a manner less embarrassing—"

"Hard-talk," said Bellanji. "Get to it!"

Laesid raised an eyebrow in agreement, and Naia felt a pinch of pleasure from seeing Tavra squirm. The Vapra hesitated, drawing her fingers in toward her palms, resolute.

"Your son and another castle guard, Rian of Stone-in-the-Wood, have been accused of treason by the Skeksis Lords. Their crime is spreading lies against the Castle of the Crystal and Ha'rar. When called to trial, instead of facing justice, they fled. Neither have been seen since. I was going to tell you on the morning, after formalities. I apologize."

Naia's breath caught in her chest, ears burning and eyes darting to her mother. The castle had been entrusted to the Skeksis since the beginning of time, and in turn they shared the ancient task of protecting it with the Gelfling. It was all part of the great Song of Thra, the endless harmony of all things existing as they should. To fall out of tune was only possible through powerful darkness and corruption. Gurjin may have been arrogant about his duty at times, but he took it seriously—it was impossible, Naia wanted to shout, that he might betray the Skeksis, the castle, and the Heart of Thra that resided there. Naia pressed her tongue firmly against the roof of her mouth, forcing herself to be still and let her mother lead.

"Well, better late than never," Laesid said, acknowledging the apology but hardly accepting it. If she felt the same defensive surprise as Naia, she hid it well, leaning back in her hammock and tapping her forefinger against her lips. "So. You came here to see if Gurjin the treasonist came home to hide?"

Tavra sighed, dipping her chin in a grave nod.

"Yes. Not even the Lords skekLach and skekOk have seen him, and they have been taking the census these past unum. Counted every Gelfling south of the Black River, and no sign—Rian and Gurjin have fled like snow in summer. If I do not find them, I am under orders to bring back one each of their closest kin to stand trial on their behalf. Should neither appear in Ha'rar within one unum to take responsibility for their actions, a notice will be released for their death."

Death? Naia looked between her parents again. Neither seemed anything but stoic, so she put on the same face, but still the news was harsh and the timeline harsher. It took almost a full unum merely to send word to the All-Maudra by the fleetest messenger swoothu; how were they to find a missing someone and make it to trial in the same time?

"Then it's not to stand on trial in Gurjin's stead, it's to stand as ransom," Bellanji said. "Say it like it is. Within one turn of the Sisters? That's all? And what happens to his kin, should Gurjin not appear?"

"His kin will be held as a witness. Should they choose to incriminate Gurjin at the trial, his warrant will only be quickened. Should they choose to defend him, the lords will have final say in the matter."

"It won't come to that," Laesid dismissed. "My son is not a traitor. Once he finds the All-Maudra is holding his kin hostage, he will arrive on trial and shortly disprove whatever treason he's accused of. Surely there's some explanation for his disappearance."

"How can you be sure he's not a traitor when you haven't spoken to him since he's been accused?" Tavra asked plainly, so direct it nearly sounded Drenchen. "There is a reason serving the castle is a duty that ends only by death. It changes you. As much as you protest, you might not recognize Gurjin as your own son, should you have the chance to see him again."

"Gurjin's interests are in hunting game and courting girls, not politics," Bellanji said. He crossed the room to stand before Tavra, the whole chamber echoing with his heavy, solid footfalls. "Those aren't likely to change his whole life, sworn to the castle or not. How I'd love to see those rosy-red cheeks on Her Silverness when she finds he's not planning treason but climbed up a tree with a lassywings somewhere."

"I wish it were the case," Tavra said, a soft huff of disdain escaping her lips.

"Then it's that scoundrel Stonewood," Bellanji insisted. "I always knew those rock-banging forest bugs were no good—"

"Bellanji," Laesid warned, and he fell silent, though his eyes still burned.

"I have been through Stone-in-the-Wood already," Tavra said. "No sign of either."

"Well, look again," Bellanji replied. "I promise you'll find it's that Rian, dragging my boy along on some reckless hoax."

Everything about Tavra hardened with annoyance. Naia wanted to be as loyal to Gurjin as her parents, but the truth was, Tavra's words had merit. It was very possible, though she didn't like to admit it, that his life outside of Sog had changed her brother, bit by bit. Had she been in his place, she would hope to have changed—grown, at least a little. Her mother had always said assignment at the castle might grow some wings on the boy, a saying that had consistently invited contest from her only son. But while Naia had grown in her training, accepting her assigned responsibilities—perhaps this was what Gurjin had gotten up to. No, she reminded herself. It was what Tavra *said* he was up to. There was no proof Gurjin was a traitor.

"If you're so sure your son is innocent, then I invite you to send his closest kin back to Ha'rar with me," Tavra said, glancing at Naia for the first time since the meeting had begun.

"I will!" Bellanji declared. "If it'll end your investigation where it stands, it would be worth the trip!"

Tavra's cheeks colored, and she pinched her lips once. Clearly, she hadn't meant Bellanji.

"Surely you're needed here in the glen," she said. "Gurjin's sister—"

"Is still in training. I'll go with you, Silverling. We'll see how sure the Court of Ha'rar is about Gurjin once a Drenchen steps foot in with some real hard-talk. We'll leave tomorrow."

Her father was so determined, he looked ready to grab his spear and leave for the home of the Gelfling All-Maudra that very instant, every hair on his body quivering with indignation. Laesid, though, didn't stop him. At least, not yet. She was still tapping her finger against her lips, deep in thought as she considered Tavra's face. Naia had to admit, the silver-haired soldier from Ha'rar didn't have a flicker of doubt in her eyes. Whether or not it was the truth, she certainly believed what she had claimed. Even Bellanji's ranting could not shake her.

"Yes, in fact," Laesid said finally. "Yes. Bellanji, on the morn, you'll go to Ha'rar and meet with the All-Maudra herself. We'll straighten this out in a civilized way . . . no need for sneaking about and sending mysterious visitors to investigate in the dark of the night."

Just as Tavra opened her mouth to protest again, Laesid continued, "Naia, you'll go with your father."

Naia straightened, hands clutching her knees, heart racing with both surprise and excitement.

"I will?"

"It's about time you left Sog, and this will be a good time to do it. You'll go with your father and see how they do things in Ha'rar." Laesid's voice dropped a bit lower, almost as if she were speaking to herself. "There's a thorny nettle growing. Between the castle and the Skeksis, tangling with the All-Maudra and the Gelfling race. As it grows thicker, we in the outreaches of the Skarith Land will need to be more familiar with those that rule us."

Bellanji huffed a ring of smoke and put up his pipe with an unruly clatter.

"Great," Bellanji said. "A final saying. Naia, we leave as the Great Sun rises. I'm off to bed."

He thumped his chest once with a fist and let out a big *brrrrruuupp* as he left. The odor carried throughout the room, and Tavra wrinkled her nose when he was gone, turning her attention back to Laesid.

"Maudra, I will accompany your daughter and husband to Ha'rar."

"Aughra bless, I'm sure you will," Laesid replied, a dubious arched brow making it clear where her trust was. "At the least, it's a way to shoo you from my sight. Get to bed and rest well. You leave in the morning, and with you goes any and all words against my son. Do you understand?"

"I may keep my lips sealed, but the truth garners singers wherever it goes," Tavra said. She stood. "Still, I thank you for your lenience. I will endeavor to escort your husband to the All-Maudra so he may make his case at Gurjin's trial, if that is what you wish. I don't guarantee its effectiveness, however."

Naia bunched up her fists at the irreverence in the Vapra's voice, but as she had all through the meeting, she held her tongue. It didn't feel good, but she knew it was the adult way and suffered through it.

Laesid shrugged and waved a hand, unaffected by the Vapra's haughty tone.

"I don't need your guarantee on anything, Tavra of Ha'rar, except one: that you'll get out of my swamp as soon as there's light enough to show you the way."

CHAPTER 4

Naia awoke early the next morning. After splashing her face with cool water from the basin outside her window, she pulled on a light tunic and tucked two *bola* in her belt. Lastly, she opened a small leather pouch that rested on her single carved shelf. It was a gift from Gurjin, something he'd brought back for her the first time he'd returned after his appointment at the Castle of the Crystal: a small dagger with a blade of real metal. Inset in the sterling hilt was a polished river rock, black as night and so shiny, she could see her reflection in it. Metals were hard to come by in Sog, though Gurjin had often told her of the many gleaming ornaments and fixtures that adorned the castle. It was the only thing he'd ever brought her, aside from all the stories that filled her with wanderlust, and what was she to use it for? Hunting in the swamp was long-distance stuff with no place for knives. But Naia had kept it, anyway, as a reminder of her brother and their shared—if separate—responsibilities.

She tried not to let bitterness cloud her memories. It was still left to be seen what had become of him, and for all she knew, he could be in danger. She could only hope he hadn't wasted the freedom she'd never had the opportunity to receive. Repeating this to herself, she tucked the dagger in her belt.

Naia smoothed Neech's quills and said a quiet good-bye to her chamber before ducking out the window and skipping along the walking-ropes to the edge of the glen. There she waited for her father and Tavra with anxious, excited flutterings in her stomach. Would she get to stand before the All-Maudra in Ha'rar while her father made his case? Would they meet Gurjin somewhere along the way and have the chance to prove Tavra wrong before they even reached the home of the Gelfling All-Maudra?

Would she see the wide, endless ocean?

It didn't seem Tavra had slept much. Dark shadows wallowed under her eyes when she appeared, her ears drooped to the side, and her hair was tied in a loose braid that was fraying and frizzing in the humidity of the swamp. She'd shed most of the cloaks and cloths she'd worn on her inbound trek and now wore only a tunic embroidered with glass beads and thread with an open back, so her silvery gossamer wings had room to move. At her hip was sheathed a short slim sword. Bellanji, at Tavra's shoulder, was in his ranging gear: light armor made of tanned Nebrie hide and sun-hardened pieces of apeknot bark. He had a travel pack strapped across his shoulders and his hunting spear in hand. With only a series of nods, silent in the awakening morning, they embarked, leaving the Drenchen Glen and Great Smerth behind them.

Naia followed her father upward, and they showed Tavra how to climb into the labyrinth of apeknot branches, ensuring the journey out of Sog would not be as grueling as the one inward. Once they reached the canopy, they picked up their pace without hesitation. Using his spear to vault from apeknot to apeknot,

Bellanji was swift and powerful despite his bulk, and Naia had to stay alert and on her toes to meet his pace. It was exhilarating to feel the wind against her skin, and the challenge of matching her father—or at least, not falling behind—brought her heart to a steady quickened rhythm that synchronized with the song of the swamp. In this way they went from morning through late afternoon, making quick headway north. Naia nodded quiet *so longs* to each apeknot she passed, still in disbelief that by the end of a day's journey, she would finally be leaving the swamp that had been her constant home since she was born.

To her surprise, Tavra kept up. Without the weight of her cloak, free of the quagmire that had sucked at her boots for miles, the Silverling was as fleet as a bog flier. Naia could only imagine how quick she might be in an open field, or maybe atop a long-legged Landstrider. Tavra's wings stayed folded tightly at her back until just the right moment—then *whissssh!* Out they'd stretch, catching the atmosphere and launching her into the air, where she'd glide, darting upward to land on another branch and resuming her pace on foot.

As the trees began to thin nearer the swamp threshold, Tavra made one particularly impressive leap, swooping high into the air and flying for some distance without landing. The clearing in the canopy let the sunlight through, and the rays caught the Silverling's wings, lighting them with a flash and sparkle of silver. Distracted by the sight, Naia swelled with envy, nearly missing her step as the earth suddenly shook. At a reverberating groan, the apeknots all around tried to curl in on themselves; the younger trees below successfully balled into knotted fists, while the older trees, armored in centuries of hardened bark, only shuddered, creaked, and cracked. Naia grabbed tightly on to the bark, digging her fingernails in and holding her breath, knowing that if she were tossed from the branch, she would have no way to slow her fall.

She heard shouting as the trembling subsided. They had made it to the Tall Pass, the great division of apeknots that marked the border between Drenchen territory and the outer swamp that would eventually give way to the grasslands beyond. As soon as she was able to do so without fear of losing her balance, Naia leaped to her feet and looked for her father and Tavra. They'd been knocked down, nearly to the swamp floor . . . but they were safe.

Safe, until a monstrous form erupted from the murky depths.

Naia pressed her hands over her ears at the deafening roar as mud and swamp slime flew in every direction, sludge falling away in a landslide off the monster that had emerged. It looked like a Nebrie, round, with tusks and dark inky eyes on either side of its bulbous head. This creature, though, was ten times larger and as black as midnight. It loomed up into the canopy with its flippers held wide like enormous thick wings. Its eyes crackled with a violet light, and the swamp around it shrank away. Even Naia could feel the energy emanating from it. Confused. Afraid. *Angry*.

As Naia drew one of her *bola*, the monstrous Nebrie lunged at her father and Tavra. Though the two leaped away, the sheer bulk of the monster broke through the limbs of the apeknots as

if they were twigs. The Nebrie crashed to the swamp floor with a thunderous *BA-BOOOOOM*, and Tavra alit on a nearby root, drawing her sword. Bellanji braced himself, planting his heels and holding his stone-tipped spear at the monster's nearest eye. The Nebrie wailed, pulling itself up and baring its tusks, each of which was easily twice the size of Naia's father. Bellanji stiffened his back and followed the beast with the head of his spear.

"What's driven you to such rage, Nebrie?" he shouted.

"It's going to attack!" Tavra warned. Her eyes darted up, and she cut the air with her hand, signaling for Naia to run, but Naia clenched her hand around the hand-rope of her *bola*, legs immobile with fear and dread, not for herself but for her father. The Nebrie reared, preparing to attack again. If it did, even as quick as Bellanji might be, there was no way he could escape the huge bulk of the creature. Without thinking, Naia swung the counterweights of her *bola* and let it fly, striking the Nebrie in one of its globular eyes. The rock-and-rope harmlessly bounced away, but she had the thing's attention.

"Naia, no!" Tavra shouted. "You'll only make it angrier! Just get out of here!"

"And let it kill my father? Not likely!"

Naia stood and darted out along the branch. The wild Nebrie turned its attention away from Bellanji and lurched toward her.

"Over here!" she called to it. "Come on, you big lug!"

"Naia, be careful," her father warned as he backed away, out of the Nebrie's shadow. From her higher vantage, Naia doubted the beast could strike her. If she could lead it away from Tavra and her father, they could ascend back into the safety of the canopy and escape. She let her second *bola* loose and struck the monster in the face, eliciting a howling squeal. It rose, taller than she had thought possible, fixing her with empty eyes that sparked with a crackle of vicious purple light. Tavra saw it, too, and asked in a shaken voice, "What's wrong with its eyes?"

Naia stared into the creature's deep orbs, sensing pain and seeing only black and flashes of violet, as if the Nebrie had looked upon something so bright and terrible that the image had burned all else from its mind.

"Naia, out of the way!"

Her father's warning came too late. The Nebrie swung its head at Naia's tree, and its tusk shattered it on impact, hurtling like a boulder and ripping through the swamp. Even old and solid as it was, the tree splintered with a deafening *CRACK* that sent hundreds of birds flying into the sky. As the top part of the tree leaned, Naia scrambled for a foothold amongst the tangled branches and overgrowth. As she reached the end of the bough, she knew she would not be able to reach the next one. Still, she leaped, knowing no other option. The leaves from the outstretched branch opposite brushed through her fingers, and then she was falling, fast, through the shadow of the dark Nebrie.

She hit the surface of a murky lake, and the shock immobilized her as she sank. Like others of her clan, she had no fear of drowning. The gills in the sides of her neck opened, and she breathed in a deep gasp of water. She sank deeper until her back touched the soft mud of the lake bottom. Neech, who had been hiding in her locs, swam around, spitting bubbles of worry. Through the murky water, she saw the shadow of the Nebrie and flashes of light. The water muffled all sounds except the groaning of the half-submerged Nebrie. All she could do was hope that her father and Tavra would survive.

Her fingers began to tingle, and after what seemed like ages, Naia regained feeling. She dug them into the mud below her, getting a handhold to pull herself up. She stopped. Something hard was under her toes. She twisted and looked, pulling away the mud and silt. Below the gray and black, there was a ripple of light—a sparkle of violet. She cleared the area and saw a crystalline vein running through the rock. Though it was only a thread's width, she found herself squinting instinctively, as if her body knew that the source—however distant it was—was so bright it might blind her.

The chaos above her seemed distant. Far away. It wasn't until a loud splash cascaded above her that she realized she had lost time, and looked up. A body was drifting toward her, blood reddening the water around it. Panic struck her, and she forgot the crystal. She planted her feet on the lake floor and launched herself upward. Her father was sinking, bleeding from a massive wound in his side.

She caught him and slowed his descent. He was conscious, but barely, spear still clenched in his hand. Naia kicked, pulling the weight of her father until they broke the surface of the lake. Then Tavra was there, trying to help haul Bellanji onto the soggy moss blanketing the apeknot roots, but one of her arms dangled uselessly at her side, and her tunic was stained red with blood. They wrestled Bellanji halfway out of the water and stopped to breathe. Tears mixed with swamp water and green bits of algae and slime on Naia's cheeks. It was quiet, and she thought for a moment that the Nebrie had fled, but then Tavra whispered, "Naia. Run."

Her mind cleared, and Naia became aware of the heavy shadow being cast upon them. Looming overhead was the Nebrie, still trembling and groaning in its rage, so close Naia could see the hairs protruding from its thick mottled hide. Froth flew from its muzzle and tusks as it sighted her. Bearing the bulk of her father's weight, there was no way she could escape. Tavra's words echoed in her mind, but she couldn't run. Her feet were useless, immobile as rocks growing from her ankles.

The Nebrie let out a deafening wail, and instead of fear, for an instant, Naia felt the agony in the creature's cry. It resonated within her so suddenly that it brought a tear to her eye. The Nebrie was in pain, and she could feel it as closely as if it were her own. Spurred by the sensation, her feet were moving of their own accord, but they were not taking her out of the monstrous shadow.

"Naia, no!" Tavra hissed. She tried to pull Naia back with her good hand, but her reach was short. Naia stepped close enough to the Nebrie to touch it. She hushed her voice and reached out, smoothing her hand along its rough skin. The Nebrie didn't move, still facing the sky, gazing with unseeing eyes. The low constant groan emanating from its belly seemed to come from beyond the Nebrie, as if the swamp itself were writhing in aching pain.

"Please," she called to it. She didn't know what else to do. She poured her honesty into her words, wishing, hoping, praying that it would reach the Nebrie. "Please, I don't know what plagues you. We mean you no harm—"

At the sound of her voice, the Nebrie gaped, tusks and teeth bared, rolling its head. Tavra cursed and struggled to move Bellanji away, giving up on trying to coerce Naia into fleeing. Naia didn't care, focusing all her attention on the Nebrie. Where had it come from? What had it seen that had changed it so? A vision wriggled into her mind, of the crystal vein in the swamp and its terrible darkness. Of shadowy shapes. Of fear. The fear bore down on her like a moonless midnight, enveloping her, but she could not afford to become lost within it. She thought of her father, her mother, her sisters, and Gurjin, wherever he was.

The Nebrie let out a high pained cry and shuddered, startling Naia into stepping back. She kept her hands at her side, watching. Out of the corner of her eye, she saw Tavra was watching, too, having given up on escape. If the Nebrie lunged, they were done for . . . but it made no move, uttered no sound. The entire swamp was quiet save for the dripping of water, and then a low rumbling moan. The cry was so miserable and pained, it brought more tears to Naia's eyes. The Nebrie shuddered from fin to snout, then collapsed in a wave of flippers, whiskers, and flesh. It heaved a breath, but the sound was ragged, deep, and hollow.

All was silent. The Nebrie was dead.

CHAPTER 5

Tavra helped Naia pull her father onto a bed of algae and moss. Naia could see that the wound, although deep, was not as bad as it had seemed in the water, surrounded by clouds and clouds of blood. Tavra heaved a sigh and fell to her knees, grasping her arm. Her shoulder seemed dislocated, and sharp pieces of daggered wood pierced her arm and parts of her torso. She must have collided with one of the many splintered branches or tree trunks that littered the Tall Pass. One of her wings looked crushed, but at least it was intact. Collapsed between two apeknots, the Nebrie was nothing but a mound of gray and black flesh. One flipper extended limply in the air, soon to be a perch and feeding ground for the scavenging animals of the swamp.

"Father," Naia whispered. "Father, are you all right?"

"Oh hush," Bellanji grunted, sitting up and pressing a hand to his side. "Of course I am."

Naia searched the traveling pack that was buckled to his belt, looking for healing herbs. Tearing cloth from her tunic, she pressed it against the wound. Tavra found Bellanji's spear and laid it nearby in case of trouble, then searched the canopy for any more danger. All the creatures had fled, afraid of the monstrous beast the Nebrie had become.

Naia put pressure against her father's wound, closing her eyes and reaching with her heart, the way her mother had taught her. It was difficult to focus, every nerve on alert for new danger. She stared intently at her father's wound and bade the bleeding to stop. In response to her effort, the moss beneath them rustled, growing. A blue light glowed from her fingertips and from her father's flesh. After a moment, the bleeding had slowed, though he was still in no condition to stand.

"Amazing," Tavra said quietly. "The songs of the Drenchen Maudra's healing ways are true, I see."

"If she were here, it would be much better," Naia said through a tight throat. She tried to push away the guilt she felt at not being able to do more. "I've only just started learning *vliyaya* from her."

Bellanji coughed, then chuckled, sitting up. Though most of it was for show, his color was returning, and Naia felt a minor sense of relief.

"Don't look so worried, little leaper," her father said. "You've done just fine. I'd worry more about our Silverling friend."

Tavra was working on fashioning a sling from the sleeve of her tunic, her broken wing hanging bent at her shoulder. Naia wasn't sure if she should try to heal the Vapra's wing, or how to ask if it was even a wanted thing. Before she could bring it up, Tavra reached back and with a swift jerk and a hiss of pain, set her wing in place. She wouldn't fly any time soon, but the break would heal. She winced as she approached them, but kept any complaining to herself.

"Naia's healing is strong, but your wound is still very bad," she said to Bellanji matter-of-factly, her coldness almost certainly masking her pain. Or maybe she was trying to hide her concern for Naia's sake. "He needs to get back to the glen, and quickly. We'll have to postpone the journey to Ha'rar."

"If your mother can lose her leg, I can be scratched by a simple Nebrie," he said. For emphasis, he coughed a forced "ha!"

Naia felt more relief at his humor, but it couldn't overpower the apprehension in her gut. The Nebrie's behavior hadn't been natural, not at all. What if there were more? If one made its way to the glen, all of the clan would be in danger.

"That wasn't a simple Nebrie," Naia said. "It was ill, I think, or possessed . . . I saw something down under the mud. It looked like crystal, the same color as the light in the Nebrie's eyes. If they're connected, it might not just be that Nebrie. There could be more creatures affected."

She half expected her father to make another joke, laugh it off, but the humor in his voice had run dry. Despite her healing, the wound in his side was taking its toll as he solemnly gazed upon the fallen Nebrie. With a grunt of effort, he braced himself with his spear and pulled himself up. It didn't seem like the best plan, but then again, they couldn't just lounge around until he healed. Tavra was right. They needed to get back to Smerth, where their medicine-makers could tend to their wounds, and Maudra Laesid could exercise her more experienced healing *vliyaya*. Naia was the only one who had suffered nothing but a few bumps and bruises.

"Tavra of Ha'rar," Bellanji invoked, glancing at the silver-haired Vapra. "What do you make of this? Is there anything we ought to know? Perhaps something more you haven't told us?"

"Not a thing," Tavra replied. For once, her voice was steady and her cheeks didn't flush with an incriminating red. She was telling the truth. "Though if what Naia is saying is true, that she saw a crystal light within the earth . . . it was no mere illness that drove that Nebrie into a rage. The veins which pulse from the Heart of Thra stretch to even the furthest reaches. Something is amiss."

Naia didn't know exactly what Tavra meant, though she did agree that something was amiss. If something had hurt Thra—injured it, put poison in its veins—had the Nebrie been poisoned, too? Bellanji jostled himself back together again, beard-locs shaking with droplets of swamp water. He shrugged out of his traveling pack—waterproof, as all Drenchen commodities were—and put it across Naia's shoulders. She suddenly realized what he was about to ask of her. Tavra noticed, too, and reached out as if to stop it.

"You can't possibly be thinking of sending her to Ha'rar alone," the Vapra exclaimed. "She's barely more than a child!"

Naia resented the implication; she could take care of herself just fine, and she was certainly more than a child, even if her wings had not yet bloomed. But there were more important things to deal with now than arguing with the Vapra. She took her father's pack, but only because she was uninjured and could bear it more easily than either of the two adults.

"Father, no," she said. "I'll help you back to the glen. When you're both healed, we can go to Ha'rar together. The All-Maudra will have to wait."

She tried to take his arm across her shoulder and turn them back toward Great Smerth, but Bellanji would not go.

"The All-Maudra cannot wait for this news," he said. He gestured with his chin at Tavra. "You, of anyone, should know that. If Naia saw flickers from the Crystal and felt something was wrong—we all saw that Nebrie, felt how out of harmony it was with Thra! And now it's dead, and we're hurt. It could be unum before I'm fit for travel, and I fear by then . . ."

No one wanted to hear the end of Bellanji's words, so he didn't bother uttering them. Naia glanced at what remained of the Nebrie. She hoped it was not an omen, but her mother had taught her all things were connected.

Tavra shrugged, grimacing.

"I will heal faster. With help of the Spriton Landstriders, I can reach Ha'rar quickly and bring the news of what Naia saw."

Other thoughts were sliding behind the Vapra's eyes, but they didn't surface in words, or even more than the frown that was deepening on her thin pink lips.

"And if you go alone, then who will represent Gurjin?" Naia asked.

Tavra snorted.

"If word finds him that his father was injured trying to defend his honor before the All-Maudra, perhaps he'll show some nerve and step forth to defend himself."

Naia sucked in a deep breath through her nose, biting her lip to control her temper. Tavra met her eyes only a moment before turning away, making to return to the canopy and begin the trek back to the glen.

"Come on, then," the Vapra said. "We don't have much time with Bellanji's wounds. We'll need to hurry to make it back by night. Naia, help your father—"

"No."

The word was clear in the awakening swamp, slowly recovering from the moaning of the Nebrie. Tavra turned, her good wing flicking in irritation. Bellanji shifted his weight, saying nothing; this was between Naia and the Vapra soldier.

"Excuse me?" Tavra said.

Naia stepped forward, resolute. She held her hands in fists to keep them from shaking, and forced her voice to be calm and controlled, but with no room for compromise.

"No," she repeated. "You're going to help my father back to the glen. I'm going on to Ha'rar. To see the All-Maudra and represent the Drenchen and my brother."

Tavra put her uninjured hand on her hip, sizing Naia up with a seasoned soldier's gaze. At first, Naia thought the Silverling might simply laugh at her. But she held firm, refusing to let her determination be made a joke. She would one day be the Drenchen Maudra. This was no time to be treated like a child, especially with Gurjin's honor on the line, and if she trusted her instincts about the crystal vein.

Tavra's appraisal ended, and she let out a sigh.

"Very well," she said. "But I assure you, it will not be easy."

Naia resisted the urge to grin. The victorious elation was short-lived, though, and in its wake was a knot and tangle of worry. For her father's safety, and for the journey she had just volunteered to take—alone. She refused to show the hesitation, though, calming herself by tightening the straps on her father's pack. Tavra raised a brow, but slid under Bellanji's arm to help support his weight. Naia's father accepted the help, though the smile on his face was not one of gratitude but rather one of pride.

Once Bellanji was stable, Tavra held out her hand. When Naia looked at it suspiciously, the Vapra sighed and gave a rare smile.

"You've never left Sog before, have you? I will show you the way."

The dreamfasting was intentional and vivid this time, so much more intense than when she had accidentally intruded during the feast. Naia saw the northern stretch of swamp end at a long ridge of forest. Beyond that were open grasslands, abutted on the west by the sea and on the east by wild woods. In her mind, Naia heard Tavra's voice:

Head north across the Spriton plains and the highlands until you meet the Black River. Avoid the Dark Wood as much as you can; speak not to spirits within it. Follow the river north to Stone-in-the-Wood, then further north to Ha'rar.

Even farther north, past the thousands of grassy hills, a ridge of mountains spanned east to west like the wedged spine of a slithering snake. At its foot was a black river that turned sharply—north again—through wilderness and wood, until it finally reached the Silver Sea. There, the river spilled into the bay upon which a dazzling, glittering stretch of Gelfling villages faced the ocean like a crust of sapphires. Seated at the crown of it was Ha'rar, the home of the Vapra All-Maudra Mayrin.

Tavra withdrew her hand.

"I will make sure your father returns to the glen safely. I hope to meet you again in Ha'rar."

Bellanji gave Naia a tight hug, though she could tell from the flinch in his eye that it pained him.

"Go to the All-Maudra in Ha'rar," he said. "Tell her about what you saw today, both above the water and below. Defend your brother's honor."

"I'll find the truth and bring it to the All-Maudra," she said.

Her father smiled, and even Tavra's eyes softened.

"Take care of my little girl, Neech," said Bellanji.

Neech burbled, hugging Naia's neck. She wiped away a tear, then darted up the nearest apeknot to the north, anxious to begin her journey.

CHAPTER 6

Naia passed into the thinning marsh that marked the final perimeter of Sog. The early evening air was already drier and cooler. As she walked, she plucked stones from the hardening mud and wound them with the stock of rope from her pack, replacing the pair of *bola* she'd lost in the confrontation with the Nebrie. When the suns set, she pulled a cape from her pack and wrapped it over her shoulders and around her neck to ward off the night's chill. She wanted to make it out of the swamp before her first camp, both because it would give her a sense of progress . . . and because she worried that, should she wake in the morning and still find herself in the comfortable, familiar surroundings of the swamp, her courage might fail her and her parents might find her back home in time for supper.

Although the changing environment kept her body busy, the physical exertion left her mind to wander. She thought of Great Smerth, and how she already missed her mother, her father, her sisters, and the hammock in her little chamber. It annoyed her that she missed it all, after so short a time away and after she had longed to leave for so long. Still, with no one else to be witness to the embarrassment, she at least admitted to herself that she was lonesome.

She felt Gurjin's dagger at her side and hoped he was safe. She hoped she might find him, and that when she did, he would have some sort of explanation for all that was happening. Together, they would stand before the All-Maudra and the Skeksis Lords and show that the Drenchen clan was loyal, and that Gurjin was worthy of his post at the Castle of the Crystal.

She thought of Tavra, and their dreamfasted visions—both intentional and accidental. She thought of the feral Nebrie, hearing echoes of its cries in her memory, and she felt the helpless pulses of guilt tingle in her fingers and toes. Every time something stirred in the trees around her, her heart beat quicker, expecting another roaring monster to come crashing toward her . . . but one never did. Aside from the usual fliers, creepers, crawlers, and swimmers, she and Neech were alone. Neech nibbled on the glow moss that felted the trees, absorbing the plants' luminescent aura so he, along with the glittering, flickering nighttime flora, lit their way. Endeavoring to think ahead, Naia stopped once or twice to pluck the glowing lichen and store it in her pack.

The apeknots receded along with the swamp, and within a few short miles, Naia trudged atop the spongy ground of a marshland that would soon disappear altogether, evaporating into the great plains ahead to the north. The Three Brother suns had vanished by the time the last of the marshland dried beneath her exhausted feet, giving way to an open field. She stood at the threshold and looked across it all, trying to comprehend the breathtaking scape of golden-green grass speckled with red flowers, undulating like waves in the wind. Far off in the misty sky were the sloped gray backs of the mountains Naia had only seen in her dreamfast with Tavra, just a ripple of color on the horizon that could almost have been a trick of the eye. Two moons were in the open heavens, one pale and mauve and the other higher, smaller, and silver. Here in the grasslands, no apeknots stood between her and the sky, and she felt dizzy looking up, realizing how big it was and how small she felt.

An intense yawn interrupted her amazement, bringing her attention back to her tired body. It was time to make camp. But where? In the swamp, any big branch would do, but she couldn't rely on apeknots any longer. Instead, she spied a small thicket only a short distance off, a cluster of bushes surrounding a trio of flowering trees. She made quick work of scaling the tree and found a bite to eat stored in her father's pack. Though there seemed to be plenty in the pack, she rationed herself. She wasn't sure how easy it would be to locate food in these new places.

"Guess we'll find out in the morning," she told Neech. She scratched him under the chin, and he gave a little purr.

That night, Naia dreamed she was lying atop a tall hill, staring into the dark heavens. Her hands were linked with another's on either side, grasping tightly yet gently as they dreamfasted together, sharing visions with each other and with Thra, below and all around. The stars twinkled like gems, arranged in constellations Naia had never seen. Only on the horizon could she make out the familiar ringed constellation of Yesmit, Aughra's Eye.

Naia woke with the Great Sun, when her body was rested. The tree's leaves provided ample shade, though through the pinpricks and rounded cracks, she saw streams of warm early light. The blossoms speckled across the branches had bloomed with the morning, twin buds opening into beautiful yellow fist-size balls of fluffy tendrils. Each was tended by an eight-legged flier with spiraling twin proboscides that perfectly matched the conjoined flowers of each bloom. The fliers buzzed back and forth between the blossoms, ignoring Naia and Neech completely. Naia watched them while stretching, massaging her feet before hopping down from the arms of the tree to the dry meadow earth.

Though she had Tavra's verbal instructions and the intense dreamfasted mental map, it would have been easy enough to head north even if she hadn't. The mountains were a constant to the grassy landscape, and at no point were there trees enough to block her view of them. Still, they were so distant yet that it was hard to believe anything—even Ha'rar and the Silver Sea—could exist beyond them. Sog was all Naia had ever known. Now, after seeing the prairie, if someone had told her it was all of Thra, she might have believed them. Smaller fliers drifted between field flowers, some stopping to pollinate while others were snapped up inside the trapdoor petals as soon as they landed. Every third step, the knee-high grass rustled nearby as something scampered away.

When the Great Sun reached its apex and no shadows could be seen, Naia stopped to climb a smooth warm rock to pluck thorns and pebbles from her sore feet. In some places her soles were cracked or even bleeding. The terrain here was so dry and rough compared to the forgiving sponginess of the swamp. The Dying Sun, just a dim purple speck within the Great Sun's light, was grazing the distance where the sky met the land, a place hidden from view within the depths of Sog. She had often heard of the tiny dying sun, and seen it drawn in calendars, but had never seen it with her own eyes. Now she watched it skim the surface of the horizon like a water bug on a still pool of water. Neech was asleep beneath the shade of her locs and cloak, and she wished for once they might trade places and *he* do the walking. This long walk was not the adventure she wanted. She was hungry and irritable, and the day was growing hot and arid.

Naia sighed, then shook out her shoulders and arms. Giving her heel a last rub, she slid down the sitting rock, wishing she could keep the smoothness of the stone under her feet even as she walked through the meadow— Wait! With a spark of hope, Naia opened her traveling pack. Out came a length of woven rope, soft to the touch yet strongly made. She coiled it in her hand and headed for the nearest outcrop of trees that punctuated the land, ignoring the stinging in her feet in the hopes that it wouldn't last much longer. Drawing Gurjin's dagger from her belt, she stooped at the foot of a tree with thick ridged bark and made two swift cuts. Off fell slabs of bark, rippled and rough on one side and smooth as the back of her hand on the other. She cut the pieces to the size of her feet, then pressed the smooth side on her skin and tied it fast with the rope.

Standing wasn't easy, but she got the hang of it. She had excellent balance, after all. Pleased with herself, Naia marched on . . . only to find that, in a few strides, the bark wriggled loose from the rope and slipped out from under her feet. The slack rope that followed got tangled and untied, and Naia kicked at the bark, rope and all, until one flew off her foot, lost in the tall grass.

"Knots-in-a-rope!" she cursed. "Now what?"

All that answered was the soft wind and the rustling of the field. There was no one to hear her frustration. No one except Neech, who merely yawned and tucked his face back under his wing. Even the mountains gazed on with seeming aloofness. With no blister-covered feet of their own to care for, they hardly had reason for sympathy.

Swallowing her frustration, Naia waded into the grass, standing over the sandals when she found them lying in a tangle in the brush. For a heartbeat, she fantasized about leaving them there and turning back. If she hurried, she could be at Great Smerth by sunset, have dinner in the great hall with her family, and tend to her wounded father all before curling up in her own hammock at the end of the night. She let herself imagine it briefly, plopping down in the grass and dirt, and drawing Gurjin's dagger.

"If I go back, then who will go forward?" she asked it, half hoping it might connect her to her brother somehow. It didn't reply, except to glint in the sun—and then she had it. Scooping the sandals into her lap, she used the knife to carve notches along the sides of the wood, just big enough to hold the rope in place. The fit was snug against her foot and ankle when all was done, and she stood and kicked, walked in a circle. Even after a lazy jog, the sandals stayed put.

She looked south toward Sog. Then, decisively, she headed in the other direction, new sandals *click*ing and *clack*ing against the earth.

"*Vas! Tamo, vas!*"

Naia halted at the sound. No, words. Most definitely, but from where? She looked in all directions but saw nothing except grass and darkness. Then it came again, this time with a word she knew.

"*Vas*, Gelfling!"

The grass on her right rustled, then parted, revealing a round brown face with big black eyes.

CHAPTER 7

It was like a little Gelfling, with arms and legs, fingers and toes, but its head was wide where a Gelfling's was long, and its nose was nothing but a rounded bump. A scraggly, thinning mess of red hair was pulled tight under a woven cap, and it wore a dirt-stained shift and a matching pair of trousers. In its chubby hand it held a gardening scoop.

"Gelfling!" it said again. When she didn't respond, only stared dumbfounded, it cocked its head and asked, "*Razumyety?* Ya speak no Podling?"

Naia let out the breath she'd been holding and let her hand fall away from the dagger at her belt.

"No, I don't. I only speak Gelfling."

"Speak only Gelfling! Ha!" the brown man said. He bobbed his head up and down and laughed. "What ya doin' out here? Why ya so green? I never seen a green Gelfling! Ya lookin' for Sami? Ya look lost!" He laughed again, and it reminded Naia of her sisters giggling.

"I'm not looking for Sami," Naia said, but hesitated. "I don't know who she is."

"She! *Prostoduzan.* Sami! Sami Thicket. The *village.*"

He pushed down the grass so he could see, though Naia was

already tall enough to follow his pointing finger. A large thicket was near to the east. She'd seen it earlier, but paid it no mind. Now that the tuber-man was indicating it, though, she could see a thin curtain of smoke rising from beyond the trees and at least one small watchtower protruding from the leaves, well disguised to the untrained eye.

"Village?"

"Yeah, yeah, the village! Gelfling village!"

Naia's heart leaped. A village! She hadn't even thought of that. Of course there would be other Gelfling communities between Sog and Stone-in-the-Wood. Perhaps they could offer her a comfortable place to spend the night.

But then came the anxiousness. She had never met a non-Drenchen Gelfling before, except for Tavra, and that hadn't gone particularly well. Tavra had been the outsider then, and this time . . . Naia's stomach grumbled and she put her hand on her belly to quiet it. Swallowing her pride, she gave her thanks to the little man and headed toward the line of trees. He waved her off, laughing and muttering "*prostoduzan*" again, but if it were to tease her, he did it with a smile on his round little face.

As Naia neared the thicket, she came across more and more of the little people, all kneeling in the dirt with trowels and other gardening tools, digging up roots and crawlers from the earth. They watched her as she passed, though they didn't really seem to care. Their inspection was casual and more out of curiosity than anything. When she reached the shade of the trees, she could clearly see the village within, nestled in the cluster of tall, well-maintained foliage and trunks. She heard talking and smelled cooking fires—then she saw them, two Gelfling, in embossed leather jerkins akin to what Naia might wear hunting, descending from the watchtower. They had dark brown skin and black hair kept in braids and threaded with beads. So these must be the Spriton. Many of the guards at the castle were Spriton, and Gurjin had mentioned their clan before—good with a *bola* and staff, tall and athletic. Yet with the way they approached, no weapon in hand, it seemed they might not have much need to defend the thicket on a daily basis. Perhaps this was the type of duty Gurjin would have preferred to the strict work he'd described at the castle—a duty he could well have done in Sog, while she donned the black-and-violet armor of a castle guard.

"Ho there, Gelfling!" one scout called. "Good travels. What brings you to Sami Thicket of the Spriton?"

"I am Naia, of the Drenchen of Sog," she said.

"Sog?" he asked, and his nose wrinkled a little. He tried to wipe the expression from his face before Naia caught it, but it was too late.

"I'm heading north to Ha'rar. One of the little men pointed me here . . ." That much came easily, but she wasn't sure where to go next. What had Tavra said, when she'd first arrived at the foot of Great Smerth? "I was hoping I might ask . . . the inconvenience . . . of your village's hospitality."

Though Naia had thought Tavra's mode of speech to be flowery and unnecessary, whatever power the words held worked with the Spriton scouts. They looked her up and down, and finding her trustworthy enough, visibly relaxed. One even walked away, waving his hand and leaving the introduction to his partner. The remaining scout gestured and stepped aside.

"Go on, then. The Drenchen have been good border allies to us. See Maudra Mera in the square. But be quick, understand? We're all a bit busy this evening."

Naia bowed uncertainly before following his directions. A wood-slatted fence bordered either side of a wide dirt path that was worn through the thicket. As she neared the center, the dirt gave way to hard walking-stones that echoed with *clicks* and *clocks* as she tread on them in her makeshift sandals.

Closer and closer to the village, she could hear voices and music. The fence gave way on either side to spears driven head-down into the earth. Streamers and ribbons wound and rippled in the gentle forest breeze. At the front gate to the village, the streamers became full-out banners and festival flags painted with the image of long-legged, wide-eared Landstriders in all colors. Naia wondered if the plains-galloping, forest-dwelling Landstrider was the totem of the Spriton clan, as the muski was that of the Drenchen.

Sami Thicket was robust, though not nearly as large as the Drenchen clan's home near Great Smerth. It comprised one main dirt-packed road that formed a large square clearing at the center of the village, where a fire pit was dug and smoldered with coal and wood. Surrounding the square were huts and dwelling mounds, some multiple stories, all formed of clay and stone and wood with round windows built into the sides. The rainproof coverings of shingles reminded Naia of the scales on the ymir-fish she used to catch with Gurjin when they were young.

Spriton Gelfling intermingled with the little people, some chatting, some arguing, some laughing, most working. Once in a while, a shadow flickered overhead as a Gelfling girl flew from one rooftop to another, landing softly before ducking in through a roof hatch. Bustling back and forth across the square, Spriton carried baskets of fruit and nuts, and all around the square, the Spriton erected elaborately decorated banner poles, wound with more ribbons, climbing vines, and huge blossoming flowers. At the opposite end of the square was a large mound of clay brick and heavy logs, far too large to be a single dwelling. Naia wondered if it was the Spriton's gathering place, just like Smerth's great hall back home.

Overwhelmed by the new sights and sounds, Naia stood immobilized, unsure where to begin. The Spriton gave her no mind except the occasional glance, more intent on their preparations. She twice stepped out of the way of a hurrying worker, the first carrying an armful of tinder and the second with a beautifully embroidered cloth, which she flung with grace over one of the several large feasting tables near the center of the square. Naia's stomach groaned again, and she adjusted her cloak and pack, held her chin up, and tried to look respectable as she approached a nearby Gelfling boy seated on a stone. Like the other Spriton, he had skin the color of dark umber and a long thick black braid that nearly reached the ground when he was sitting. He stared intently into his open hands and jumped when Naia cleared her throat.

He closed his hands just before Naia could spy what was in them, and her curiosity overcame her original intention to ask about the Spriton *maudra*, and instead she asked, "What are you doing?"

His startled green eyes brightened like a leaf with the sun shining through it. He was tall but thin, slender where other Spriton his age were growing into their athletic way of life. Where the scouts at the entrance to the thicket had worn and callused hands, this boy's fingers were artful, woven together in his lap. The moment of quiet that nibbled at the end of Naia's question dangled like a blindfish on a line, and the boy suddenly gave a little cough and opened his hands, responding simply, "A nut."

Lying in his palms were two halves of a split nut. The outer shell was tan, with the inside nearly white. At the center was a red seed, and in the meat between the seed and the shell were thin green lines in concentric waving circles and ovals. The patterns were a perfect mirror, identical on both sides. It was interesting, but only to a point.

"Ah," she said, trying to be polite. She'd been the one asking, after all. "I'm wondering if you could direct me to your *maudra*."

The boy cleared his throat and pocketed the nut, ears turning back in embarrassment.

"Oh, of course," he said. "Maudra Mera is at the hearth."

He pointed to the cooking fire at the village center, visible below a whisping plume of smoke that twisted lazily into the sky. There, an older Gelfling was seated, surrounded by children as she gave instruction to the two boys who were much closer to the fire, holding forked branches over the smoldering flame.

"Thanks," Naia said. "Um . . . enjoy your nut."

She left the boy to his own business, following his direction and her nose. She smelled food, and as she drew closer, she could see that there were roasting cherry-squashes on each of the forked prongs. Her mouth watered at the sweet rich scent of the cooking fruit as she listened to the *maudra* call out orders across the square, directing the Spriton that dashed around like busy scully-bugs.

"You Drenchen always know how to be in the right place at the most inconvenient of times, don't you?" said the *maudra* as Naia approached. She smiled, though a bit coldly, and held out her hand as Naia had seen her mother do. Naia took the *maudra*'s hand and focused to keep from dreamfasting by accident. "Welcome to my Sami Thicket. I am Mera of the Spriton. Are you here with your mother? Naia, isn't it? You look just like old Laesid!"

"No, Maudra," Naia said, startled that Maudra Mera might recognize her as the daughter of the Drenchen clan's *maudra*, much less know her name. "I mean, no, I'm not with my mother— yes, my name is Naia. I was traveling to Ha'rar with my father, but he was injured, so now I bear his journey alone."

"Injured! That's just like Bellanji. Well, you are a brave girl to continue alone— Lun! Not so close, don't you see it's smoking? They must be *perfect*! If it burns, I'll see you eat it yourself!"

Naia watched Lun pull the fork farther from the fire and yearned for the squash, even if it was singed. She tried Tavra's approach once more, as it had worked so well with the scouts.

"Maudra Mera, I was hoping for the hospitality of—"

"Of course," Maudra Mera said. "I couldn't very well say no, though the night couldn't be worse . . . Well, what's there to do about it. Lucky girl, though. The Podlings harvested the cherry-squash for tonight, and if these boys don't burn them to crisps, we'll have more than even the lords can eat."

"Oh, thank you—" Naia began. Then the blood drained from her face. "The lords?"

Maudra Mera let out a big sigh and waved her hand.

"Yes, my little soggy one, the lords. For the census. Now listen, they'll arrive soon, so if you're going to be here in the evening, I'll need you to help prepare, and then when they arrive, stay *out* of the way."

Naia's heart beat with excitement and with a little pinch of awe-inspired fear. Only one council of creatures on Thra might be called *lords* by a Gelfling Maudra. They were coming to Sami Thicket? How lucky! To think, only her second day outside of Sog and she was going to see the Skeksis Lords with her very own eyes.

"Of course!" she exclaimed. "I'd love to help!"

"Good girl, then I'll give you a place to start. There's a stream just outside the village to the east. Please see to it that you bathe before supper, would you? You smell of Sog, and I wouldn't want anyone's appetite ruined."

CHAPTER 8

The stream was just outside the village limits, a small trickling thing that was big enough to leap over, should she have a running start. Even at its deepest, the water came up only to her thighs, so she left her clothes, pack, and sandals in sight and sat on a half-submerged rock to let the cold river water run over her. In the swamp, most water was slow and sluggish, full of life. Here, it was quick and so clear, she could see the pebbles and sand at the river floor. Though it gave her a chill, the cool water felt refreshing on her feet, washing away the dirt and pieces of grass that clung to her skin. Neech sniffed the streaming ripples once before puffing up his spines and gliding away to the safety of the riverbed, cowering under the folds of her rumpled cloak.

Naia slipped into the water and knelt so it ran over her shoulders, splashing her face and taking a sip to quench her thirst. Finally, she tilted her head back and fully submerged herself, letting her gills open and taking a big drink.

After she felt clean enough—she hoped—she dressed and squeezed her locs until they were dry. Bathing was largely unnecessary in the swamp, as most of the time the Drenchen were in and out of the water all day long. Naia raised an arm and gave herself a sniff—she didn't smell *that* bad. But if it was Spriton custom and Maudra Mera asked it, she would do it. Embarrassing the Spriton in front of the lords was the last thing she wanted to do, especially as someone who would one day be *maudra*.

She shivered again as she made her way back toward the village, picturing the towering Skeksis with their rings and scepters, gathered in their gargantuan castle. Though she had never seen one, Gurjin had described their feather-adorned mantles and ruby-coated jewelry and gilt crowns encrusted with precious gems. Though they were lords over all of Thra, it seemed they had a particular interest in the Gelfling over other creatures. Gurjin had remarked that they were willing to pay heed to even the poorest or meekest of their race. Their council ruled Thra with a strong hand, full of wealth and bounty that they shared with the Gelfling through All-Maudra Mayrin. They had given the Gelfling people technology for agriculture, for mining, for inventions from wind ships to wheelbarrows. It seemed only proof of their protectorship. They were guardians of the Castle of the Crystal and the keepers of the Heart of Thra, yet they were coming all the way here, to little Sami Thicket, *tonight*.

What kind of faces did the lords bear? She had heard of their long black plumes and ebony beaks, and their omnicient-seeming intelligent eyes. Gurjin had spoken of hardly anything else when he'd last visited. The lords looked straight through you and into you, he'd said. As if they saw a universe inside.

Naia's heart gave an uncomfortable squirm, thinking of her brother. He'd been so full of pride before, telling the stories and filling her with envy, but now he was nowhere to be found.

The Great Sun had all but set, taking the Rose Sun with it, as she returned to the Thicket square. The village was gathering at the center hearth for dinner under the open sky. The roasted cherry-squashes were cut into slices, skewered on sticks, and set on wood trays beside diced roots, leafy greens, and bowls full of fruit. The Podlings scurried around with the Gelfling children, carrying dishes from the hearth to the serving table. A small band played on lutes and forked *firca*, though they had only a single drum. Only the music filled the square, as the rest of the Gelfling whispered anxiously among one another, many standing to the side and holding wrapped baskets and bundles of gifts.

All around, the villagers appeared, each with an offering to add to the table. Her stomach growled and she put a hand over it, hoping it would stay quiet while she waited behind two athletic Spriton girls with smooth ebony hair done in beautiful loops and braids, accented with feathers. Their open-backed bodices let their wings show, long and narrow for speed and agility, whereas Drenchen wings were shorter and webbed, better used for gliding and swimming in the deep of the swamp. Naia swallowed a little sigh and turned her eyes to the front of the square, where Maudra Mera was pacing back and forth, shouting last-minute orders and waving a gnarled old staff back and forth. The *maudra* was robed in a voluminous cloak that ballooned around her thin body. With the staff in addition, she looked like an overturned cup-flower caught in a wind eddy. A gentle giggle chimed like a chorus of bells from the lovely Spriton girls, and Naia smiled with them— until she realized their mirthful eyes weren't on Maudra Mera, but on Naia's feet. Naia looked down; both of the Spriton wore dainty tailored shoes, beaded and strapped to their slender ankles with dyed leather. When the girls saw they had been noticed, they covered their giggles and moved elsewhere. Flushed with embarrassment, Naia quietly slipped off her sandals and hid them in her pack.

"They're here!"

The two words spread like spring rain, first in pairs and then across the entire square in a hushed pitter-patter of whispers. Every Gelfling stared eager-eyed and ears-forward, watching the gate at the Thicket's entrance. The band started up with a ceremonial processional, and Maudra Mera stood solemnly at the end of the main road, hands folded around the neck of her staff. At her left and right were two youngsters, her children, ready to partake in the welcoming of the lords—just as Naia had partaken in the welcoming of Tavra of Ha'rar.

Naia held her breath as ten Spriton guards bearing leadway torches entered in two rows. In the center of the well-lit aisle lumbered two big riding phegnese, resplendent in their brilliant azure plumage. The ground shook under the heavy plodding of their three-toed feet, each with black nails as big as Naia's arm. Their wedge-billed faces were masked and reined, driven by a single Gelfling each, seated where the big birds' necks joined with their lean shoulders. The Gelfling attendants wore light armor, violet cloaks, and adorned helmets, for they were guards from the Castle of the Crystal. Behind, on the saddled backs of the phegnese, were what looked to be crowned heads protruding from

an extravagant mound of lush brocades, velvets, furs, and feathers. They were beaked, with bald heads and narrow-set otherworldly eyes: the Skeksis Lords, Two of Twice-Nine, holders of the castle and protectors of the Crystal.

The Spriton crowded forward with cheers and praise, and Naia lost sight of the lords and their mounts as she fell to the back. Instead, she found a bench and climbed atop it, watching from farther away but higher up as Maudra Mera beckoned the lords to the square.

"Scroll Keeper Lord skekOk! Census Taker Lord skekLach!" she cried. "Come, come! Welcome to our humble Sami Thicket! Please, we have prepared—"

The *maudra* was interrupted by a harsh resounding guffaw that burst from Lord skekLach's barrel-thick body. As sturdy as it was, his phegnese was strained from bearing his weight, no small portion of it made up of the beautifully crafted armor and dazzling adornments he bore on his hefty broad-shouldered body. He kicked a leg over his saddle, and after he dismounted with a thundering *BOOM*, the riding bird nearly toppled in the opposite direction from relief. The second lord, skekOk the Scroll Keeper, remained atop his steed. Unlike his companion, Lord skekOk was thin, his face pointed and narrow, almost like Neech's. He was robed in a bright magenta brocade accented with an extravagantly frilled white-lace ruff. Finely crafted metals were bent and soldered in complicated spirals around gems bigger than Naia's eyes that glittered on the bangles and cuffs up the lord's wrists.

Lord skekLach threw his cloak back into what appeared to be

a plume of red and black, seeming to double his already massive size. There he towered, the village falling still as he cast his gaze upon them, panning slowly to take in every Gelfling face. Then he raised his beak and took a harsh, hard inhale, scenting the thick aroma of the prepared feast. He exhaled and immediately drew breath again, sweeping his head through the air and giving a deep hungry rumble of satisfaction.

"Something," he said, "smells delicious."

"Come," Maudra Mera said, leaping into action. "Will the lords take sup at the head table? This way, this way!"

Lord skekLach grinned broadly, knocking his cloak back at the elbows. His companion, fingering the rim of the shining spectacles perched on his pointed nose, finally dismounted as well, and the two of them followed Maudra Mera to the front of the square. Until this moment, all Skeksis had looked alike in Naia's imagination, but now she saw they were quite distinct from one another. Where Lord skekLach was wide and powerful, Lord skekOk was narrow and shrewd; where one had a beak blunt like a boulder, the other's snout was fleshy and straight. Together they made quite the pair, approaching the head table surrounded by mounds of Spriton offerings. Maudra Mera seemed like nothing but a skittering crawly, zipping back and forth between them, barely avoiding a heavy squishing.

When they finally reached the table, Lord skekLach threw himself into the fat bench prepared for him, skekOk taking a more calculated seat beside him. With great ceremony, Maudra Mera gestured over and over to her sons who stood nearby with a large dish of squash. At her bidding, they hurried forward and placed the offering before the two lords.

"Sweet cherry-squash, my lord," Maudra Mera said, bowing yet again from lack of another position to take. "A specialty of the Spriton clan. Sweet, in thanks for the kindness the lords have shown us, and sour, for the sharp strength of our loyalty to the castle!"

Both lords leaned forward to smell the platter. Though skekOk made a cluck of disdain, turning his head away, skekLach found the roasted vegetables more appetizing. Without further ceremony, he grabbed a fistful of squash, shoveling it into his hooked maw.

The Spriton fell quiet as they waited for his review. Maudra Mera stood before them, hands wringing one another, with every Gelfling in the square holding their breath. The air grew hot and tense in anticipation, and Naia felt an ugly chill crawl up her back. Lord skekLach plucked a final wedge of the stringy vegetable meat, and Maudra Mera tried to hide a tremble while the last wet sounds of Lord skekLach's feasting echoed through the silent square.

The silence was broken when skekLach let out a thundering roar. Naia's heart plummeted in fear. Was he unhappy? What would this failure entail? How might Maudra Mera and the Gelfling of Sami Thicket atone for the displeasure of a Skeksis Lord?

"GWAAAHHHH-HA-HA-HA!"

With a gulp, Naia realized the terrible sound was laughter. Following a collective sigh of relief, the Spriton band started up, and Maudra Mera turned away, wiping her forehead with her sleeves. The reception had passed, and the feast had begun.

CHAPTER 9

Naia sat alone on one of the many benches in the square, eating carefully with a pronged fork that a Podling had offered her. She ate slowly, though she wanted for all the world to scarf it down by the handful in her hunger. No one joined her, and that was fine, or so she told herself. She fed small pieces of food to Neech, but he spit them out, finally gliding free of her shoulder and off into the night to find prey more to his taste. For Naia, the Spriton food was palatable, though she longed for a sliver of fish or wort beetle. For the others—even the Skeksis Lords—it seemed scrumptious. Even well into the night, the two lords continued to call for more platters of food and goblets of wine. She watched them from the far end of the square, determined to stay out of their attention for the duration of their stay in Sami Thicket. This was Maudra Mera's affair. If it were somehow spoiled and Naia was within the village bounds, there would be no hearing the end of it from her parents.

After supper, the children and the Podlings collected the dishes in a barrel of water for rinsing in the river. Naia tried to help, ready to carry a barrel to the river herself, but she was greeted only with cautious glances, so she surrendered her dish with a quiet thank-you. Turning back to the square, she saw a long line of Spriton had formed, leading up to the head table where the two lords were still seated. The platters of food had been cleared and replaced with only a large decanter of wine. Lord skekOk placed before him an enormous stack of paper, bound together with sinewy twine between two heavy leather covers. She'd heard of books before, but this was the first one she'd ever seen. He split it open to some page near the center and, when one of his castle attendants offered them, took a quill and pot of ink and set them to his right. From the distance, Naia watched as each Gelfling stood before him, one at a time, speaking to the lord as he moved the quill across the paper, staining it with a long stream of black ink. Naia jumped when a hand landed on her shoulder. Maudra Mera had joined her.

"The lords are taking count of all who live in Sami Thicket," she said. "Since you do not live here, my little soggy pet, you needn't join the line."

"Why does he take count? The lords have never taken count in Sog."

In fact, Naia wasn't sure the lords had ever *visited* Sog, let alone taken count. The question was probably inappropriate, diving into the Spriton's business, but Naia asked it, anyway. The *maudra* could always refuse to respond. She touched one of Naia's locs absentmindedly, as if she'd never seen a thing like them before.

"It's only worth counting what's valuable," she said, and Naia swallowed the jumble of words that rose in her throat. The *maudra* went on to smooth her cowl, arranging it and setting her black braids just so at her shoulder. "Now, listen, dear. I've put up a cot for you in my chamber to sleep the night. It's a bit cool now, but Mimi will get the fire started soon enough. You're welcome to turn in at any time. But, but, I thought you might like to know, Kylan always tells a song after sup."

In the deepening evening, Naia saw the pointed roof of the dwelling Maudra Mera indicated. Though she wasn't particularly interested in hearing a song, she also wasn't a child, ushered off to bed so early in the evening by her mother.

"Thank you, Maudra," she said. "I'll just need to find Neech, then I'll be over. I don't want him to get lost."

"That *eel?*" Maudra Mera asked. When Naia nodded, the *maudra* sighed but shrugged. "Yes, yes, of course . . . Well, we will see you soon for bedtime. Good night, my soggy dear."

Maudra Mera took her leave, returning to Lord skekLach's elbow as he continued his interviews with the Spriton. As the line dwindled, the children and Podlings came back from dishes duty. Naia walked the perimeter of the square, whistling and calling quietly for Neech as the little ones gathered to sit on the wide walking-stones near the hearth where the cooking fires had died down to glowing red embers. With Lord skekLach's earthshaking voice and Lord skekOk's tinny wobbling one as the backdrop, the children whispered among one another with excitement, and Naia couldn't help but pay attention when a slim Gelfling boy her age approached. It was the boy who had been staring at the split seed-nut when she'd arrived. He held a lute in one hand and took a seat on the bench facing the audience.

It figured such a strange one would be a song teller. Song

telling wasn't popular with the Drenchen. Weaving fantasy stories was a waste of time, according to her mother, who favored hard-talk and action. Stories were only good for distractions. While Naia peeked in between houses and in bushes for Neech, Kylan the Song Teller stood on the hearth and faced the Skeksis Lords, giving a deep well-practiced bow before taking a seat and tuning his instrument. Before long, he launched into a melodic overture on its thin harmonic strings. It was nothing like the Drenchen drums, but it was still beautiful, and he played well.

Naia finally found Neech draped from a small potted tree beside a hut's doorway, crunching on some night bug with happy snaps of his jaw. She gave him a kiss and let him take his place on her arm, making ready to spend the night as quickly as she could in Maudra Mera's home, out of the gaze of the census-taking lords and, as much as possible, out of the *maudra's* as well. With the lords to entertain and their *very important* people to be counted, Maudra Mera had little time for Naia and that was fine enough. She would accept the hospitality for what it was and say her polite good-byes on the morrow. In the meantime, though, she felt more alone in Sami Thicket than she had in the wild field beyond it.

Well, it's to be expected, she thought. *They are Spriton, not Drenchen. Their maudra was very different indeed, so of course their clan was as well.*

From the hearth, along with the melody on the stringed instrument, Kylan began to sing:

Let me tell you a tale of Jarra-Jen

Who flew Thra once over and back again

Met a four-armed monster with half a heart

Jarra-Jen and the Hunter, and the Leap in the Dark

Naia paused to listen. The words sounded peculiar coming from his otherwise gentle voice. The awkwardness that had guarded him before, when she'd spoken to him first, had vanished, and now when he spoke, his tone was alive with energy and confidence. Even the Skeksis Lords turned their heads, Lord skekOk tilting his beak until it was pointed almost straight at the shining Sisters in the night sky.

Now the Great Sun is waning as the Rose One takes chase

Thra's Winter ninet as it drifts us through space

The nights long and chilly, the days short and shy

The Brothers scarce seen all three in the sky

Now traveling by foot through the Dark Wood alone

Making way through the bramble to Stonewood, his home

Fair footsteps fall firmly as he fasts through the fen

Lightning-born, Gelfling hero, our brave Jarra-Jen!

Now Jarra-Jen, by the Skeksis, was truly adored

And this eve he was laden with gifts from the lords

Thanks for telling them tales of his travels abroad

From Ha'rar to the North all the way South to Sog

Now the Three Sisters rising, two bold and one meek

Light the way for our hero as he reaches Black Creek

But the cold wind dies still and he hears in the dim

Monstrous breath heavy through pointy-toothed grin!

Now Jarra-Jen, yea, he turns and he peers through the dark

To see writhing black shadows in the tangled tree bark

And out of the night hover two burning eyes

The wicked horned mask that's the Hunter's disguise!

Now the Hunter, he laughs with a hook-beakéd smile

Picking his teeth with a bone all the while

He steps closer and closer! Stars shine on his face!

Jarra-Jen crouches ready—now the Hunter gives chase!

Now through the Dark Wood, Jarra-Jen, yea, takes flight

'Twas not in his plans to be dinner tonight!

And the Hunter's sharp maw snapping close at his heel

Snatching with claws bent to make him his meal

Now to the high hills of Dark Wood they fly

Jarra-Jen, thinking fast, up an incline he'll climb

Now his toes at the edge of the cliff into black

Seeing nothing below him, he—panting—looks back

Now the Hunter waits behind him

Jarra-Jen, he looks before him

Knowing not what lies below him

He looks to the stars above him

Now holding his breath, Jarra-Jen drops his pack

And slowly, before the dark Hunter attacks

He handfuls of treasure and gifts from the lords

Flings over his shoulders and into the gorge

Now his bag has run empty, and the Hunter comes forth

Jarra-Jen, his ears straining, now prays for his worth

Eyes closing, mouth smiling, "I've heard you!" he breathes

Now jumping outward, into freefall he leaps

Splash!

Up ahead now, above him, the Hunter cries "No!"

Jarra-Jen, yea, he cheers up from far down below

Drifting down the safe landing for which he'd prayed

Where he'd heard treasure falling on calm river waves

Naia hadn't realized she'd been holding her breath. She exhaled slowly and drew another one in. The song was over, and the Gelfling and Podlings alike threw their hands in the air and cheered for the triumphant Jarra-Jen. Even the Skeksis Lords had listened with keen interest, their counting finished. Lord skekLach had his big meaty hands steepled on the table before him, exchanging glances with Lord skekOk and finally giving a low guttural chuckle.

Kylan turned and gave another flourishing bow to the head table where Maudra Mera stood with the lords, then gave a littler bow to his audience of children and Podlings. He handed his lute to one of the youngsters to play with until the children were, one by one, called home by their parents. With as sharp an eye and ear as they had listened to Kylan's story, the lords at the table watched the children disappear in singlets and doublets, ready to be tucked in by their parents within their warm and cozy huts. When the square was nearly clear, with only Kylan and the single hearth keeper's dark silhouettes against the nighttime fire, Kylan packed his lute on his back and approached the head table.

"We counted this one, hm?" Lord skekOk said, leaning toward his fellow as Kylan stood before them with another formal bow.

"Thank you for your ear. I'm honored that . . . ," Kylan said. Some of his confidence had escaped, but Naia couldn't blame him. Even her own courage suffered some withering in the presence of the Skeksis Lords, and she wasn't even the one standing before them.

"With the mother-family, yes," Lord skekLach said, as if Kylan hadn't spoken at all. "Just two, just two in his old house."

"Yes, my lords," Kylan said. "My parents were taken by the Hunter when I was young."

Maudra Mera, standing near the end of the table, stiffened and grabbed the sleeves of her cloak, quickly shuffling forward to take Kylan's shoulders in her hands and begin escorting him away from the gaze of the Skeksis Lords.

"I'm sorry, my lords, he's—"

Lord skekOk held up a hand, the ruffles at the end of his

sleeve flaring like webbed quills. He leaned forward so the tip of his needly nose nearly touched Kylan's. Naia felt her whole body tense, imagining herself in Kylan's place.

"This . . . Hunter. From song," the Scroll Keeper said. "A myth? Some story, made by Gelfling?"

"It's not a myth," Kylan said, but Maudra Mera laughed nervously and clutched his shoulders tightly.

"A story, yes," she added. "To teach the children not to leave their homes after the Three Brothers have gone to bed. You know, they listen to the song tellers more oft than they do their own parents!"

"Songs of brave heroes, thwarting villains," skekOk said, almost humming the words. "Gives a Gelfling hope, eh? Gets a Gelfling through the night? Very well, very well."

Lord skekLach dug his claws under the front cover of his tome and, with an unceremonious gesture, flung the cover forward so the book shut with a cloud of dust and a resounding *thump*. He rose, leaving his quill, inkwell, and the tome to be taken away by one of his attendants.

"Lodging!" he cried.

Rising with the Census Taker, Lord skekOk gazed at the song teller standing uncomfortably before him, clacking his beak and sucking his teeth. When Maudra Mera laughed, much louder than seemed necessary, Lord skekLach jostled her by the shoulder with another clanking, ear-rattling guffaw.

"Lodging, little Gelfling mother! And more wine."

"Yes, my lords, yes— Kylan, run on home now. Good night."

With a peal of coaxing laughter, the *maudra* led the two lords off, and that was the last Naia would see of them. They entered the town hall that adjoined the square, the only place still lit by torches and alive with music and the sounds of wine barrels and clinking cups.

Kylan, left standing at the table, let out a big breath. He held out his hand and looked upon it. It was shaking, nerves not yet calmed from his meeting with the lords. He pushed both hands into his pockets, looking around and meeting Naia's eyes only briefly before departing the square, presumably to wherever it was he called home. Then all was still and the square was doused in silence, so Naia took her time making her way to Maudra Mera's home.

There, on the main floor of the generous two-story hut, she found a stack of blankets and cushions laid out for her by the hearth and curled upon their flat softness. She longed for her hammock, the sounds of her sisters whispering between themselves in the adjoining room, and for the distant echoing footsteps of the Drenchen tapping through Great Smerth.

What were her parents up to? Her mother, tending to her father's wounds, no doubt. Her father, trying to laugh off his pain and discomfort, telling jokes, flirting with Laesid while she told him to stop moving around, lest his wounds reopen. Pemma and Eliona, complaining that it was too early for bed. All this in the warm heartwood of Great Smerth, so far away, it seemed like a dream, or a song someone else might tell.

Her mind inevitably wandered to Kylan and his tale. Jarra-Jen's adventures took place all over Thra, though some songs spoke of his home in Stone-in-the-Wood. She wondered if Jarra-Jen had ever missed home or felt lonely on the long journeys alone. Naia snorted and rolled to her other side, her back sore between the shoulders no matter which way she lay. It didn't matter—Jarra-Jen was a folk-hero, likely not even real. And even if he had been real, so what? The songs might be fun to listen to while they were being sung—but after they were said and done, the song teller's lute was packed away. They didn't help her now. In a way, they were nothing but soft-speak, huff-puff only good for distraction, children, and the curious Podlings.

No, what had been real were the glistening beaks and crafty eyes of the Skeksis Lords. Their coats and cloaks and robes and mantles all layered upon one another in opulent richness, in colors made of dyes Naia had never seen before, most likely cured from the fruits and vegetables all across Thra. And their ornaments! How had they cast such intricate shapes, in twisted metals? And that *book*, that counted all the Gelfling in Sami Thicket, and probably villages elsewhere. How many numbers were within it, and to what end? For whatever end, Maudra Mera would spend the night and the following days pursuing it, that was to be sure. Naia, however, would follow the opposite path, treading alone to stand on trial for her missing brother before the Gelfling All-Maudra.

Well, she would bring honor to her people, if Gurjin would not. Before long, she told herself, the names of the Drenchen would be marked in the thick pages of Lord skekLach's tome, and their number would be recorded in history. That held in mind, Naia stared at the wood beams of the ceiling for a long time, watching the shadows sway until their slow dance finally lulled her to sleep.

CHAPTER 10

The following morning, Naia woke early. Though her body was tired, she was eager to leave Sami Thicket. On the road toward her destination, there would only be plants and animals to deal with. She made her bed and folded the blankets, though in her light sleep, she really hadn't disturbed them much. From the calm quiet that had settled on the square outside, it seemed the lords had taken their leave. When Naia peered out the front-facing window, through a soft cloth curtain, she saw no sign of them, their feathered steeds, or their decorated attendants anywhere. She sucked in a breath when she realized she was not alone in the common room. Maudra Mera was mending pieces of leather with a short tough needle and sinew thread, rocking slowly in a finely finished chair. Her fingertips glowed blue with *vliyaya*, though it wasn't the same healing magic as Naia had learned from her mother. Maudra Mera's power infused itself in the thread with which she sewed, binding it tightly to the fabric through which it wound. Maudra Mera's attention was on her hands, but her voice was for Naia when she said, "Eager to leave, my dear?"

Naia straightened her tunic and brushed off her knees. "Thank you for your hospitality, *maudra*. But I have important business in Ha'rar, so I should be going."

Maudra Mera set aside her craft and walked Naia to the door. Naia's pack was waiting for her, though it looked fuller than it had been when she arrived. Inside she found packed food and a skin of water. Hanging from the side by the laces were a pair of Nebrie-skin shoes.

"Oh!" Naia exclaimed, almost too touched for words. "Thank you . . ."

Maudra Mera tightened the drawstring at the top and hefted it for Naia, helping her sling it over her shoulder. For once, Naia thought the *maudra* might finally reveal some secret fondness for her—but instead, all the woman did was pat Naia on the arm and say, "You'll tell your mother I took you in, won't you? What good care we took of you?"

Naia bit back a sigh and nodded.

"Thank you," she said shortly. "I will."

Sami Thicket was still sleepy in the early morning, the main street empty save for the hearth tender stationed in the center of the square and two night guards relieved of duty, returning home. None paid Naia any mind, not even to stare, as she left. Once she had crossed through the wood that shrouded the village, she paused to sit, digging out her handmade sandals from her pack. She held them in her hands, pride full to the brim as she compared them to the expertly crafted moccasins gifted from the Spriton. She didn't need their charity—yet they were beautiful, in a way, with delicate beadwork and finely cured leather dyed a deep red. The inside was lined with clover fleece, soft and insulated.

Swallowing her pride, she slipped the new shoes on, pulling

the laces taut so the shoes fit snugly. The toes and heel were open, and she imagined she could climb in them—feats impossible in her clunky sandals. Reluctantly, without room in her pack, she left her old sandals on the side of the road behind her. There was no point in holding on to two pairs when she only needed one.

The dirt path cut through the grassland, something she hadn't been able to spot from the long route she'd been taking from Sog. The path had mostly footprints in its sandy wake, though here and there were long ruts made by wheels of wagons and carts. Once and again, Naia heard the voices of Podlings in their Podling tongue, working in the grass and digging up tubers, tossing them into the carts, singing and laughing. The prairie was maintained by them, it seemed. The grass was shorter here, less wild, the flowers growing in rows. As she rounded the big thicket, she saw posts circling a wide field, and far across the gently rolling acres she glimpsed a fleet of white wing-eared animals loping in the distance on legs as tall and narrow as saplings.

Naia's ears perked at the sound of Gelfling voices, calling to one another in the early morning. Up ahead, she saw a second cleared area in the field where the grass had been rolled flat. Several target posts had been driven into the earth there, each painted with different-colored stripes. Four Spriton Gelfling were standing about, three with rope-and-rock *bola* in hand. The fourth was standoffish, eventually dragged closer by one of the boys.

Naia stopped to watch one of the girls hold the *bola* by the handle-weight—a fist-size rock at one end. She swung it over her head so the two counterweights—one at the middle and one at the far end—whipped around in a quickening circle. Finally, she let out a yip and released it. The rocks cartwheeled through the air and snapped around a distant target, the counterweights tying the rope in knots and securing it midway up the post.

The girl cheered and gave a little jump of victory. Two of her companions cheered with her, though the fourth was not so enthusiastic. Squinting, Naia recognized Kylan the Song Teller as the last, stiff like a stalk of grass as a *bola* was shoved into his arms, pushed up to the toe line from which he was to swing. The others chided and hooted at him, and from the way he held it in his hand—at the wrong spot, with the wrong hand—Naia could tell *bola* swinging was not one of his gifts. Reluctant, but jeered into it by his companions, Kylan twirled the weapon. When he let it loose, it was at the wrong time, before the counterweights had fully reached their peak—the *bola* went crashing into the earth, blowing up a chunk of dirt before falling to a pitiful rest not ten paces away. His companions exploded into laughter.

Naia shook her head and re-shouldered her pack, looking ahead to the mountains. She had a long way to go, with no time to waste teaching Spriton youth how to swing a *bola*. She'd had a *bola* in hand since she was a child. One of her first toys, her father had often joked, was a tiny *bola* made of floating wood and vine. Kylan the Song Teller had plenty of his own people to teach him.

The Gelfling voices drew her attention again as the curved road brought her abreast of their target field. The three Spriton had gathered around Kylan, and though Naia couldn't make out all the words, she could hear their tone nudge from teasing to mean-spirited. Kylan went to retrieve his *bola*, but it was so sharply embedded in the earth that he had to use both hands to release it. Even then, when it came free, the recoil sent him stumbling backward, nearly losing his footing and eliciting another round of laughter from his companions. Naia watched for a moment more, until the oldest of the group, a boy with long braids bound with red and purple smimi feathers, reached out to shove the chagrined song teller.

"Hey!" Naia shouted, interrupting the boy before his hands could make contact. "Don't you think he's had enough?"

"Mind your own business, *Drenchen*!" the boy called back, but he turned to face her. While he had his side turned, Kylan snatched up his bag and made a quiet escape toward the road ahead. When the boy with the braids finally noticed, he hissed and shook his head. To Naia, he repeated, "Mind your own business and go back to the bog you crawled out of!"

That got a good response from his friends, though Naia wasn't impressed. She waited until Kylan had gained some distance before taking one of her own *bola* from her pack. From the road, she was twice the distance from the posts that the Spriton were. Swinging with a well-practiced arm and grounded stance, she brought it to full circle in only two orbits, then let loose on the third. The rope-and-rock sailed through the air with perfect precision, latching snugly onto the highest colored band on the center pole.

"That's what they teach us in the *bog*," Naia shouted, grabbing her ears in her fists and sticking out her tongue. Speechless, the Spriton only looked back and forth between her and the tightly knotted *bola* at the top of the post. Neech, who had launched eagerly from her shoulder the moment she'd thrown the weapon, perched on the post in short order, taking the counterweight in his mouth and skillfully unwinding it. From the high vantage, he easily glided back to her with the *bola* dangling from his jaws like a pendulum. By the time he dropped it in Naia's open hands, he was chirping with little pants. She smiled and kissed him when he settled on her shoulder. He wasn't quite big enough to do his job tirelessly yet, but his effort had paid off in front of the Spriton, who gaped as if they'd seen two suns collide. Contented, Naia put her nose in the air and carried on down the trail, confident she'd have no more trouble from their lot.

Up ahead, where his path through the field met the road, Kylan was leaning with hands on knees. When he heard Naia's footsteps, he straightened, brushing his braid over his shoulder and taking in a big deliberate breath.

"Thank you for your help," he said with a trained formality. Naia noted that the woven pack strapped to his back was full, and not with *bola* or whatever else a song teller might take on a normal daily excursion. He had on traveling shoes as well, the same kind as she, but with less beadwork and more stitching. His gaze lingered at her shoulder. "Is that a muski? I've heard of the flying eels of Sog. I've never seen one before. My thanks to you, too, little one."

"You could've helped yourself if you'd fought back," she said, letting Neech's sudden self-contented preening speak for itself. "Those kinds are all talk. Give them a little fight-back just once and they'll leave you alone forever."

Kylan looked warily down the road from where they'd come. Then he straightened his vest, paying it more mind than it required.

"I'm not good at fight-back," he said. "I know I'll have to learn to be, on my journey . . ."

"Journey?" Naia nodded to his pack. "Where I come from, I think we'd call it running away."

"I'm not—!" he exclaimed, but the outburst was sudden with guilt.

Naia chuckled.

"Good luck to you, song teller. Don't let others pick on you like that anymore. A rock's good for one of two things: throwing or hiding under. Pick whichever you want, but the more quickly you decide, the better."

She waved a good-bye and headed down the path, leaving the chagrined song teller behind. The cleared ground was easy to walk on, flattened and free of stickerplant-filled grass. She wondered if it would go all the way to the mountains—if only she could be so lucky! The sky was clear, perfect weather for a long day's journey, and . . . She heard footsteps behind her. Kylan, though a few strides back, was nevertheless on the same path, heading in the same direction, at more or less the same speed. They walked at a constant distance for some time until his eyes on her shoulders became so distracting that she slowed her pace enough for him to walk side by side. He smiled, and she didn't smile back, unsure whether she wanted to become attached to a song teller on a journey like the one she was on.

"Where are you headed, then?" Kylan asked.

"Ha'rar, at the coast of the Silver Sea," she replied. Hoping he'd take it as a warning, she added, "It's a long way, through wilderness."

"Ah!" Kylan said. "*North toward the misty peaks, through the Darkened Woods we creep, along the Blackened River deep. If I remember right, Stone-in-the-Wood is along the way, isn't it?* That's where I'm going."

Naia shrugged in agreement. She knew from her dreamfast with Tavra that Stone-in-the-Wood was the halfway point between Sog and Ha'rar.

"Would you mind if I joined you?"

The question was so polite that Naia very nearly agreed on principle, but she imagined any number of dangers they might encounter on the way. In her mind, each scenario was made more dangerous when she pictured protecting a Spriton song teller who couldn't throw a *bola* to save his life.

"Well, I'm not sure . . . ," she began. She tasted soft-talk forming on her tongue, and before the flavor could overwhelm her, she stopped and turned so they were facing each another. It wasn't fair to either of them, really, and she knew better than to try to sweeten the inevitable.

"Listen. Song Teller. I need to reach Ha'rar as soon as possible with a message for the All-Maudra. I don't know how long it will take me, but I don't have time to waste—"

He held up his hands. "You won't have to take care of me. I promise, I—"

"You can't even throw a *bola*!"

Again, his ears folded and he curled his lips in. A flush of guilt hit her cheeks, but she stood her ground. It was the truth, anyway.

"Maybe not, but I can be useful in other ways," he said. "At the very least, I promise I won't slow you down. I may not be good at hunting, but I'm a good cook and I tell a good song."

"Songs won't help on the journey I'm on," Naia said. Although it was true, her belly rumbled a little, as if whispering to her in protest.

Kylan caught the bit of hesitation and insisted, "I can record our journey in exchange for your protection from ruffnaw and—and fizzgigs!"

Naia barked one accidental laugh at the thought, shutting her mouth quickly after, but it was too late; the smile was already on her face. She tried to lose it, but it haunted her lips.

"Firstly," she said, "I don't need my journey recorded or songs during camp. Secondly, I would hope there isn't a Gelfling alive who'd need protecting from a fizzgig!"

"But in *Jarra-Jen and the Maw of the King*, the Fizzgig King eats Jarra-Jen whole," Kylan said. If anything, he was determined, and he'd seen that smile. "*To escape the huge maw was no easy feat; Jarra-Jen, yea, he tickled the King's throat with a leaf—*"

"It sounds stupid," Naia interrupted, but the smile was returning at the idea of a fizzgig swallowing someone whole— what nonsense! Jarra-Jen would have had to be an awfully small hero indeed. But Kylan's words were strong, putting the ridiculous image in her head: a red-and-orange fluffy ball of fur big enough for a Gelfling hero to stand in. Before she knew it, she was almost laughing at the idea. Trying to hide her mirth, she turned away, hearing Kylan following.

"And when the King wouldn't burp for his part, Jarra-Jen tickled backward and King let out a big—"

Naia burst into laughter, unable to contain it. The story wasn't even *that* funny, but she hadn't laughed since leaving home, and the feeling was so good, she didn't want it to end. It was like a friendly fire, growing stronger with every round. She knuckled the laughing tears from the corners of her eyes, chuckled some more, and kept walking.

This time, Kylan didn't follow, seeming as if he'd finally gotten the message. He stood there, quiet and solemn, holding the straps of his pack and looking forlornly after her. Just when he was about to disappear on the trail behind her, she stopped and turned back with a little sigh.

"Well, Song Teller?" she called. "We're still a long way off. We don't have time to stand around like sticks in mud!"

His head popped up, ears pointing to her, and she saw a grin grow on his face. He quickened his long-legged gait to meet her, and then, elbow to elbow, they were off into the rolling golden hills.

CHAPTER 11

Kylan was quiet while they traveled, holding the straps of his pack and looking left and right, constantly absorbing the scenery with an active focus. It made Naia feel more comfortable in her own keen curiosity. For her, their surroundings were foreign, but out of pride she tried not to seem *too* interested. Together they watched the clouds spiral in the sky, the hills crawling with grasses and roaming shrubs, the wind come alive with the voices of the prairie creatures. True to his word so far, Kylan kept pace with Naia on his skinny legs, breath never growing short, never once complaining for rest even after a long day's journey. It wasn't until much later that he finally broke the silence, and then only with a question.

"How do the Drenchen fly?"

The question brought Naia's gaze out of the clouds down to Kylan's inquisitive green eyes.

"What do you mean? With wings, like all Gelfling."

He nodded to her pack, held tight on her back and shoulders by two arm straps. Naia's cheeks warmed. If she *had* wings, wearing a man's pack like her father's would make it very difficult to use them indeed. She was glad for her dark skin, imagining how bright her blush would have been had she a complexion more like Tavra's.

"This is my father's pack," was all she said.

"Oh." She half expected him to pursue the topic, but instead, he simply asked, "Your mother is the Drenchen Maudra Laesid, the Blue Stone Healer?"

Eager to change the subject, Naia nodded. That Kylan knew her mother's name endeared him to her, though she hated to admit it.

"Yes. I'm the eldest of her daughters."

"So when your mother retires, you would become the *maudra*."

"Yep," Naia said, wondering what he was getting at. "That's how it works."

"Doesn't that scare you?"

She laughed. "My family has been the *maudren* for as long as there have been Drenchen. I'm learning *vliyaya*, and I'm trusted with a spear and *bola*. I know Sog blindfolded, above water and below. What's there to be afraid of?"

Kylan shrugged.

"Maudra Mera often laments the matriarch's burden. She struggles to maintain order in Sami Thicket and the other nearby Spriton villages. I suppose if it's not so difficult in Sog, it wouldn't be such a trouble."

"There are plenty of difficulties. When I was young, I didn't understand, but in my training, I'm learning. Being *maudra* is a responsibility and a blessing. I always wished I had been able to explore Thra—see the Silver Sea, the Caves of Grot—but . . ."

Naia trailed off when she realized what she was saying. Kylan was thinking the same thing, nothing but a smile on his thin lips.

She snorted and waved the idea away, changing the subject yet again, taking her turn asking questions.

"Have you traveled beyond the Spriton lands before, Kylan the Song Teller?"

Kylan shook his head and pointed. Up ahead, on the horizon between them and the mountains, was a growing dark line that Naia took to be a huge expanse of wood.

"No farther than where the wood begins," he said. "The trail till then runs easy, but the Dark Wood . . ."

Tavra's warning about the Dark Wood tickled the back of Naia's mind, and Kylan's nervous unended statement did nothing to calm her worries. It didn't matter, though. All they had to do was skirt the wood as much as possible. If it were too dangerous a route, Tavra would have said so.

"Isn't there a way to the Black River without going through the wood?"

"Yes. There's a trail that leads above it, through the highlands," Kylan said. "And it's just a forest, after all . . . But I always think of the songs."

"Jarra-Jen and the Hunter? Aren't those just songs? I'd never heard of the Hunter before I left Sog, but everyone's heard of Jarra-Jen."

"Songs carry truth," he replied. "Jarra-Jen was a real hero, and the Hunter is a real villain."

Naia remembered what Kylan had said to the Skeksis Lords about the Hunter and his parents.

"So . . . you've seen him?" she asked quietly. "The Hunter?"

He clenched his hands into fists.

"Yes," he said. "No one will believe me. Everyone thinks he's just a tale to frighten children. Maudra Mera thinks my parents were taken by a hungry forest creature while they were in the Dark Wood—or that they fell in the Black River and were swept away. She thinks I imagined it—the four-armed shadow with the bone mask—but I know what I saw. Even after we dreamfasted, she doesn't believe, and saw only darkness in my memories."

"I'm so sorry," Naia breathed. She imagined herself in Kylan's place, how alone it would feel to have lost her loved ones and then have no one believe. It was hard for her to think that a monster as terrible as the Hunter he'd described in his song could possibly exist, but the Dark Wood was no small thicket. There was no telling what lurked within its mysterious depths.

"I dreamed the song of Jarra-Jen and the Hunter afterward," Kylan said. "Maudra Mera lets me tell it because it keeps the children entertained. She likes the idea of the Hunter as a story, but she'll never admit he's real."

"So you're going to Stone-in-the-Wood to prove it?" Naia asked, completing the circle. "Are you going to find him and try to avenge your parents?"

"I don't believe in vengeance," Kylan replied. He looked up. "But I don't want what happened to my parents to happen to anyone else. I don't know what I'll do when I reach Stone-in-the-Wood, but someday, I'd like to find the Hunter and stop him."

Naia smirked.

"You'll have to learn to throw a *bola* if you ever want to do that," she said. "Or find one big enough to hide under."

Kylan didn't respond to the lighthearted tease, probably thinking about the Hunter and his parents, so Naia left him alone. She hadn't given the Hunter much thought, but now ... did she believe Kylan, after what he'd told her? She thought of asking him to share the memory with her in dreamfast—but she didn't want to ask him to relive the moment he lost his parents, whether or not it proved the existence of the Hunter.

"Maybe if you don't find what you seek in Stone-in-the-Wood, you can come back to Sog with me," Naia chirped, hoping to lighten the mood. "I could teach you to throw a *bola* there, in the apeknots where I taught my younger sisters. You could tell songs at the drum feasts ... It would be a rare occasion!"

Naia smiled in relief when a bounce returned to Kylan's step.

"You don't have a song teller in your clan?" he asked.

"Not really. We keeps songs of historical importance, of course. Mesabi-Nara's first steps into Sog, the founding of Great Smerth. That sort of thing. But we don't waste time and breath with fanciful stories every night 'round the hearth."

"I see," Kylan said. "Ah, Mesabi-Nara is the Maudra of the Deep, is she not? *Blue stone Gelfling, born in the sea, with lungs as well as gills to breathe?*"

"You've heard of her?" Some of that clan pride crept into Naia's voice, whether she liked it or not. Kylan nodded, and a big smile warmed his face now that he'd gotten even a little excitement out of his otherwise quiet companion.

"Of course, the first Drenchen, the inventor of healing *vliyaya!*

Oh, you must tell me the songs you know. I'd love to hear them. I'll sing them at the hearth . . ." This time, Kylan was the one who let his sentence wither. He glanced over his shoulder, back down the path, though the Spriton town was long behind them.

"You can still go back, you know," Naia said. "No one will even notice you left if you turn back now."

She stopped when he did, wondering if their companionship would end so quickly after it had begun. If he went back now, maybe she would miss him—no, that was silly. She'd hardly even gotten to know him—but it didn't matter, either way. Kylan shook his head and turned toward the north with a stern grunt of decision, walking ahead. Naia followed him, and that was the last either of them said on the matter.

The mountains seemed just as far-off as ever, even by the time the sky darkened. Naia wondered if they were only an illusion. They made camp in the lee of a boulder, shedding their heavy packs. Kylan made a fire—quickly, at that—and Naia took up a couple *bola* and her knife. Neech was waking, every quill alert, gliding nearby in short swoops before resting on Naia's shoulder again, ready to hunt for supper. Nighttime critters rustled in the tall grass, all around, and before too long, she struck one with her *bola* and called for Neech to find it. He did. It was a furry little shrub beetle with six jointed legs. Naia picked it up by the hair on its back and carried it back to camp. Kylan yelped and recoiled when she pushed it at him, slowly squirming legs and all.

"Dinner!" she declared.

"How do you know we can eat it? What if it's poisonous?"

She held it to her nose and gave it a big sniff. It smelled earthy and a little bit like grass. Her stomach grumbled.

"Anything you sniff and still want to eat can't be poisonous," she said. "Drenchen motto: Trust your gut. Anyway, weren't you saying you were a good cook? A good cook should know a great dinner when he smells it."

Kylan assumed a stern expression for the first time since she'd met him, a little bossiness creeping into his voice at her challenge.

"What if smelling good is just a trick? Or what if something smells good to one person, but terrible to another? What if it's not just poisonous to eat, but poisonous to touch?"

"Well, what do you expect me to do?" she asked. "It's the best I could catch. Would you rather just go hungry? There's no other way for us to know."

He held up a finger, and the fire glinted in his eye.

"There is another way," he said.

Naia sighed and held the wiggling shrub beetle while he dug through his pack. From its bulk, she'd thought it to be full of traveling gear or rations, but now she saw it was mostly papers and papyrus, scrolls, and *books*. Kylan withdrew one of the folios and paged through it, carefully turning the sheets of thick paper with two fingers.

"Ah! Here, it says this is a burrowing noggie, and it's safe to eat if we shuck off the outer shell. Often prepared roasted and seasoned with herbs."

"That's what I said: safe to eat. This gut doesn't lie!"

Kylan snorted and snatched the noggie. "It says here that if we don't shuck off the shell, we'll be bedridden for a week, and smell of lumproot for twice that. Did your gut tell you that much?"

Naia grinned, taking her own turn at feeling a bit sheepish, but enjoying seeing a bit of assertiveness from the Spriton boy. She sat by the fire while he laid the noggie down on a flat area of the boulder nearby, killing it with a swift blow from a smaller stone. When he set the rock down and closed his eyes, Naia did so as well, taking part in the solemn silent prayer they offered in thanks to the noggie that had given its life for their supper.

Afterward, Kylan shucked the shell as it instructed in his book and prepared it for the fire. They sat in silence while supper sizzled, the creature's under-shell popping every once in a while under the heat. The smell of the roasting noggie meat was woody and savory. Kylan sat with the book on his lap, smoothing the pages and looking upon them in the flickering firelight.

"How did you learn to read?" Naia asked, impressed.

"I learned from Maudra Mera, so I could read all the tales of Jarra-Jen," he said. "Our clan doesn't have a dream etcher, and since I'm no good at anything else, she thought maybe I could take that place . . . I suppose her efforts are wasted now that I've left."

"You know writing *vliyaya?*" Naia gasped. Reading was one thing, but dream-etching . . . "Words that stay?"

In answer, Kylan spread his hands above the book, where the picture of the noggie was already etched alongside rows and lines of swirling, intricate markings. Naia sidled closer to watch.

"Maudra Mera is stern and often cranky, but she is a dream etcher, and she taught me after my parents died. Even when I tried her patience. I practice whenever I can."

He stretched his slender fingers and held them over the book, focusing. His hands brightened with a gentle blue fire, and as he moved his hands, delicate spirals, lines, and dots lit the air in the path his fingers took. The shapes he drew settled into the pages, smoldering into deep lines of charcoal black. The enchanted shapes flowed from his fingers like music from his lute, all intertwined in long lines across the pages. It was like an intricate tapestry and so mysterious, for Naia could tell that the shapes were not only beautiful but meaningful.

When Kylan was done, he pointed to a string of intricate swirls and loops, straight lines, and dots.

"I wrote about the noggie, where we found it and how we prepared it. That way, if someone else reads it later, they'll have our experience to learn from as well. And that's your name. *Naia.*"

He pointed to a special shape among all the others. Naia tried to memorize it—the shape of her name, right there for anyone to see, long after she'd gone. She traced over the drawn words with her eyes, afraid to touch lest she smudge them.

"What did you write about me?"

"I wrote your words," he said. "Always trust a Drenchen's gut!"

Then he winked and Naia laughed.

"None of our people have mastered dream-etching *vliyaya*," she said. "Long ago, our elders did. They left behind some tablets, and some old things written in Old Smerth's halls . . . but we only remember the meaning."

"The Drenchen are known for their words and feats of strength," Kylan said. He looked upon the etching. "I suppose the Spriton are known for their spears and *bola*, but . . . if I could choose, I would like to be known for this."

"I get the feeling you will be," Naia said. She smiled and, in return, got a smile out of her companion. From the mouthwatering aroma, she could tell their dinner was done, and pulled the skewers from the fire. She handed one to Kylan, and when he sniffed it, his stomach gave a loud growl that made them both giggle.

"Trusting my gut," he said, and took a bite.

She grinned and picked a twig from the ground and poked at the fire with it, letting loose a *pop* and a flurry of twinkling sparks. Content, with bellies full, they watched the embers dart back and forth on their way into the night sky.

Later, after a rest much more restoring than her previous night in Maudra Mera's home, Naia packed while Kylan snored a little while longer. She rekindled the fire to dry the dew from their packs, and by the time she'd just about finished preparing to put out the fire, Kylan finally stirred. He rolled onto his back and stretched.

"Time to go?" he asked.

"Unless you want to travel on your own, stick-bug," Naia chided. She kicked him playfully, and he sat up. He carefully folded his sleeping roll. She expected him to complain and ask if they would need to maintain such a schedule every morning, but all he did was dutifully pack his things until he was standing beside her. Together, they pushed dirt on the fire and headed back to the trail. At first it was quiet, and Naia reveled in it, watching the Rose Sun join the Great Sun on the horizon, adding its pink hue to the palette of the cloudless sky. The air was full of flitting bugs and territorial calls of fliers and crawlers. Kylan walked off the path, meandering behind and to the left, behind and to the right, carrying a twig in hand and poking at grass and the occasional shrub or animal. Naia took the more pragmatic route along the flattened earth, hardly interested in any of the wildlife that surrounded them until it was time for dinner.

"May I ask about your business in Ha'rar?"

Kylan's question, interrupting the silence, was innocent enough. Still, Naia pressed her lips together, thinking. There wasn't anything wrong with telling Kylan about Tavra, was there? After all, it was Tavra who had come to Great Smerth looking for Gurjin. It wasn't as if Naia had anything to hide. Still, she didn't feel like telling Kylan that her brother had been accused of treason, fled, and left her to stand trial in his place.

"I'm looking for my brother, Gurjin," she said instead. "He's a guard at the Castle of the Crystal and he's gone missing. The All-Maudra is looking for him, too." And then there was the darkened Nebrie, and the crystal veins in the mud . . . "I have a message for her from one of her soldiers."

Kylan stood straighter at just the mention of the All-Maudra, though her land was farther away than even the mountains ahead.

"I didn't realize . . . ," he began. When he looked at her this time, a new respect had settled on his features—chased by a worried wrinkle to his brow. "Is something wrong?"

Telling him *no* would be a lie, but Naia didn't particularly want to tell him *yes*, either. After all, she didn't know exactly what was going on. Even Tavra had been surprised by the Nebrie, though from the urgency with which she'd sent Naia to Ha'rar, it seemed the All-Maudra's soldier might have an inkling as to what it meant.

"I don't know, but I do know that not everything is right," she said, kicking a pebble as she walked. When her companion didn't answer, she looked to see what he was thinking, and halted with a lurching feeling.

Kylan was gone.

CHAPTER 12

"Kylan? Kylan!"

Naia trotted back a few paces, looking left and right. In the open field, he should have been easy to spot—but there was no sign of him. Not even his pack or a shoe. She hoped he hadn't stumbled and fallen into the tall grass, or worse, been carried off by some animal.

"Over here . . ." He somehow sounded both distant and close by, but—most importantly—safe. Naia let out the breath she'd been holding and followed his voice, stepping off the trail when he called once more. His words were muffled, hard to make out—and then she heard him clearly.

"Watch out!"

Too late. Naia's breath leaped out of her lungs as her foot met air. Instead of the mound of earth she was expecting beneath the thick, tangled grass, there was nothing but a hole. She lost her balance and was falling, and although it was only a short distance before she landed solidly on her rear end, she knew she'd have bruises from it later. She coughed at the dust that had clouded up from her fall and heard Kylan doing the same.

"I told you to watch out," he said.

Naia waved the last bits of dust haze away, standing. She

had landed, almost on top of Kylan, in a dug-out cavern. Roots lined the walls, and the smell of soil and vegetation was thick in the air, but from the makeshift shelves and wicker furniture that lay in neglect, it was clear the burrow had been someone's home. Up above, the hole they'd fallen through let in the remaining daylight from outside. Naia glanced at Kylan as he rose, rubbing his backside. He seemed fine, though the dry red dirt that now coated his tunic and hair gave him the appearance of an unamoth that had just come out of its cocoon. She expected him to sprout antennae any moment.

"Who lived here?" she wondered out loud, touching the wall nearest and then crouching to inspect a little wooden rocking chair. The seat was much too small for an adult Gelfling, but a child might have used it—or, she noted, one of the little Podlings. The wicker was dry and cracked, overgrown with a pretty turquoise plant. From the color and shape of the leaves, it seemed the same sprawling flora covered almost every surface of the little room, from the walls to the ceiling. It was quiet and gentle, with delicate white flowers and coil-like tendrils dangling like curled ribbon.

"Looks like Podlings," Kylan said. "Yes, see. This is one of their gardening scoops. But it's so old and dusty . . . I wonder where they went?"

"And left all their things," Naia added. She moved through the room, poking and prodding at the shelves filled with decorative stones caked in dust, carved wooden talismans, and clay pots whose contents had long since dried and been eaten by crawlies. A doorway, half-covered with a brittle woven curtain, was dug into the room at the far wall. Naia pulled the curtain back and peered down a dark hallway blanketed ceiling to floor with teal leaves and twinkling, pearlesque blossoms. Though the flowers gave off some light, the tunnel was otherwise drenched in shadow. She grinned.

"Let's see where it goes!"

Kylan hadn't moved far from where he'd landed, still brushing dust from his front and patting it out of his braids. He followed her gesture with a little curiosity, but his feet didn't move. She realized as he stared into the blackness down the tunnel that he was afraid. Before she teased him about it, she remembered the fate of his parents. Perhaps the fear of the dark wasn't so silly after all.

"You stay here and find a way out, then," she said. "I'll be back soon."

He didn't want her to go, but he didn't protest. He nodded nervously and said, "Be careful."

With no openings to the world above, the tunnel began dark and grew darker still as Naia followed it away from Kylan in the main chamber. The ceiling was low and rounded at a height for creatures of smaller stature, and Naia had to creep with bent legs to keep from bumping her head along the top of the corridor. She trailed a hand across the overgrown wall to keep her bearings, feeling the soft spongy tendrils and leaves of the life that had taken root in the cavern's abandoned insides. The leaves and coils shivered as she passed, crowding around her fingers to take in her scent, kissing her knuckles and fingertips.

Tilting her head, she looked closer at the surface of the wall. Beneath the overgrowth was a faint light, and she parted the tangles of the plant to look closer. It was dirt and rock beneath the lacy roots, but there was certainly *something* . . . She dug with her fingers, pulling at the dry soil and old clay until a crumbling handful fell away. What she saw beneath sent an icy lance through her: A bright mineral shimmered deep in the darkness of the earth—something crackling, glimmering. Dark. Violet.

"The crystal veins . . . They're spreading . . ."

"Naia! Help!"

She shook off the fear-struck numbness, sprinting down the hall to find Kylan facing the wall, one hand pressed over his mouth. At first she saw nothing, but then she heard it: the sounds of scratching and digging. The leaves of the plant that covered the burrow shivered, and then sand and small pebbles trickled down the wall. Naia could feel a growing tremble under her feet. Something was making its way through the earth, and it was *big*. The cavern steadily filled with a familiar disturbing sensation, as if the song of Thra was being drowned out by something darker, more chaotic. It was the same as she had felt in the swamp, standing in the shadow of the darkened Nebrie.

"It's the Hunter," Kylan whispered, grabbing her arm in terror. "He's here. He took the Podlings. Now he's come to take us!"

A brief imagined vision of the wall falling around them to reveal the bone-masked monster from Kylan's songs sent a shock of panic through Naia's body, but she stayed calm for her companion's sake.

"It's going to be all right," she said. "But only if we can get out of here. Soon."

"Can you fly us out? Quickly!"

Naia swung her pack down and knelt, searching feverishly for the length of rope she'd packed, but it was buried in between food and *bola* and—there! But it was tangled, and as she struggled to straighten it, the grating, deafening sounds spread to all their surroundings. She yanked out spans of rope, but before she could straighten more than her height's length, the wall cracked, then buckled, then crumbled. The earth fell away in huge rocky chunks to reveal a black furred monster, twice as tall as Naia and many times bigger around. Though it was a predator—its enormous claws made that clear enough—Naia felt the heavy weight of panic drop from her chest. It was not the Hunter.

"A ruffnaw?" Kylan squeaked, naming a beast Naia had never seen before. They froze instinctively as the monster halted, disoriented in the open air of the Podling burrow. It had thick oily fur coated in dirt and mud, and its eyeless face was spiked with hundreds of long whiskers. At the end of its pointed nose was a red flanged cluster of nostrils that flared when it took in the open air, flashing a warning crimson. The color was a sign of danger, and so were the huge hooked claws that made up the creature's front paws.

Behind the ruffnaw, sheets of the glass-like violet mineral glowed hot in the earth where the soil was falling in damp dark clumps.

Naia reached out and grabbed Kylan's hand, dreamfasting to avoid making any noise. He accepted her link with a rush of warmth.

It's darkened, she whispered into his mind, sweeping aside his other thoughts and fears and memories in order to focus on simply communicating. *It's been enraged by that crystal in the earth—we can't expect it to behave normally!*

Kylan swallowed, and his hand shook in hers, but his chin dipped in a little nod of bravery.

If—if we stay quiet and don't move, it might leave us alone. Ruffnaw hunt by sensing movement, not by sight . . .

His advice was obvious and belated, probably from some song, Naia guessed, instead of out of common sense. Even so, she wasn't sure common sense mattered right now. The ruffnaw crouched before them in the entrance it had made, breathing heavily through its glistening star-tentacled muzzle. Little drops of mucus flew from its nostrils, and its sides heaved with its panting, its slick fur standing on edge. Seeing it in such a state evoked such a heavy dread that Naia felt as if she were sinking into it, stuck with both feet, unable to move. The Nebrie was not the only darkened creature, and the crystal vein, deep in Sog, was not the only instance of the cursed mineral. Wherever the sickness had begun, it was spreading.

What would happen if it spread all the way to Thra's heart?

Kylan released her hand and slowly backed away, but there was nowhere to escape. Naia clutched the rope in both hands, calculating how hard she'd have to swing the counterweight, and at what angle, to get it out of the opening overhead and far enough away that it would—hopefully—catch onto something. Then they could climb to safety.

The brief opportunity of stillness expired. Sensing their movement, the ruffnaw lunged, claws spreading. Kylan yelped as the furry beast fell on top of him. Naia grasped after it, not knowing what else to do except try in vain to keep it away from her companion. She felt the thick strands of the ruffnaw's fur race through her fingers, and then her grip held, firm around its sinewy pink tail. Though she couldn't restrain the huge creature by force, her grasp distracted it long enough that it turned back at her, letting out a high-pitched hiss and spraying her with saliva. She thought of grabbing Gurjin's dagger from her belt and plunging its blade into the ruffnaw's vulnerable muzzle, but the memory of the Nebrie in the swamp stayed her hand. Instead, in desperation, she reached out to the ruffnaw with her mind. She first felt a searing, blinding light, then saw a dark jagged silhouette floating in a tunnel of fire, and finally felt the groaning of Thra itself—creaking and moaning in agony.

A piercing whistle reverberated through the tiny burrow, and the ruffnaw went still from nose to tail. Naia felt its fur raise, going all on end, and something in it changed. Her hand felt hot where she had touched it—*dreamfasted* with it—and its fur slid away from her grasp as it backed away. The whistle came again, and the ruffnaw needed no more incentive. It was gone, back down the tunnel from which it had come.

Naia fell to her knees and held her hands over her breast, wishing she could calm the pounding of her heart with pressure of palms alone. She squeezed her eyes shut and saw glimpses of the vision . . . the dream the ruffnaw had shared with her, whether it had done it intentionally or not. The darkness in the earth and the electric violet light—the same she had seen with the Nebrie. Only this time, to her relief, the encounter was over and no blood had been shed. Her ears were ringing, but through it she heard someone kneel beside her. Kylan touched her shoulder.

"Naia," he was saying, "Naia, are you all right? We should get out of here."

Naia felt numb, but Kylan was right. She felt around in the dirt and rubble until she found the length of rope, and stood. The ruffnaw might come back, and the next time, who knew what might happen. She gave a soft grunt and launched the rope's counterweight overhead, letting it land before tugging. When she felt the line was secure enough, she tightened the straps on her pack and held the rope for Kylan to climb first. While he did, she took in the abandoned burrow for the last time . . . then pulled herself up to daylight.

They sat in the grass to catch their breaths and put themselves back in order. Naia wound the rope around her elbow and thumb to still the shaking in her body.

"What happened? With that whistling call . . . Was that you?"

Kylan put his small fingers into his mouth and curled his lips in, then blew a loud, bold whistle that carried across the plain. He put his hands in his lap and shrugged.

"The ruffnaw fears the hollerbat call," he said. "I heard it in a song."

Naia sighed, but whether it had come from a song or not, it had worked. She couldn't deny that. She focused on stowing the rope, then checked her pack to see if anything was missing. At the very bottom of it, hiding in a bedroll, she saw a trembling tail, and pulled. Out came Neech, ears flat along his body and eyes big and alert. She stroked his head and scratched his chin until he relaxed.

"It's all right. It's over. No thanks to you, little spithead." To Kylan, she said, "Are you hurt?"

"No. Are you?"

"I don't know . . . I'm not hurt in body. But . . ." She shook her head, trying to put into words what had happened. It had all been so quick, and powerful, and her head was still spinning. She sat down, feeling weak, pressing her hands against her face. "I think I dreamfasted with the ruffnaw . . . I saw within its mind, and it saw within mine . . ."

"You dreamfasted?" Kylan gasped. "With the ruffnaw? Is that possible?"

Naia shook her head.

"I don't know. All I know is my head hurts."

Kylan squatted beside her, hand on her shoulder, lips pressed together, and brows furrowed. Then he stood.

"I think we should call it a day," he said. "Come on. Can you make it to that tree?"

The tree Kylan had picked wasn't far off, and he helped her by taking her pack and bearing some of her weight while she leaned on his shoulder. She tried to keep her mind trained on the path and the fields, the rustling of the nearby trees and the pastel sky overhead, but it all blended together. Even the big breaths of dry meadow air left her exhausted. In her weakened state, some dreams passed between them. She saw the fear he'd felt, looking in the face of the mindless ruffnaw, but within it she also saw the flicker of strength. What she shared with him in return were muddled visions of looking up toward the exit to the burrow, the heavy weight of shame at not being able to save them with the wings she didn't yet have. The rest she kept hidden from him, though the effort left her dizzier still.

By the time Kylan lowered her to a patch of soft grass beneath the shadow of the tree, her wits were returning, but she still felt tired. She stayed quiet while he settled their packs and kicked grass aside to make a fire.

"I can't help but feel like there's something you aren't telling me," he said, mostly to himself, as if he didn't expect a response at all. "You didn't seem surprised at the way the ruffnaw was behaving."

Naia was half inclined to let his words become lost on the cool wind, but maybe he was right. They had been in danger—real, dire danger, and for Naia, it wasn't the first time since setting off. Kylan wasn't her ward, but they were companions now. Maybe even friends. Maybe she owed it to him. Making up her mind, she held out her hand to him. Recognizing the gesture, he clasped her hand in his, and she felt the link of the dreamfast warm again. At first it was a trickle, like water drops gathering on a broad leaf, but soon the memories flowed like rain filling a river.

Naia showed Kylan her home in Sog, the sunlit apeknots and the lush, living wood of Great Smerth. She showed him the morning Tavra had arrived, the feast that had followed, and the

hearing they'd had in her mother's chamber. Their departure and their confrontation with the Nebrie—the crystal veins buried in the swamp bed, and the haunting loneliness and rage in the Nebrie's heart. She showed her father's wound and Tavra's message, but through it all, she kept back her secret about Gurjin—that her brother was accused of treason and that she was going to Ha'rar in his stead.

Kylan showed his parents, raising him in a little hut on Spriton land near the Dark Wood, tending the crops that fed their bellies, and playing in the rolling hills of the grasslands. She saw Kylan's father teaching him to play the lute, his mother harvesting the tall, wide grass and weaving it on a loom to make their roof. She saw a winter night with no moons, so cold, little Kylan had gathered two quilts and wound them tightly around his body. He jumped when the shutters flew open, banging against the inside wall with a startling clatter, freezing wind gusting in and bringing all the black of the night with it. His mother went to close the shutter, but it was too late. The dark wind extinguished every candle in moments, and then *he* was there. The Hunter, in a cloak so black, he was one with the night, pierced only by hateful red eyes behind a bone mask. He snatched Kylan's parents in his inky embrace. His claws muffled their screams as he disappeared, leaving Kylan alone in the howling night.

The dreamfast ended, and Naia felt Kylan's hand draw away from hers. They sat in quiet and stared into the fire, letting the silence be. The memory of the black wind that had taken Kylan's parents stuck in Naia's mind, the phantom chill of the winter night clinging to her skin though a warm breeze blew upon it. No wonder he had feared the dark tunnel in the Podling burrow.

"The crystal veins . . . they're a sickness in Thra," Naia said. "They darken the hearts of creatures. I worry what might happen if the sickness reaches the Castle of the Crystal. That's why I've got to reach the All-Maudra, whether or not I find my brother."

"The Skeksis will protect the Crystal," Kylan assured her. "Ancient gods gave them the power to protect it when the castle was entrusted to them."

Naia nodded. She sighed and turned her eyes to her present surroundings, stroking the top of Neech's head where it rested on her knee. The great waves of grass around them looked afire with gold, and they stopped to watch as the flickering of night bugs sparkled across the horizon.

Though it was beautiful, above and all around, Naia couldn't help but wonder what else hid below and up ahead, waiting in the shadowy arms of the deep.

CHAPTER 13

When the morning fog cleared the following day, Naia raised her hand to her brow and squinted. Under the quickening daylight, she could make out a ridge of stony highland within the day's distance, lying like the back of a serpent between them and the still-distant mountains. It had been invisible in the dim of the previous evening, but now it was unmistakable. Kylan, following her line of sight, let out a quiet sound of astonishment under his breath.

"What is that?" Naia asked.

"The Black River's Spine. Were you not expecting it? That's where we'll meet the river that will lead us to Stone-in-the-Wood . . ." Kylan's voice faded as he realized what Naia was just understanding. Her cheeks warmed, and he said it, out loud. "You didn't think we were traveling all the way to those big purple mountains, did you? Those are the misty mountains! It would take unum to get there if we didn't ride the river!"

She pressed her lips together and gave him a sock in the arm.

"I've never been this far north! How was I supposed to know one ridge of mountains from another?"

Kylan held his arm and laughed. It wasn't mean-spirited, though. He was only enjoying *not* being the embarrassed one for once. She let him have the moment. Even if she felt silly now for thinking the mountains were their midway destination, the relief of knowing they would reach the prickly ridge within the day was worth it. They might even touch toes with the legendary Black River in the evening. Naia's mouth watered, thinking of the swimmers that they might roast for dinner and how much Neech would enjoy the well-missed moisture of running water.

"We could reach the river by evening, I think," Kylan said, and Naia agreed, picking up her pace in anticipation.

The great Spriton plains began to give way to a more arid region, though nestled against the Black River's Spine, Naia could make out a dense line of lush trees. The clouds were full of white sweeps and vapor as the humidity from the Dark Wood beyond fell in sheets of rain and rainbows, leaving little left as the winds blew south. Naia was ever thankful for the shoes Maudra Mera had given her. As the grasses gave way to drier weeds and shrubs, the earth became salty and golden. Walking it barefoot, or even in her first set of bark sandals, would have made the journey near impossible. Even the little Pod people had worn shoes, she reflected. It seemed Sog might be the only place in the Skarith Land where shoes were more a burden than a blessing. Then again, Naia had never seen a Podling before she'd left. Perhaps shoes were common to all but the Drenchen.

"Are there many Podlings in this area?" she asked, and Kylan brightened at the question, eager to share the overflowing trivia he had stored in his mind.

"There used to be dozens of communities, all throughout the

area. But their numbers have been dwindling, and many families end up living with Spriton communities when their colonies become too few. Some say it's poor crops."

From the abundance of wildlife around them, both in the wide grasslands and even here in the deepening highlands, it seemed strange to hear of failing crops. Although Naia was used to the bounty of the swamp, even she could tell there was plenty to eat and build and live off in the Spriton plains. How were they struggling in a land of such natural wealth? The answer was what Kylan wasn't saying, which was that the troubles the Podlings were facing might not have to do with crops at all.

"I believe the Hunter hunts more than Gelfling," he said quietly. "Though Maudra Mera would not have it said aloud."

Naia shivered.

They ate lunch on foot—dried fruit and the tender sweet cores of thick red grass. By the onset of evening, the ground began to slope upward into the smooth, layered rock of the ridge highlands. There, the path split: one way down into the wooded valley and the other ascending into the ridge. Up they went. Between boulders and steep cliffs, their path narrowed until only one of them could fit abreast, winding through carved stone arches and along wide steps that took them higher and higher. At first, Naia worried about Kylan slipping and falling, but he fared well, occasionally more nimble even than she. Though he couldn't throw a *bola*, his balance was keen, and the two of them made their way through the warm reds and oranges of the ridge, overgrown in places with woody vines and tangled overgrowth. As they climbed higher into the steppes, Naia marveled at the forest teeming with foliage and the calling and squabbling of fliers and buzzers. Once, when she set a hand down to steady herself, a tentacled shrub leaped up in alarm, rapidly rolling away and down the slope before disappearing into the wood below.

When the Great Sun eased downward, they paused to watch its vibrant descent. Clouds mottled the sky, heavy with rain that reflected the wash of colors with added iridescence. From the high spot where they stood, Naia could see south across the huge area they had already crossed. The plains so wide, Sog was not even a spot of black on the horizon.

"There," Kylan exclaimed, grabbing her shoulder and pointing. "There, see that?"

Up ahead, to the west, a sparkle of reflected sunlight glittered amid the dense wood. Naia strained to follow it, and as the Great Sun's last light struck at just the right place, she could see it: a snaking line of dark water that carved its way through the shelves of the highlands. Rushing from its origin in some spring high in the ridge, the river flowed to its—and Naia's—final destination to the north.

"The Black River," she said. A smile came over her face. "We're so close! We'll build a raft and ride it all the way to Ha'rar. Are there any falls?"

"Ha! How would I know?" Kylan asked. "This is new to me, too."

"No songs about Jarra-Jen and the Black River?" Naia was teasing, but when he shook his head, she felt some disappointment even so. She knew how to build a strong raft, but no raft would be strong enough to carry them over a waterfall. She sighed, dreaming of how easy it would be to reach Ha'rar if they could simply float there on the easy current of the river. She'd be before the All-Maudra in no time.

"Not aside from the one I already told, back in Sami Thicket."

"I guess they'll tell songs about us, then," Naia teased. "Come on!"

Energy renewed by the sight of the river, the two treaded on, using the numerous bulky roots and branches that tangled with the earth as hand- and footholds. The large viny growths were all of the same green-brown color and rough woody texture, though they were covered on top and in every nook and cranny with other plants, flowers, and grumbling, crawling, squeaking critters. The huge vines snaked up from the forest below like tentacles, gripping the highlands and rocks as if the wood itself were climbing over the ridge. It reminded Naia of an apeknot, in a way, and she hummed to herself as she hopped over the roots with a hand and a gentle jump.

Their path abruptly ended, some way down the ridge. The highland dropped off in a steep cliff, the opposite side much more than a leap or vault away. The constant thick vines that wrapped around every corner of the bluffs ended here, too. Though one large branch, big enough for two Gelfling to walk side by side, jutted out over the ravine just a few steps before it ended in jagged, broken splinters. Across the ravine were the remains of the other end of the branch, broken just the same, the length of the branch dangling at the break by the last remaining fibers of old wood.

"It was a bridge," Kylan said as they stared at it. "But . . . it's not anymore."

Naia stepped closer to the cliff, out onto their side of the broken branch path. The valley below, between them and the other side and so, so far down, was flooded with dense forest, so overgrown, she could only see the tops of the trees. The calls of fliers and other wildlife echoed through the red stone ravine, carried along by the face of the cliff and the steady buffeting wind.

"We have to cross to get to the river," she said. "I can't believe this! We're so close, I can practically feel the river's water on my toes. I wanted to make it there by night."

Kylan curled his lips in, quiet. There was nothing to say, anyway. Naia kicked a pebble over the side of the cliff and tugged at her locs. If only she had wings! Yet there was nothing at her back but soreness and a heavy traveling pack that would probably weigh her down too much to make the crossing, even if she had been able to fly. And what would become of Kylan, then? She pushed down her frustration and turned away from the broken branch pass. Heading back from the direction they'd come, they searched for a way down the side of the cliff.

Backtracking led them eventually to the fork they'd passed much earlier, and Naia swallowed any words about the time they'd wasted. She stopped when Kylan's footsteps halted behind her, turning to see him standing before a flat boulder face and holding out his hands. Before she could ask him what he was doing, he showed her. The blue dream-etching *vliyaya* lit from his fingers, burning words that stayed into the face of the rock. When he was done, he stepped back to inspect his handiwork before jogging to catch up.

"Warning any other travelers about the pass," he said.

Naia held her tongue, though she wanted to remind him no one else was likely to come this way any time soon, and even if they did, most Gelfling could not read. Then she realized there was no harm in it and she was only frustrated with their unexpected detour. The bridge wasn't Kylan's fault, nor was it anyone's, really, and so as they began their descent, Naia left her frustration on the cliffs of the highlands.

By the time they reached lower ground, the vines had grown thicker and taller, sprouting up into leaved trees in more and more places. In the darkening evening, the forest was alive with the hoots and hollers of nocturnal creatures, resounding with the song of night. Neech coiled again and again on Naia's arm in anticipation as they stood where the trees grew in a weaving line, dividing the bluffs from the wood. Though their eyes had already adjusted to the night, Naia stooped and went into her pack, drawing a pouch of glow moss. She held it out to Neech, who devoured it eagerly. After a few moments, the glowing green of the moss saturated his oily skin, the light shining from his body brightly enough to illuminate their path. Kylan watched with delight; she was sure he would record it in his scrolls later.

Tavra's warning about the Dark Wood and its dangers came once more to Naia's mind, but she pushed the words away. She couldn't afford to lose more time after their day-long detour.

"Ready?" she asked. Kylan met her eyes, and she saw memories in them. Memories of his parents and the Hunter and all the songs of the Dark Wood. But though she saw fear, she also saw courage.

"It'll be all right," she assured him.

"I just wonder if it would be better to go during the day. You know, once the Brothers are out and it's not quite so . . . dark."

Naia looked back into the wood, her friend's words changing how she saw it. It was dark indeed. The Dark Wood had certainly earned its name. Though she wasn't afraid of the dark, she knew the wood could be dangerous if they entered it carelessly . . . but even so, she was no stranger to wilderness and they had wasted too much time.

"Just think what Jarra-Jen would do," she suggested.

"I don't know if you were listening, but the Dark Wood at night is when Jarra-Jen met the Hunter and was chased until he had to leap off a cliff into the Black River," Kylan retorted. The huffiness crept from his words into his posture, and he put his hands on his hips. Naia grinned. That was the attitude he needed. Sometimes, a little confidence was all it took to chase away uncertainty.

"But wasn't he also alone? That isn't the case for us."

Kylan peered into the wood for a long time. Naia waited, watching his ears rise from a wary flatness to a more determined form, pointed forward. She smiled. Though she had been eager to write him off as a soft-talking song teller in the beginning, she was glad she had let go of the thought. He had a spark of courage in him, and she was pleased to see it.

"I guess if I never see him, I can never confront him," he said with a resolute nod. "Let's go."

And so together, using the two rising Sisters as guides, into the Dark Wood they went.

As a Drenchen and a Spriton, and of course as Gelfling, neither Naia nor her friend were unfamiliar with forests. Still, the density of the trees was unlike anything Naia had ever seen. The strong pillars of ebony bark and dark turquoise leaves were interrupted only by thick brush, shrubs, spiny rocks, and flowering land corals with huge white night blossoms. The earth was padded with layers and layers of leaves and moss, rippling over the forms of the ever-present roots that sometimes arched from the land in swooping forms that created hoops and arches under which they walked. Though Neech's body, glowing with his dinner, lit the way, there were other night flowers with their own sources of light, breaking the darkness with dreamy spots of blue, white, and green. Though it was beautiful, Naia reminded herself, it was also dangerous, endless in its mysteries. A twig snapped nearby, and Naia looked—but nothing was there except shadows and quiet.

"Do you know the name of these large vine roots?" she asked quietly as they made their way through the bramble. Kylan ran his hand along one of the big hulking trunks, shaking his head.

"Maybe you could ask?" he suggested, nearly whispered, as if there were someone listening—and in the wild wood, there probably was. "Have you always been able to dreamfast with creatures beyond other Gelfling?"

"I don't know. It's never happened until recently . . . Until the

Nebrie in Sog. Though sometimes I have trouble controlling my dreamfasting. Makes for some embarrassing encounters with soldiers of the All-Maudra, I'll tell you that much."

"I envy you. I'd love to be able to share dreams with the trees, with the furry beasts and the scaled ones. See what they've seen— share what I have! But I guess I'll have to settle with learning as many languages as I can."

"That's not so bad," Naia replied. "At least you won't touch minds by accident."

"Oh, plenty of things are said in language by accident—"

Naia was going to laugh and tell him he had a point, but a low eerie moan interrupted her first, as if the earth below their feet had heaved a deep pained sigh. The chirping and chattering of the night critters ceased at the sound of the cry, and then all in the wood was silent. The only thing Naia could hear was the wind tickling her ears—but then the moan came again, reverberating through the wood of the big root she was leaning on to guide her steps.

"What is that?" whispered Kylan.

The glowing flowers were closing up, lights dipping into darkness one by one, the ethereal beauty replaced by inky blackness. She snatched Neech from the air, hiding his glowing body in the front folds of her tunic. In the heavy silence that followed the chilling sound, she felt an itch at the back of her neck, as if she were being watched. Yet everywhere she looked, she saw nothing but shadows—shadows that could be hiding anything, she thought with a gulp, her heart beating a faster rhythm. Her skin crawled at another spindly *snick!* of a branch, this time much closer than before. Kylan edged closer to her, eyes wide and ears twisting to and fro.

"Could it be—"

"Don't say it," she said, shushing him. "Don't . . . say it."

Something *definitely* moved to her left, something long and heavy that slid along the ground and rustling branches. Naia put her hand to Gurjin's knife but did not draw, hoping she wouldn't have to, but crouching just in case. The creature's serpentine body bent aside bushes and rocks as it pushed through the earth, coiling around them in a broad arc. Kylan backed up against Naia and they stood together, breathing in sync. When Kylan's fingers snaked around Naia's wrist, she tried to brush him away.

"Don't grab me now. I need to be able to move."

Kylan jumped, moving away from her, though the warm grasp on her wrist only tightened. Voice piqued with surprise, he said, "I'm not . . ."

Naia looked to her arm just as she was suddenly yanked to the side. Instead of a hand gripping her, she saw a cluster of tendrils encircling her arm and gathering in mass, dragging her through the brush, and then she was in the air, tossed upward, Kylan's shouting voice dropping away from her. When she began to fall, responding to the call of gravity, a shivering, shaking rustle of plant life exploded from the canopy of overgrown trees, another tangle of vines darting out to catch her, only to swing her and release again, carrying and launching and throwing her through the maze of the wood. She could hear Kylan's voice, sometimes farther, sometimes very near, in yelps of dismay that echoed her own.

The journey ended as abruptly as it had begun. The grasping vines loosened, sending Naia tumbling to the earth. No sooner had she regained her footing than she heard something rushing toward her. She ran as roots and branches lunged for her, scratching her arms and legs in their attempt to catch hold of her once more. Her ears burned as a flock of hollerbats burst from within a knotted old tree trunk, screeching and flapping their clawed wings as they thrashed past, but she couldn't stop to curse them. She knew she was running deeper and deeper into the wood, but she had no other choice. If she stopped, she would be caught, devoured by the Dark Wood. Tavra had been right—it had been foolish to come at night, and now she was paying the price.

The vines suddenly disappeared, slinking back into the canopy and the brush, though she could sense them all around her. She slowed, laboring to catch her breath and hoping perhaps the wood had grown tired of chasing her. Kylan was nowhere to be found, and she couldn't find Neech, no matter how many pockets of her pack and clothes she checked. She could only hope he was with Kylan, and that his keen sense of smell would bring him back to her soon.

"Hello?" she asked quietly, into the night. "Kylan? Is anyone there?"

Someone was there, of course: hundreds of trees and fliers and buzzers and crawlers, but none answered. Wherever Kylan was, he was not close enough to hear her, and so she straightened herself and tried to get her bearings. The Dark Wood felt infinitely darker now that she was on her own, and she wondered at how foolish and impatient of them it had been to attempt the journey to the Black River at night. Every bit of movement caught her eye and caused her a moment of alarm as she reoriented using the glimpses of the moons she could see through the crowded trees. If she could make it to the river, she could meet Kylan there eventually, she hoped.

Her footsteps crunched alone as she made her way, and the night came full into its prime. As the shadows grew even darker, she sensed something else lying in wait within the belly of the Dark Wood. It had a presence, of course—all things of Thra did—but this was different, somehow. Its melody did not fall in perfect harmony with the rest of the song of Thra, but Naia could not yet put it into words. Alone, without Kylan to worry about, nearly blindfolded by the night, Naia felt her inner eyes opening, seeing, sensing. Yes, the Dark Wood sang the song of Thra, but notes were off-key, as if it had forgotten parts, or was too distracted—too disturbed—to fall back into tune. As she listened to its song, it brought a familiar scent to her mind—a dark and primal hollow scent that quickened her heart and her step, urging her silently to find Kylan and reach the Black River as soon as she could.

"Naia?"

The voice paralyzed her, a wisp of cold air tickling the backs of her arms. She turned toward it, wary in disbelief but unable to deny what all her senses were telling her. A Gelfling boy stepped out of the tree cover, exactly her age, with matching clay-colored skin marked with Drenchen spots and speckles. His locs hung at his shoulders, and he wore a beautifully embroidered black-and-violet soldier's uniform. Naia's breath was stuck in her throat, her heart leaping.

It was Gurjin.

CHAPTER 14

"Gurjin, wha-what are you doing here?" Naia asked, running to hug her brother. She frowned when she felt his arms against her shoulders. His embrace was cold to the touch, almost like stone, even through the fabric of his tunic. She pressed her hand against his arms, but the coldness refused to dissipate. "What's happened to you?"

"I've been lost in the forest for days," he said. "I'm trying to find my way back to the castle."

"But you're a soldier, shouldn't you know . . ."

Naia trailed off, stepping back. Something had flickered in Gurjin's eyes, deep within, invisible except to the eyes of her heart. She could feel something was wrong. He didn't react to her retreat, remaining where he'd been standing, arms at his side. The wind ruffled the trees above, and moonlight fell through, hitting spots on his tunic and face. In that brief moment she saw his skin was pale, his eyes deep and hollow, and his tunic, so recently resplendent in its ornament and fine embroidery, lay in tatters.

"You looked upon the crystal veins," she whispered. "Oh, Gurjin . . ."

"Naia, there's something I have to tell you," he said. "I must return to the castle."

His voice was as cold as his touch, empty and withered. He spoke the words with a sightless gaze, and Naia turned away, not wanting to look deep enough into his eyes that she would see the flickers of darkened light.

"The castle," he repeated. "Do you know the way?"

Naia knew what she had to do. She took her brother's arm in hand and shook him.

"Gurjin, you need to come with me. We need to find my friend and we need to leave the Dark Wood. We can help you . . . I don't know how, but we can help you. All right?"

He fell behind her as she tugged him by his cold hand, resuming her course for the Black River. She could only hope her sense of direction was strong enough to get her there. With her brother's stone-like feet and disinterested gait, she would not be able to rely on him, though this should be territory he was most familiar with. Though Stone-in-the-Wood was at the center of the Dark Wood, the Castle of the Crystal lay in the western branch of the sprawling forest. Surely the soldiers that guarded its halls also knew the wood by which it was surrounded!

But she'd found him—and with him, they could stand before the All-Maudra and clear his name, and the name of their clan. Everyone would know the truth.

"Everyone will be so glad to know I've found you," she said, smiling suddenly. "We can show everyone you aren't a traitor to the Skeksis—"

"He is a traitor."

Naia stumbled when Gurjin's hand slipped out of hers.

When she turned, she cried out in surprise. Gurjin was gone, and standing in his place was Tavra of Ha'rar, though her white and silver robes were in the same state of disrepair as her brother's tunic had been. Her broken wing dangled uselessly at her back, and her expression was void of any life save for a grim, rising look of anger.

"He's not," Naia said, backing away. "Where's Gurjin—who *are* you?"

Tavra did not attempt to close the distance as Naia took another step back, though her voice seemed just as loud when she repeated the four terrible words.

"He is a traitor."

"No," Naia said, refusing to be bullied by the Vapra. "It was someone else, or . . ."

"Are you so sure?"

Now Gurjin—or whatever ghostly creature had taken on his appearance—stood behind her, and she spun before she collided with him in her retreat. His uniform was complete again, no longer in shreds, though the jewels that lined his collar and breastplate were cracked, glinting in the dim light with shimmers of violet.

"I'm sure," she said. "Who are you? What do you want?"

"I'm the traitor," he said.

Naia's breath left her when he grabbed her by the shoulders, holding her firmly in place with fingers that constricted around her body like vines. He fixed her with his blackened eyes, and she could smell the earth on his breath, soil and crystal and fire from the deepest reaches of Thra. When he spoke, it was as if he pulled the words from the corners of her heart, from the dark spaces where she'd hidden her secret fears.

"I'm the traitor," he repeated. "Traitor to the castle. Traitor to the Crystal. Traitor to all of Thra."

"No," she pleaded. She tried to close her eyes against his gaze, but he had locked her into it, and within she could see the Crystal. Its song was a drowning call, pulling her toward it, whispering echoes of the doubts that lay within her, numbing her fingers as she tried to draw the dagger from her belt.

"You cannot save me," Gurjin hissed. "You'll meet with the All-Maudra empty-handed. You'll stand before her alone. Our clan will be marked as traitors, and it will only be a matter of time before the Skeksis come for retribution—"

"*No!*"

Naia's fingers found purchase on the hilt of her dagger, and she thrust . . . but the blade met only the trunk of an upright root. Gurjin had vanished, and where the blade split the bark of the root, dazzling purple light poured out. Naia yanked the knife free and spun to face Tavra, toes digging into the dirt of the forest floor.

"You're not strong enough to save him," Tavra said with a sneer of disdain. "Now run. Just like he did."

Though the implication filled her with dread, every nerve in Naia's body was telling her to take the opportunity and escape this awful place filled with the nightmarish apparitions. She bolted, acting on instinct, sprinting as fast as she could away from the ghostly Vapra soldier. Vines and roots reached for her as she ran, scratching and grasping after her, but she tore free of them, refusing to be caught again. Tears came as she heard the echoes of Gurjin's words in her mind, but the breeze on her cheeks as she ran dried the saltwater away, and she tried with all her might to leave it behind her in the wood.

"Why?" she cried, knocking away another branch as it reached to ensnare her. "Why is this happening? What do you want?"

In the forest to the right and the left, she saw figures, more shadowy shapes, taking on the forms and faces of people she knew. Her mother, her father. Her sisters. Maudra Mera, Kylan—and then she heard voices, shouting, crying, echoing through the depths of the wood as she raced to escape it. Some she recognized, and some were strange—

You cannot save me . . .

I won't accept it . . .

Through the din she heard Gurjin's voice. It was unmistakable, and the words it uttered struck her like stones:

I'll tell everyone the Skeksis are villains. I'll turn them against the castle. Even the All-Maudra.

"No," she cried, but her voice was growing hoarse. "No—"

Her brother's voice did not let up.

Just you wait and see.

Amid all the other faces, she saw one creature she didn't recognize. It was a hulking spidery thing, looming above the other Gelfling ghosts, with four monstrous arms and long square-tipped fingers. On every surface of its body grew sprouts of trees, weaving in and out of its flesh and bursting into branches and diamond-shaped violet leaves. The being stared into her with piercing otherworldly eyes, and when it tilted back its long-necked head and opened its mouth, it let out a sonorous moan so loud and miserable, it shook every tree in the wood.

I must rejoin the Heart of Thra.

Terrified by the vision, Naia misstepped and yelped in surprise as the earth gave way to a sudden valley. She tumbled in a ball of arms and legs and locs, finally landing with a groan on a hard rippled surface. Unsure if she was broken, or maybe dead, she remained still, waiting for her head to stop spinning. She wanted to cry, but she didn't have the time. She had to find Kylan and Neech, and get out of the forest before it brought an early end to their journey. The phantoms . . . Had they been real? Some enchanted creature taking on the forms of Tavra and her brother? Or had the shadowy figures been an illusion caused by her own mind—her fears taking form under the power of the crystal veins that plagued the land?

"Naia?"

Naia leaped to her feet, holding her dagger before her with energy she hadn't realized she still had. Almost close enough to touch, Kylan crouched, hands up to protect himself. They faced each other, both breathless, both prepared to fight or flee.

"Stay away from me," he warned. "Who are you? What do you want?"

"Kylan, it's me!" she said. "Naia . . ."

"How do I know you're not another shadow?"

"How do I know *you're* not?"

He moved away from her. The sorrowful, haunted look in his eyes was emotive—living. She felt the rigid muscles in her body relax as she recognized the expression. He'd seen the forest's phantoms, too. Carefully she lowered her dagger, and a *chirrrup* came from his sleeve and out flew Neech, still glowing gently, gliding through the air to Naia's shoulder. Relieved and exhausted, Kylan let down his guard. She reached out and squeezed his shoulder to prove it, to both of them. When she did, she could feel he was warm to the touch. Naia could only imagine what nightmares the forest might have brought Kylan. She hardly wanted to think about the ones it had conjured for her. The voices. The four-armed monster. She pushed them out of mind, hoping to clear her senses enough to get them out of the wood safely.

"From the look of it, you've seen what I've seen, or something like it," she replied quietly. "Are you all right?"

He let out a long breath and curled his lips in, then out.

"I think so. Where are we? What is this?"

The clearing was made entirely of the thick roots here, tightly packed against one another in a huge spiraling basin, squeezing out all other plant life. At the very bottom of the bowl grew a warped angular tree. It had leaves that matched the shoots and saplings Naia had seen in the highlands and throughout the forest, but this one was different. It was bulging at the base, in lumps and protrusions that looked like half-formed limbs or faces. Four knobby branches sprouted from it, two on either side, spread wide as if the tree were grasping toward the sky with four arms and hands full of diamond leaves. In the dark of the night, lit only by the moons and stars overhead, it looked as if it were moving, slowly reaching toward them.

She thought, inescapably, of the monster she'd seen in the wood. She hoped it had only been a vision. She shivered to think that it was a real thing, somewhere out there, watching them with its penetrating eyes.

Rejoin the Heart of Thra, it had said. What did that mean?

"What is that?" Kylan asked, shying away from the four-limbed tree. Naia wanted to do the same, but she was reluctant to look afraid in front of her friend.

"I don't know," she said. "A better question is why did the trees bring us here to see it?"

The clearing had been quiet for a beat, but now the rasping sounds of the crawling roots and vines simmered up again. Naia felt the roots shift beneath her feet as the entire basin constricted like a knot of rope when one end is pulled. The echoing moan they'd heard before they'd been carried away came once more, but now it was so nearby, Naia could feel the sound vibrating against her chest and making her whole body shiver. As scared as she felt, though, there was something apart from fear in her.

"It's in pain," she said, her mind clearing with the realization. "The tree—the forest—or something—it's calling for help. I saw those shadows, the phantoms—but I also saw inside the root of the tree, and it was the same as the crystal I saw in Sog and in the Podling burrow . . . Look."

Naia knelt and cut into one of the roots at their feet, prying back the thick bark so Kylan could peer inside. As she expected, the tightly packed grain within the core of the root was veined with traces of the violet mineral. It looked like filaments of purple ice had frozen inside, spreading in forks and webs almost like the embroidery Naia had seen on the cloak of Gurjin's shadow.

"The crystal vein," Kylan gasped. "It's here, in the wood. It's darkened this tree . . . this tree that makes up all of the Dark Wood?"

Naia thought of running, of escaping. Of getting out of the wood with their lives. But then she thought of the Nebrie and its mourning wails just before it had passed. How lonesome it had been in its rage, just before it had died through no fault of its own. Afraid, but resolved, Naia shouldered off her pack and sat cross-legged beside the root, placing both hands upon it.

"I'm going to dreamfast with it," she said. "And then I'm going to try to heal it."

"That's a bit dangerous . . . ," he began, but shook his head, thinking better of it. Instead, he said, "Can I do anything to help? The last time you did this, it didn't work out so well."

Naia nodded to her pack. "If there's danger, grab a *bola* and make the best of it."

Her friend hesitantly drew the rock-and-rope weapon with a stern-faced resolve. He stood over her with the *bola* in hand, looking back and forth into the wood that surrounded them. Should anything actually come for them here, she hoped he would find it in him to swing the *bola* heroically, but in reality she hoped she would be able to sense it from within the dreamfast quickly enough to rescue them both. Still, his determination to do his part was endearing . . . and maybe a little charming.

Leaving Kylan to protect them, Naia turned her attention to the smooth-barked root before her. It was quivering, as if trying to yawn but unable to find its mouth, humming with the unvoiced cries of anguish that coursed through the miles and miles of the plant's sprawling body. Even as ready as she thought she was, hands pressed against the tree's skin, the recent memories of the ghosts that it had manifested made her reluctant to make contact. But she wasn't going to let reluctance or fear stand in her way. She had let the Nebrie down, and the ruffnaw—she wasn't about to let the Dark Wood down, too. If she could calm the chaos in its heart, they could finish their journey in peace . . . and maybe, she hoped, come a step closer to understanding just what was happening in their world.

Bracing herself, Naia closed her eyes, opening her heart and mind to the tree. It sensed her contact, and with a hungry, maddened surge of energy, it lunged to swallow her whole.

CHAPTER 15

In a rush of memories and emotions, feelings and experiences that were unlike anything that could be felt by a Gelfling, Naia fell into the tree's consciousness as she might ride a raft over the side of a waterfall. The texture of the earth. The fluid breeze. The warmth and cool of the days and nights.The crawling of creatures and the tickling of their breaths as they lived and died within the forest, the predators and the preyed upon—fliers, buzzers, diggers, even walkers—with their Gelfling-light footsteps through the spongy understory. Then the fall was over, plunging her deep into the basin, suspending her in time as she sank deeper and deeper into the heart of the tree. Ninets seemed to pass like seconds as Thra orbited its three suns—some trine cooler and some warmer as the suns changed configurations at the center of the system.

When Naia regained her bearings, she was still floating. She felt the forest all around; the tree *was* the forest, she realized, with roots that crawled every inch of the rich wood, and branches that reached between and above even the highest sentinel trees. It had been the first sprout to grow here, in ancient Thra. Its name was Olyeka-Staba. The Cradle-Tree.

For the moment, drifting in the dim current of the great tree's memories, it seemed calm, hardly the dangerous pulling aura that had conjured the tumultuous phantoms she had seen. Being within the gentle memories reminded Naia of the naps she would sometimes take in the pools in Sog, dozing underwater in the cool shallows. She felt almost as though she might fall asleep . . . but that thought alone sparked her wariness. The Cradle-Tree might have been the foundation of the Dark Wood, but it had been calling to her, sending nightmares to her in its torment. Lashing out in the madness awakened within it by the crystal shadows. It had tried to deceive her before, and nearly succeeded—this comfort was likely another attempt.

Cradle-Tree, she called to it. *Show me your pain. I want to help.*

Naia could only feel. This was the perception of a tree, she realized, with no Gelfling eyes or ears or mouth. She closed hers, then, and reached into the current of the tree's dream, feeling as a tree might . . . listening. As she did, she felt the pulse of the tree's life force, uneven and wild, growing louder and more anguished. It was like the Nebrie and the ruffnaw. It was like the empty void she had glimpsed herself, staring into the crystal veins before she had known they were the cause of the hollow darkness.

I must rejoin the Heart of Thra . . .

Though Olyeka-Staba's voice was haunting, it gave Naia a burst of hope.

Let me help you, she pleaded. *How can I bring you peace?*

I must rejoin . . .

Naia cried out as a flash of memories rained upon her. The Cradle-Tree's roots, growing deep as they were meant to and cultivating the soil throughout the lush area of the forest, braided

through pure white crystal veins that radiated from the Castle of the Crystal. The veins in the memory were like ribbons of sunlight, warming the Cradle-Tree with the harmonic life-song of Thra.

Then, without warning, Thra cried out, and its song, for a moment, went quiet in shock. The white veins of crystal bled, melting into the dark amethyst that made Naia shudder. The soil blackened, and where the Cradle-Tree's roots touched the veins, tiny sprouts of darkness blossomed. Thra's song resumed, but it was injured, confused. Broken. Flaws, somewhere, from a deep wound that bled emptiness into its eternal refrain.

I was not strong enough, Olyeka-Staba cried in its silent voice.

And so the tree raged, poisoned over trine and trine by the darkened veins, until nearly every inch of it was blackened with regret and remorse. Naia remembered the words the shadows of Gurjin and Tavra had spoken to her. Had they merely been echoes of the tree's guilt? Echoes, perhaps, though they had resonated against the walls of Naia's own doubts and fears. But she couldn't let those get in the way now, not while she was linked within the dreamfast with the tree. Its memories were growing chaotic now, just jumbles of panic and anger and loneliness—guilt and hopelessness, compounded by the discordant song of Thra.

It's not your fault, she urged, fearing she might lose her connection and everything else with it. Was this the source of the darkened veins? Some injury, deep in the Dark Wood? What had happened in its murky depths? Whatever it was, it was only a matter of time before the sickness reached the Heart of Thra where it resided, so nearby within the Castle of the Crystal. When that happened, there was no telling what might happen.

With all she had in her, Naia strained her ears and listened for the song of Thra. It was there, all around, though distant. Holding it in mind, she carried its song through her body and offered it to the Cradle-Tree. For a moment, its anger ebbed. For a heartbeat, the shadow of hopelessness that had consumed it flickered. Taking the opportunity, Naia brought the song within her to her fingertips, and they glowed blue with healing *vliyaya*. She saw it both within the dreamfast and without. Her physical body's hands channeling the healing magic into the hard wood of the tree's roots while her body within the dreamfast became the light itself, illuminating the darkness of the Cradle-Tree's heart.

With a gasp, she fell out of the dreamfast, body and mind aching from effort. Kylan caught her as she nearly toppled over, but she didn't have time for rest. All around them the forest was reacting, moving, slithering. But this time it was not in darkened rage, but in vigor, as if waking from a terrible nightmare. The Cradle-Tree let out a long cry . . . but this time, it was in anguish of relief. With a monumental tremble, the Dark Wood gave an exhausted sigh. A deep purr resonated from the earth, and in response the night creatures of the wilderness took up their calls, filling the night with the song of life.

"What did you do?" Kylan asked.

"I tried to heal it," Naia said. "I think it worked—"

The sound of cracking wood drew their attention over the rising song of the awakening forest. At the bottom of the basin, the contorted, four-limbed tree was splintering. At first, Naia thought perhaps it would burst into growth in the wake of the Cradle-Tree's rebirth, but as she watched its limbs jerk to and fro, she realized that something else was breaking free. Splinters and jagged panels of bark and wood split and fell, and Naia's breath caught in her throat when a giant hand erupted from one of the four limbs. Then another, and another, and another.

With a deep rumble, an unearthly monster stepped out from the remains of the brittle gray wood encasing. It had a long maned neck hunched down between four sloping shoulders, ending in an oblong head nearly as big as Naia. At the end of its four spidery arms were enormous hands with big blunt fingers shielded with square yellowed nails. It shook its entire body, releasing a low resonant cry, and Naia saw that it was the four-armed monster from her vision, during her flight through the wood.

It shook itself free of the remaining splinters of wood which had imprisoned it, until only one clay-like piece remained upon its brow, hiding its face like a mask of bone.

CHAPTER 16

Naia's hand had moved to her *bola* the instant the monster emerged, but she held it in check. The creature, grunting in disorientation and flicking any last chips of wood from its gray cloth robes, had been released when the spell on the Cradle-Tree had been lifted. Why would healing the Dark Wood end in releasing a dangerous monster?

"Kylan," she breathed, not wanting to say it, but needing to know, "is that . . . ?"

The monster twitched, moving an arm. The movement fired an instinctive response in Naia's body and she stepped once, launching the bola in her hand forward. It shot from her hand, on target toward the monster's narrow-set eyes—but quicker than she could see, the thing's hand darted forth, snatching the center *bola* stone before it could make its mark. The counterweights flailed uselessly, spinning in open air, striking nothing. Trying not to lose determination, Naia raised the dagger, lowering herself into a defensive crouch.

A counterattack never came. The big creature under the broken tree skeleton dropped the *bola* with a casual wave of the hand. It made a sound like a cough, dry and airy, and Naia realized it was chuckling. It finished the motion it had been making when Naia had attacked, lifting its square hand to remove the last piece of bark from its face. It made no move for them, thumping its chest with a fist until the coughing ceased. In the moonlight over the basin clearing, she could see nicks and cuts across the creature's whorled, textured skin from breaking out of the tree's skeleton shell.

"Should we run?" she whispered.

Kylan underlined the unfortunate truth when he replied, "To where?"

She had another *bola*, and a knife, if she needed it. If they were in danger, perhaps the Cradle-Tree would come to their aid. Even now she could feel the tree's vigor reviving, renewed with its healed heart. She hoped it would last, and that there would be no more fear-singing phantoms. She had seen enough of those for the night.

The monster tilted its oblong head at the sound of her voice, its long and ragged mane swaying in the night wind.

"Sounds like Gelfling breathings," it mumbled in a voice that sounded like many tones all at once, speaking the Gelfling tongue with an unfamiliar accent. "That Gelfling urVa sees there? Two? Ah! The one who healed Olyeka-Staba."

"urVa," Naia repeated. "Is that your name? What were you doing, trapped in that tree?"

"Mmm . . ." urVa looked over one of his shoulders to the remains of the tree prison. "Came to help Olyeka-Staba, I did. And I failed. Seems the Cradle-Tree could be healed by Gelfling hand, or else by none."

When he turned back toward them, though his story had the

possibility of truth, Naia couldn't shake how similar in form he was to her imagination's painting of the Hunter. Though his cloak was more clay and brown than black and made of shadows, she imagined a true shadow hunter could always use magic to take on a different form. urVa—if that was his name—bent to pluck a remaining tree branch from the brambles at his feet, holding it with his two upper hands and leaning on it as a walking staff.

"Having thoughts?" he asked. "Thoughts . . . that I'll eat you?" He chuckled.

"Well, you look like you might," Kylan snapped. "What are you doing here? Why were you trapped in the tree?"

urVa sorted through the pieces of wood that lay at his big feet. In the moonlight, he looked like a ghost. Perhaps he was some spirit like the phantoms, entrapped by the Cradle-Tree for good reason. Naia banished the thought, though. There was no point in letting her mind go to frightening places without proof.

"The wood is dangerous," urVa said. He tilted his head and smiled, his teeth glinting in the moonlight. "Come with urVa, little Gelfling. Come with urVa, for supper. Been a long time inside that tree . . . Very hungry."

With no more than that, urVa turned and ambled out of the basin, using his staff to climb the ribbed wall. Soon he would be out of view, gone into the Dark Wood. Naia exchanged glances with Kylan.

"What do you think?" she asked. "Supper sounds great, but not if we're the ones in the pot. Do you think he's . . . you know . . . the Hunter?"

Kylan's ears went flat, though she could hardly believe he hadn't already been thinking it. Giving the thought words and saying them aloud was different, though.

"Since when do you believe the songs?" he asked. Naia felt her cheeks warm, but Kylan went on. "The Hunter is ruthless. He isn't a trickster. If urVa were the Hunter that took my parents, he wouldn't have given us a false name . . . He wouldn't have spoken with us."

Reservations aside, urVa was nearly out of sight, and Naia's stomach rumbled. She was exhausted from her dreamfast with the Cradle-Tree, and although she had wanted to reach the river by the end of the night, it seemed an unrealistic goal. urVa's invitation of food and rest sounded more alluring than she wanted to admit. If he could be trusted, perhaps they could spend the night somewhere safe. But if they couldn't . . . Naia didn't want to think about roughing it after what they'd been through.

"Maybe . . . we should see where he's going. Just to find out."

Kylan hugged himself with a shiver.

"Do we have a choice?"

"Yes. Our other choice is to sleep here in the wood and see what other monsters come crawling out of it."

Kylan took a look behind them, into the wood. Even if the Cradle-Tree's heart had calmed, bringing the wood into a new state of life and wildness, it didn't mean predators might not still be lurking. The cycle of life was not a form of evil, after all, but one that proved the forest was healthy.

"All right," Kylan said. "But we should be careful."

They hurried after urVa, up the wall of the Cradle-Tree's basin where new green sprouts were growing in throngs to replace what had so recently been dark and barren.

urVa traveled at a steady pace, and Naia and Kylan were able to catch up without too much effort. They walked the Dark Wood for some time, one on either side of urVa's long heavy tail, and by the time urVa finally pulled back a curtain of frothy vines, Naia was dizzy with exhaustion. In a small glen was a dirt hovel, teeming with every plant Naia could think of. The trees that surrounded the modest clearing were strung with lines and lines of chimes—made from wood, metal, bone, shell—giving out low hollow droning sounds amid the other groans of nature.

The hovel itself was hardly more than a few ancient stones holding up a mound of earth. The dusty rocks that made up the entryway were dream-etched, reminding her of the doorways in Great Smerth, back home. urVa entered without a word, leaving the two Gelfling to follow of their own will. Naia's heart thumped with discomfort, and she felt a tingling in her fingers and toes, but she calmed the impulse. Trading nods with Kylan, she drew her resolution and entered the strange den.

Within they found a single dimly lit room with a sand-packed floor, just as overgrown and under-maintained as the exterior. A cracked wooden chair sat near a latched trunk caked in dust and moss, and a small dirty hearth with one clay pot. A wooden staff with a long piece of cord connected at the top leaned beside a satchel full of thin spears with feathers on the ends, each stick longer than Naia was tall. Beyond that, the only accents to the room, save for a lone shelf with a few glass vials, were the lines and lines of writing carved across every space of wall.

"Hmm . . . Left the door open too long and time came in, I see. Ha-ha." He waved a hand, clearing some of the dust but stirring up just as much in the process. "Apologies, little Gelfling, for the time inside. Had I been meant to be found, I would have been more prepared."

urVa was illuminated by a dim fire he was starting in the simple hearth. Naia stepped in, drawn to the large circular shape that covered most of the far wall. It showed ten globes in a vertical line, connected by arcs of intertwined pathways, curving in swoops and circles. Extra-orbital bodies were placed outside the core, and between three in particular were straight lines, connecting them in an equilateral triangle that she had seen before, inscribed on charts and sundials.

urVa busied himself setting a kettle to boil, filling it with water drawn from a large stone well built into the ground outside of his hovel. He went from vial to vial on his shelf, finding some had been spilled and emptied by wildlife since he had last been home. What contents he did find, he added to the pot, stirring it occasionally. Naia and Kylan found spots on the floor to sit, watching the big creature move almost gracefully within the confined space.

"A Drenchen, aren't you?" urVa said suddenly. "I remember Sog . . . yes, ah! And that little sapling, what was it? Smerth. I suppose it's grown enough now to climb, hmm? Do the younglings dangle from its branches like alfen fruits?"

The thought was nearly comical. Naia said, "Not exactly."

"Smerth-Staba and Olyeka-Staba," urVa said, facing the pot as if he were incanting the names of the two great trees into a potion. "Pillars of the world. Protectors of Thra. I suppose it was inevitable that the shadows of the crystal have stretched so far as to fall upon the Cradle-Tree . . . but I must stay out of such things. Have for a long time, will for a long time yet . . . Soup."

urVa reached with two hands and gently plucked crudely carved bowls from a stack. In a third hand, the ladle danced back and forth from the pot to the bowls, and by the time he was through, he turned with three bowls, offering two to Naia and her friend. She could still see the cuts and scratches he'd gotten escaping from the Cradle-Tree's prison on the backs of his hands and fingers. One particularly bad cut, a series of two overlapping in an X, still bled a little, but urVa didn't seem to be in any long-lasting pain. He only gestured at his Gelfling guests with the bowls.

"Now, eat, eat, little Gelfling. Gelfling like to eat. Yes."

Naia didn't know about all Gelfling, but she knew stew when she smelled it, and her stomach did, too. Neech poked his head out from her pack and chirped twice—his quills lay flat and calm, bright eyes curious of their mysterious host, who waited with his hand outstretched.

If Neech isn't worried, then I won't be, either, she thought, and took the bowl in both hands. Savory-smelling steam rose from the red-and-green broth, and her stomach ached again in anticipation. Their hunger overcame their apprehension, and the stew was delicious. The longer they stayed, the less anxious Naia felt. By the time her bowl was empty, she felt almost cozy in the firelit den, ready to fall asleep at any moment. urVa reclined on his stool and took up a long staff pipe, propping the smoldering end over the fire and puffing at the mouthpiece with the occasional ring of blue-gray smoke.

"Do you live here all alone?" Naia asked. "In the wood?"

"No, no. Plenty of trees and rocks."

Naia couldn't tell if urVa was being intentionally obtuse, so she clarified: "I mean, are there others like you . . ."

urVa tilted his head and rubbed his chin with a big hand.

"Yes. But we all went our separate ways . . . after the separation. Divided, then divided again."

He smoked his pipe and said nothing more on the subject. It was less than Naia wanted to know, but at least she didn't have to worry about being surprised by another hulking four-armed monster any time soon. She focused on her soup. Kylan, who had been transfixed by the markings on the wall, broke the silence next: "What is that sign writ on your wall? I don't recognize the word."

urVa craned his neck to glance at the triangular emblem Naia had seen earlier, to which Kylan now pointed. urVa gazed at the triangle and the three concentric circles it contained, then rubbed the bottom of his throat with one of his hands as if he wasn't sure what it meant, even though it seemed clear he had been the one who had put it there.

"It is a time, I suppose?" he asked, as if Naia or Kylan might be able to answer him. "Or a door? A time or a door or an awakening. Yes. Something like that."

"Those aren't nearly the same thing," Kylan muttered under his breath. "Perhaps he's not the Hunter, but he certainly may be mad."

"He makes a good pot of stew, even so," Naia replied with a yawn. She was about to suggest they try to sleep, but Kylan was transfixed by the writing. Rising, he approached a cluster of the shapes, tracing the symbols with his hand. Naia burned with a tiny ember of admiration as he read pieces out loud.

"Turn your eye forward in time now . . . It is the day of the Rose Sun." Here, Kylan turned back, his hand still against the writing. "But that day has already passed. The Rose Sun is waning."

urVa moved his head from side to side, making a long low *hmmmmm* sound and continuing to stroke his chin with his fingers curling in, one at a time in rolling sequence.

"Yes, but that was writ when what is now our past was then our future."

It made sense when she thought about it, but Naia wondered if it was necessary to say it in such a confusing way. She kept quiet, considering whether she could serve seconds to her bowl while Kylan continued to read, his lips moving and the occasional word escaping on his breath. She wondered what kind of words the wall held. Songs. Messages. Perhaps a record of history or a prophecy of the future. The circles and spirals looked like star charts, but for all she knew, they could be something else altogether.

"The Great Conjunction," Kylan said, and then he stopped. Naia didn't know what he was referring to or what the words meant, but she shivered. "When single shine the triple suns."

"Mm," urVa agreed, though he added nothing despite Kylan's querulous expression. Instead, he waved the Spriton boy from the wall and toward the corner of the den where a pile of folded robes lay upon a stack of old hay. Though it smelled musty from age, it was soft and dry, and Naia felt herself nodding off almost the instant she settled upon it. Kylan yawned and wrapped his cloak around himself, settling beside her.

"When single shine the triple suns," he whispered, so quietly it had to be to himself. And then she heard nothing but his breathing as he fell asleep. Soon after, she followed.

CHAPTER 17

Even on the hard floor, Naia slept soundly for the first night since she had left the swamp. She dreamed of flying through the awakening branches of the Cradle-Tree, and when she woke, her back and shoulders ached. urVa was nowhere to be seen, though a kettle of water was heating over the hearth, and Naia smelled herbs and spices steeping in the iron pot. Kylan was already awake, sitting in front of urVa's wall of writing and studying it with such intensity she thought new words might be dream-etched from his gaze.

She rose, stretching the rest of her body and looking across urVa's etchings and writing again, now that morning had come. Golden sunlight lit nearly every corner of the sparse cozy den. She wondered if there were others of his kind nearby. From the limited belongings he kept, it was hard for Naia to believe he was completely solitary. Life in Sog was very different, with every family keeping their own stock of meat and preserves, ranging gear and ceremonial garments, spears and *bola*, trinkets and family treasure. The Spriton had lived in communion with one another, too, each village hut full of material evidence of life and family and the village as a whole. Even the Podling burrow they'd found had had that same proof . . . but should urVa one day pass away, or leave for another place, the only thing left of him would be the bare walls with the writing Naia couldn't read. And even then, it wouldn't take long for the wild and the elements to eat away those as well, and then there would be no record he had existed at all.

"Have some *ta*."

Naia nearly jumped at the sound of urVa's voice. Despite his size and dragging tail, he was surprisingly stealthy and was already halfway across the small den's space, heading toward the kettle. As he walked, his spine snaked in a liquid motion from his head to his tail, giving his entire body a limber movement that contradicted his bulk. He lifted the hot iron kettle in his bare hand and poured the steaming water into three stone cups arranged in a triangle on the windowsill. As the water hit the herbs within, the steam changed from white to a powder-red, and Naia's mouth watered at the sour, sweet, spicy scent. She accepted the cup urVa gave her, holding the warming stone in her chilly hands.

"Did you sleep well?" When she nodded, he added, "I wake to watch the Brothers rise. All three were in the sky this morning. For but a short time . . . though it will grow longer, mm."

"Is it that strange for all three to be in the sky?"

"Strange?" urVa echoed, tilting his big head. "No, very natural. It may seem strange in the short time, but in the long time, it is no stranger than day and night."

"In the long time . . . Why? How often does it happen?"

urVa pointed at the shape that Kylan had called the Great Conjunction, then took a sip of his *ta* and said nothing more. Whether he didn't know, hadn't understood the question, or simply wouldn't answer, Naia wasn't sure. She tried a sip of the hot drink and was rewarded with a tangy flavor similar to the alfen fruit back home. Though she knew in the back of her mind that time—and Gurjin's trial—would not wait for her to enjoy every chance to pause, she set the thought aside for just a moment of rest.

"We're headed to the Black River," she said. "Do you know if we're very far? Could you give us directions?"

urVa looked out the window.

"Yes . . . ," he said. Naia waited to hear the directions she hoped would follow, but instead of words, urVa picked up his stringed staff and the satchel of spears and rose from his stool. "Shall we go now?"

Naia grabbed her pack and shook Kylan by the shoulder as urVa left without so much as a "come along." Scrambling to gather their things and shake off the sleepy warmth of the morning, they darted out the door after their four-armed host.

urVa was not a fast mover, but he was not by any means a slow one, either. Most importantly, he was consistent, never seeming to tire, though they crossed a huge stretch of land within the Dark Wood. In the daylight, now that the Cradle-Tree was recovering, the wood seemed an entirely different being, full of life and the joyous singing of all the creatures that dwelled within it. Naia's heart sang, light and in tune with the forest she had helped heal.

Kylan finally asked if they could stop for lunch, as they hadn't eaten breakfast. Although Naia's own stomach had been grumbling quietly to her for several miles, she hadn't been about to be the first to say anything, not with one of her companions a Spriton song teller and the other a tireless hermit. urVa agreed right away, finding them a spot near a pool of freshwater and taking his staff and spears. Naia watched keenly as he pulled the cord taut between the ends of the staff, so tight the entire length of the limber wood bent in a more pronounced crescent.

"What is that?" Naia asked. "A way to catch some lunch?"

"Its name is *bow*," urVa said. "These, in this quiver, are arrows. Would you like to see?"

Naia was already on her feet. "Kylan, do you mind?"

Kylan had already taken off his shoes and was massaging his sore dirt-caked toes.

"As long as you bring back something to eat," he said, waving them away.

Naia followed urVa into the wood, Neech drifting beside her, until they came to a rocky ledge overlooking a steep hill of moss-covered boulders. Trees jutted out between the black rocks, and from somewhere deep within the rock, a tiny trickling stream wound between and over, all the way down to the next step of the wood below. Naia kicked a pebble down and watched it bounce back and forth between the jutting ledges and narrow crevices. A cool draft rose, heavy with the scent of green and rock. urVa stood close to the ledge and held the bow in his two left hands, taking one of the arrows from the barrel-like quiver that contained them. Naia watched urVa place the notched butt of the arrow against the taut string in the bow. The arrow's feathers would offer the stick a better flight, Naia realized.

"Bow—two ends connected by a single string. Arrow—head and tail connected by a single shaft."

"For hunting? They look like spears."

"Bow and arrow do not hunt; a hunter hunts. I am not a hunter."

He pulled the end back and tilted the stone arrowhead upward, and on release, the arrow disappeared so quickly into the wild below that Naia barely had time to follow it with her eyes.

"It's so simple," she said. urVa handed the bow to her. Though it was nearly as tall as she, it was light. When she tried pulling back the bowstring, it was very difficult, even without an arrow. Upon reflection, she realized urVa had twice her number of arms, not to mention his size and weight.

"It is, isn't it?" urVa replied, with almost a hint of surprise. He notched another arrow, this one with a bone head and wound with string, and held the bow for her, gesturing for her to try drawing. With both hands and urVa's help steadying the arrow, Naia drew back the string, using her entire body to do so. When the tension became too great, the string slipped from her hands, and the arrow flew with a rackety *TWANG*, shooting away with an unsteady, audible wobble. It clattered into a rock and ricocheted away.

Neech, responding to his instinct and training, puffed and waited for Naia's command to retrieve the arrow, though she wasn't sure the flying eel had even been able to track the shooting spear's final landing spot. She calmed him with a wave of her hand, and he settled on a rock nearby, fussing with little chirps. urVa chuckled.

"We need a Gelfling-size bow."

Naia let a few more arrows loose with urVa's help, getting better and better at holding the string steady with each release. He let her hold the bow itself, after, and she memorized the way the string was tied in the notches at either end of the bow—the degree of curve and flexibility the piece of wood required. She set the bow aside and sat cross-legged to look at the remaining arrows from urVa's quiver. Each was unique, with a different engraving or colorful adornment. Some had glittering sea-green scales along the sides, some had feathers or barbed orange leaves. The arrowheads were an array of hard materials, from stones and claws to bone and ancient wood. One even appeared to be made of a tooth. Every arrow was different, made with painstaking care and detail.

"Shall I retrieve the others, from earlier?" she asked. Although they had fallen a long way down, she wasn't afraid of heights, and with Neech's help, she hoped they might find the arrows with not too much trouble.

urVa waved a hand. "I'll make more."

Naia looked at the arrows in the quiver, knowing it may have taken days just to weave the feathers into the shafts. Ornaments like these were displayed with love and pride in Sog, and even *bola* were retrieved with the help of hunting eels. To think they were lost forever in the Dark Wood gave Naia a pang of guilt, and she prepared to climb down the mounds of boulders, anyway. Before she could begin the descent, however, urVa put a hand on her shoulder and gently pulled her back.

"Ah, Gelfling, little Gelfling," he said. "Let them go. They were made of Thra and have returned to Thra. Now that my quiver is nearly empty, I have room for new arrows."

Naia considered waiting until urVa wasn't looking and going down the rocky valley, anyway, but he fixed her with a placid gaze, and she realized he was truly uninterested in reclaiming them. In fact, he was already gathering handfuls of leaves off a bushy purple and green plant. Furry berries dangled from the tips of the leaves, still wet with dew. This was their lunch, not any hunted quarry. urVa patted her shoulder with his fourth hand, as if he were trying to shake her from her fixation, and said, "A stone in each hand leaves no room for a fifth . . . Mm, or in case of Gelfling, a third. Holding on to things too tightly will prevent you from moving forward."

It didn't feel right, and Naia said so, though she also stooped to help gather their leafy lunch.

"If I let go of the things I care about, then what's the point of going forward? I understand stones-in-hand, but there are things more important than stones."

"Little stones, pebbles," urVa said. "Big stones, boulders. Even bigger, Thra itself. Stones come in all shapes and sizes. All things are connected. What we surrender, we may be given. What we lose, we may find again. For every one there is another."

"Well, I'm trying to find the truth about my brother. That's not some stone I'm going to throw out into the wilderness."

urVa didn't argue, simply bobbing his head from side to side. Though she hadn't really expected to change his mind, Naia felt a pinch of frustration when he didn't reply at all, but she kept it to herself. It was fine to disagree, after all, so long as neither of them held the feeling in contempt. As they returned to Kylan, Naia felt crowded in her own mind. She had pushed so many thoughts away in order to make her way north. That was the best thing she could do, she had told herself. It was better than dwelling on all her fears, anyway. But now, as she couldn't shake urVa's parable from her mind, the worries were surfacing. The same worries that had been projected into the words of the phantoms created by the guilt of the Cradle-Tree.

You aren't strong enough.

"urVa," she said, pausing. She wanted to ask her question while they were still alone. urVa slowed his gait, swinging his big head around to peer down at her. She pushed her toes into the dirt and squeezed her locs. "I heard voices. Last night. Saying horrible things. But . . . those were just part of the Cradle-Tree's magic, right? Echoes of my fears, trying to scare me into loneliness, the way the crystal veins had done to the tree."

"Hmmm," urVa murmured. "Yes, and no."

"Yes and no are opposites," Naia said, though it pained her to state the obvious.

"Some things are . . . Listen. Olyeka-Staba's magic can only show us what is already there. What *was* already there. If you heard it, someone said it. If you saw it, something did it. But remember. Words can take on many forms."

Naia tilted her head, bordering on the edge between wanting to understand his riddles and wanting to give up on them.

"Then are you saying what I heard was true? Or are you saying it was only in my mind?"

urVa smiled and nodded, and she wondered if he was hard of hearing.

"Words can take on many forms," was all he said before he looked away and continued his ambling walk.

When they returned, Kylan was sitting cross-legged on a stone, his tablet and book in hand, dream-etching. From his concentration and the amount of words he was enchanting, Naia guessed he was writing about what he had read in urVa's den, making a copy of the words he could take with him, so he might never forget.

"Smart one, this one," urVa said with a chuckle. He set his bow and the nearly empty quiver against the rock and began tearing the thick leaves into bite-size pieces. "What words are for, you know. Passing along a message from one place to another, even when the original dreamer has, himself, passed along and gone."

Kylan put away his writing and rose to help them prepare their lunch.

"Did you learn to use that thing?" he asked. "Did it, eh . . . help you catch this feisty wild shrub?"

Naia snorted. "No. urVa doesn't use arrows for hunting."

"What for, then? Picking his teeth? Doesn't he have bones for that?"

She didn't answer, stuffing her mouth with leaves, and Kylan got the hint to leave her alone. She didn't want to talk about arrows that weren't used for anything but shooting out into the wood. She didn't want to talk about opposites being the same, or whether or not words needed to be spoken aloud in order to be true. The leaves and berries were bland but filling, and even Neech nibbled on one or two. Before long, their hunger was sated, and they picked up their things and continued on their way.

Without urVa's help, Naia imagined the Dark Wood would not have been completely impenetrable. However, she recognized that had she and Kylan tried to make the journey alone, it certainly would have taken them much longer. urVa knew every tree, every lump of moss, every disk-shaped fungi growing on every slime-backed slug. He was passive, blending into the forest seamlessly, sometimes so much so that Naia feared she would lose sight of him. Fliers landed on him in pairs, pecking at his robes once or twice before fluttering onward. Though he didn't use the bow for hunting, Naia remembered the speed with which he'd caught her *bola*, back in the Cradle-Tree's basin. Should urVa ever find need to use his bow for quarry, she was sure he would be a stealthy, deadly hunter.

urVa slowed sometime later in the afternoon, waiting until Naia and Kylan had caught up before remarking, "Someone is looking for you."

Naia stiffened, turning her ears in all directions, but she heard only the cacophony of the wood. Kylan came up with the same as well, because he said, "How can you tell?"

urVa pointed up, and Naia looked. With a gasp she recognized the cliff pass above them, the limb of the broken bridge dangling like an inverted tree. She could see now that the bridge was just another limb of the Cradle-Tree, broken and fallen at some point during the great tree's possession by the darkened crystal veins.

Now there they were in the valley between the two cliffs, nearing the opposite side. Naia's heart leaped. If they were here, the Black River couldn't be much farther off. Perhaps her journey to Ha'rar could finally continue, detour and all.

"What are we looking at?" Kylan asked, reminding Naia why she had turned her face to the cliffs overhead. urVa stretched his arm up, giving his point more definition, and when Naia followed the direction, she saw the silhouette of a figure traveling along the ridge. Beside it was a larger figure, loping in long-legged strides. Squint though she might, the brightness of the sky and the distance made it impossible for her to see anything else worth recognizing.

"Could just be a traveler," Naia said. "How would you know they're looking for us?"

urVa shrugged and lurched into motion again.

"An archer knows the path of an arrow from either end."

Another way of saying a hunter knows when he's being hunted, Naia thought. At least sometimes his riddles made sense to her. She took a last look up the cliff where the figure had moved out of view, then quickened her step. *Even if he says he's not a hunter . . .*

"Come on, then," she said. "If they're skilled enough, we'll meet them sooner or later. No reason to slow our own steps waiting up."

urVa brought them through the valley, over little streams that grew more robust the farther they walked. They saw no more of their follower upon the ridge, and Naia didn't dwell on it. If they were being pursued, it would eventually come to a resolution one way or another, and she didn't have time to worry about which way it would be. Her mind inevitably returned to the frights of the previous night, but when she tried to pick any meaning from it, all she could come up with was that she had no grasp of the truth. And that, she reminded herself, was why she was on this journey in the first place.

When they reached the other side of the gorge, urVa stopped alongside one of the streams and placed his two top hands upon his bow.

"If you follow this stream, it will take you to the river," he said. "There are falls, down into the deeper wood, but Gelfling should be able to climb on foot. After the falls, the river flows through Gelfling Stonewood, then onward north."

Naia committed the directions to memory, clasping her hands and bowing.

"Thank you, urVa. And for showing us the way to the river."

"May we meet again," urVa replied. "Even be it in a different form."

Then Naia and Kylan waved their farewells as urVa turned, vanishing into the forest from which they'd come. The wood folded around him so completely, it was as if he had never been there, just another ghostly projection of the Dark Wood.

"What do you think that meant?" Kylan asked.

"I don't know. He seems very wise, but what good is wisdom when it can't be understood? I didn't understand half of what he told us this entire time."

"Maybe it will make sense later," Kylan suggested. "Sometimes it can take a lot of time before things come together, but when they do, there's no missing it."

"It was about time you said something like that, Song Teller," Naia teased. "Now come on. Most of urVa's words were in riddles, but his directions to the Black River certainly weren't. If we hurry, we can make it before sundown."

CHAPTER 18

They walked for another quarter day before the light pattering of rain started. Though it was gentle—hardly there—it did not let up and was only a warning of what type of storm was to come. Instead of taking shelter, Naia and Kylan did their best to stay close to the gorge cliffs, avoiding most of the rain and the occasional buffet of strong wind. There was no sign of the figure they'd seen on the ridge, and Naia hoped it would stay that way.

"Hey, Naia?"

She stopped and looked back to where Kylan stood behind on a boulder. She faced him and waited, though she half expected it to be nothing, or close to nothing, as it had been in the past. He huffed a sigh and skipped down a few steps, nearing her so he could speak without raising his voice. When his words came, they were serious, and full of the weight of respect.

"When we dreamfasted, after we saw the ruffnaw in the Podling burrow. I could tell you held back. But in the forest—I heard . . . things."

Naia shivered, looking back at him, searching his face in an attempt to know exactly what things he'd heard. The same things she'd heard? She didn't know what she might do if those echoes, preserved forever in time by the Cradle-Tree, had reached his ears.

Kylan stepped closer, keeping his voice gentle.

"I know it was probably just my imagination, and things made up by the tree in its darkness, but I . . . I was wondering if you'd tell me. Whether or not what I heard was true . . . that your brother has betrayed the Skeksis Lords."

So he'd heard it after all. Naia's heart sank in dread, but she couldn't escape it, or Kylan. That wasn't the honorable thing to do, and anyway, no matter what Gurjin had done, his actions were his, just as Naia's belonged to her. As she read the loyalty in Kylan's face, she knew she could trust him. Especially after the journey they'd undertaken so far.

"I don't know," she said finally. "The truth is, the All-Maudra sent a soldier to my clan looking for my brother because he had been accused of treason by the Skeksis. After they accused him, he suddenly went missing, which only made things worse. Now I don't know whether he really is a traitor, or whether something bad has happened to him. That's why I'm traveling to Ha'rar . . . to represent my clan before the All-Maudra, and also, I hope, to learn the truth."

Her confession brought nothing but a nod from Kylan.

"So the voice I heard in the wood . . . the one that sounded like a soldier saying . . ."

"Saying those awful things about the Skeksis?" Naia finished, throwing her hands up in frustration. "I don't know! I asked urVa, and all he did was tell me more riddles. This and that about how the Cradle-Tree only echoes words that were truly spoken—but then he went on to say words don't need speaking to be true. All I wanted to know was whether Gurjin said those things or whether he's been falsely accused . . . all I want to know is whether he is really a traitor or not."

"Words don't need speaking . . . maybe he meant words of the heart," Kylan said. "But then, whose words? The fears of your heart?"

"Or spoken words from Gurjin's mouth, said somewhere in the wood? The Castle of the Crystal lies within the Dark Wood, just as Stone-in-the-Wood does. There must have been days or nights when Gurjin spoke near a branch of the Cradle-Tree. I just don't know, and I can hardly stand it."

Naia grunted and kicked a rock, sending it bouncing down the path ahead and into the creek. The sound of it was hard, hard, hard . . . and then *soft.* They had nearly reached the bottom of the highlands. Spongy turf crept up between the rocks, blanketed with moss and vines, spiked here and there with tube-shaped red flowers full of sugar-tipped pistils glistening in the daylight. She left the topic behind and so Kylan did, too. There was no use in talking it over and over. The longer Naia thought about the dilemma—the truth about Gurjin—the more she knew there was only one way to find out, and that was to find him herself.

It wasn't long before Naia could hear the sound of water, slow-moving but deep, and she could smell the cool earthy scent of the riverbed. Beyond the nearer *plunks* and *brrr-blunks* of the raindrops falling on the river was a distant white noise, growing ever closer—the falls urVa had mentioned. Naia's pace quickened in excitement, and she pushed back the circle-shaped fronds of the lusher riverside plants. As the leaves gave way and the scaled tree bark tightened away from her, the view became clear. A sparkling obsidian river moved steadily to the west, where it poured over the last of the highlands to a frothy lake far below.

At the sight of it, Naia let out a whoop of joy and, despite their tense words earlier, threw an arm around Kylan and gave him a hug so tight, he laughed. They had arrived at the Black River.

They stowed their shoes in their packs and rolled up their leggings, wading into the strong cool current. Along the bank, the riverside was carved with pockets of shallow water and smoothed stones, full of speckled green and blue swimmers. Each faced up-current, swimming in a lazy S shape, seeming perfectly still, though in reality they were in constant motion to avoid being swept down the river to the falls. Neech zipped out from Naia's pack and dived, dipping into the water and resurfacing with a spray of water droplets, one of the swimmers thrashing in his jaws. He landed on a nearby rock and gulped the swimmer in two bites, shaking drops from his fur and chattering happily.

"It's beautiful!" Kylan exclaimed while Naia filled her cupped hands with water and took a fresh cold drink. Though the river appeared black from far away, up close she saw that it was the hard black gravel and stone that lined the riverbed and gave it its midnight color. When the sunlight hit the bottom of the river, she could see thousands of diamond-shaped facets glittering with dark blues and purples. Even the silty sand at the shallow portions was black. A handful of the stuff looked like the night sky, twinkling with silver speckles when the light hit it just right. Naia poured some into one of her empty water skins, hoping to gift it to her parents when she eventually returned home.

Their meeting with the river added some necessary levity. For a moment, Naia forgot all she had before her and could instead appreciate how far she'd come. They dried their feet and put their shoes on before carefully making their way down the jutting rocks that comprised the front of the falls. The rocks were damp from the rain and spray from the falls, coated in a thin layer of slippery algae that made finding a safe handhold more difficult than it would have been otherwise. Still, the drop was not too far, and before long they had reached the basin, all sounds drowned out by the thundering of the falls. The air was thick with mist and the dark flickering shapes of bats darting in and out of their roosts within the cliff face. Naia gave the highlands a last glance, and then together, she and Kylan headed into the dense forest.

"Let's follow the river a ways. Then we'll need to make a raft . . . and from that point, we can rest."

"Jarra-Jen once made a boat from half a shell of a giant skorpus," Kylan said. When Naia gave him a sidelong glance, he grinned and for a moment held her gaze with just a smile. Then he broke away and said, "But I think we can do with logs."

Before Naia could come up with some teasing response, they heard an approach from within the depths of the wood—quick and loud and coming closer. Before they could take cover, a tall white beast burst into the clearing. It reared before it trampled them, wheeling around with a whistling trumpet as Kylan cried out, falling back. Naia held her arm in front of her face, standing between the long-legged animal and Kylan, but there was no need. A familiar voice called out over the din of the beast's cry, "*Doye, doye*—at last, I've found you!"

At the call, the creature turned, planting all four hooves on the soft ground and snorting with an agitated gurgle. Naia lowered her arm and took in the creature's large gray ears and wrinkled pug-nosed face punctuated by a long red proboscis. It was indeed a Landstrider, a creature she'd only heard of and then glimpsed along the wide Spriton plains. Seated on its gray-furred shoulders, arm in a sling and sleek silver hair flowing between her folded wings, was none other than Tavra of Ha'rar.

CHAPTER 19

"D oye," Tavra shouted again, but it was more to calm the Landstrider than anything. She soothed the beast with a pat on the shoulder, and it grunted, the pink in its ears fading. With an agile leap, she dismounted, wings outstretched just enough to ease her landing to nothing more than a soft step.

"Naia," Tavra said. "Thank Aughra you're safe."

Though Tavra looked relieved to see Naia, her mouth remained a tight pale line, and her eyes and ears were alert. Her broken wing was on the mend, held in place with a light splint. The Landstrider, outfitted with a Spriton riding harness and a saddle strapped with traveling bags, moved away to take a drink from the river. So this was the one that had been following them! Naia wasn't sure whether she should be relieved.

Tavra nodded at Kylan with a quick tilt of her chin.

"This is the dream etcher? I saw his words on the stone near the bridge and knew you'd come this way."

"Yes," Naia said. "He's accompanying me to Stone-in-the-Wood. We've come from Sami Thicket together . . . So much has happened since I saw you. Is my father well?"

"Indeed. When I left him, he was still bedridden, but your mother is unmatched in healing *vliyaya*." Tavra looked both ways, up and below, then leaned in and lowered her voice. "We need to speak, and quickly. First, you're truly unharmed? Were you within the wood at night? Did you meet anyone, or anything—did you hear anything?"

The questions were rapid, wary, and instead of bringing answers out of Naia's throat only made her hold on to them more tightly. What was Tavra worried about? Maybe she was merely concerned for Naia's well-being, but maybe it had to do with the echoes of Gurjin's voice in the wood. Naia felt every muscle stiffen as a thought crossed her mind. According to Tavra, the Skeksis had only accused Gurjin of spreading traitorous lies, but they had not stated what exactly those lies had been. Did Tavra know the truth? Did she know something she wasn't telling?

"Yes," Naia said, choosing to answer only the first two questions. "We traveled the wood overnight, but we survived safely."

Tavra's eyes narrowed. "As I was tracking you in the wood, I saw prints from another. Were you with someone?"

"We were following the tracks, hoping they would lead us to the river," Naia said. Again, it was half-true. If she told the soldier about urVa, she wondered if she might be putting the riddle-ribbing old Mystic in danger. Why was Tavra so intent on knowing if they had been alone? The Silverling leaned back slowly, every feature on her face tight with suspicion.

"I told you to beware the creatures of the Dark Wood," she said quietly. "Even those that seem good are connected to those that are not so good. Connected in ways we don't understand."

"For every one there is another," Naia said. As little sense as it made to her, the words had an impact on Tavra, who sighed.

"Listen. We received a message by swoothu in Sog. Gurjin is alive, but he's been taken captive."

"Captive?" Naia repeated, just to make sure she'd heard the news properly. Alive was good, but captive was not. "Captive by who? Where?"

Tavra shook her head.

"That is not for you to know. I have orders from your parents to send you home to Sog. They asked me specifically not to tell you any more than I have."

"Because if I know where he is, you know I'll go to him," Naia huffed. "He's my brother, Tavra! I'm not a child—let me go with you to rescue him!"

Tavra's eyes flashed and her jaw was set.

"You will return to Sog," she repeated. "And that is the end of the matter."

"But I've come all this way! I'm not about to turn around and go all the way home, not when I know my brother is being held captive somewhere. I don't need you or my parents protecting me!"

"Naia—"

"I'll have you know, I saved this wood," Naia said. "It was under a curse—it had looked into the blackness of the crystal veins, deep in the earth. But I healed it by dreamfasting, without your help or my parents' protection. Something is terribly, terribly ill in Thra—something that started somewhere in the Dark Wood—and it's related to all this with Gurjin. I don't know how, or why, but I feel it in my gut. And"—Naia dropped her voice to let Tavra know she was absolutely serious—"I know what Gurjin was saying. I know what he said about the Skeksis."

Naia's words had hardly any effect on the Vapra soldier. Tavra leaned in, her expression so stern, it was as if she were truly made of silver.

"If you know what he said, then you'll understand this is much more dangerous than one Gelfling can handle alone."

Naia knew then that what she had heard echoed by the Cradle-Tree was true. Somewhere in the Dark Wood, Gurjin had spoken high treason against the Skeksis.

"You are under the orders of your parents and myself to return to Sog," Tavra added. "An order from a soldier is an order from the All-Maudra, so I hope you'll take it seriously."

It was all Naia could do to lower her chin in half a nod.

"I understand," she whispered, knowing that arguing with the Vapra would get her nowhere.

Tavra took in a big breath and let it out slowly, then pinned the same stern gaze on Kylan.

"That goes for you, too, Spriton," she said. "You'll take my Landstrider, both of you, and fly from this place as quickly as it can take you."

"What about you?" Kylan asked Tavra. He had been quiet during the entire exchange, though Naia was confident he'd made out every word of it. Anger boiled in the Drenchen's stomach, though she tried to hide her feelings. How long had she known about Gurjin's treason? Tavra had acted as though she knew nothing when she'd arrived in Sog.

"I've traveled many paths by foot," Tavra replied. She walked the Landstrider to Naia and pushed the reins into her hands. Naia took the heavy straps, immobilized by frustration and betrayal. She held her tongue, though, knowing the soldier would not be swayed. As if in apology, Tavra put her hands on Naia's shoulders.

"I will find your brother," she said. "And I will do the right thing."

Naia could only find the restraint for three words, and so she said them, as calmly and evenly as possible. "As will I."

Tavra met Naia's eyes for a moment, as if trying to dreamfast without dreamfasting. Then, with a grim but understanding nod, she strode quickly into the wood.

Naia waited until the sound of Tavra's steps had faded before she dropped her pack to the ground with a bitter huff and started pulling out only the essentials—rope, *bola*, food, water. After checking that Gurjin's knife was still strapped to her belt, she bent to tighten the laces on her shoes, her sore shoulders and back appreciating the stretch.

"What are you doing?" Kylan asked. "You can't get back to Sog without your pack—it's got your kindling stones and such."

"I'm going to the Castle of the Crystal," Naia said.

"But you just promised Tavra—"

"That I would do the right thing. And I am. Don't you see? The castle can't be more than a day's journey here, so of course she can make it on foot. She didn't deny what we heard of Gurjin's words. There is only one place she could be going."

"The castle . . ." Kylan reached out and caught her sleeve. "Wait, Naia. You can't be sure of that. And she's trying to keep us safe, isn't she? Don't you think that if she's worried, you should be, too? What do you think you can do that Tavra can't? And she said your parents want you to come home . . ."

Naia pulled out of his grip.

"You heard the same words in the wood that I did! Were they lies or not? No one has the answers—no one will tell me! Even when I thought I'd heard it from Gurjin, I couldn't be sure. So now the only way is to find out myself."

"Even so, we shouldn't go barging into the Castle of the Crystal—"

"You want me to just give up?"

"No, but what you're planning is reckless, and dangerous. There has to be another way!"

He was shouting now, and she shouted back over him, clenching her hands in fists.

"There *isn't*. It's either go to the castle or run back home, and I'm not letting go of my brother so easily!"

Kylan let out a loud annoyed groan.

"You're so stubborn, I'm surprised you can let go of a *bola* long enough to throw it!" he cried.

"Says the one who couldn't hit a target if his life depended on it," Naia shot back. "I let go of how I felt about you *Spriton* back in Sami Thicket, you know—so that you could travel with me. And look how that's working out, eh!"

Kylan jerked as though she'd struck him. He looked down,

and she knew she'd won the argument. He gave up.

"There's no other way," she said again. "So this is *my* way."

Naia pushed past him and entered the thick brush after Tavra, away from the Black River that would have otherwise taken her all the way to Ha'rar. The journey would be meaningless if she had to stand before the All-Maudra and represent a brother she might not even truly know. Kylan's voice was already fading behind her, muffled by the thick leaves and the early sound of rolling thunder.

"But the heroes always find another way," he said.

Her response was in a mutter she doubted he could hear. "Maybe in tales, but this isn't a song for telling."

Any minute, she expected the distressed sighs of Kylan picking up his things, tromping into the woody brush after her. Hearing nothing, she turned halfway, looking to see if he was coming—but he wasn't. There was nothing but green and purple leaves, red and brown branches, darkening light, and thickening rain.

She was alone.

CHAPTER 20

Naia trekked between dark-leaved trees with huge barrel-size trunks, and rocks covered in wriggling purple moss studded with hairy polyps. Black-winged scaly things swooped and flapped in the canopy overhead. The purple rocks eventually gave way to lumpier rocks that grumbled and moved as she walked by, shifting away from her and burrowing deeper into the mulch- and leaf-covered forest floor. Naia's footsteps were loud and harsh as she stomped her way through the brush, although she hardly cared who heard her. At the very least, it frightened the crawlies and hundred-legged armor-ants from her path so she didn't have to worry about stepping on them. Though her sense of direction was good, it was getting dark, and the storm clouds were moving in, hiding what little was left of the Brothers' sunlight in the sky. Still, she had to continue, and she no longer had the clear Black River to guide her safely to her destination. She broke a branch off a tree she passed, snapping the twig into smaller and smaller pieces until it was merely splinters, and then she tossed them away in disgust.

Thunder broke overhead, like an egg cracking and pouring out huge endless drops of cold wet rain. Naia looked for shelter nearby but found none, and all she could do was pick up her pace and move forward. She thought briefly about Kylan, but pushed the thought from her mind. He'd made his choice not to come with her. Anyway, by now he was probably halfway back up the falls. Maybe he'd even make it to urVa's before long—that would be nice for him, safe and warm next to the hearth with a hot cup of *ta*. Naia, however, would be stranded in the muddy, cold, dark, shadowy forest on account of doing the right thing.

The rain came harder, streaming in soupy rivulets as the land sloped downward, carrying leaves and twigs as if they were tiny boats on a raging river. As the slope steepened, going from a gentle decline to a deep hill, Naia had to grab on to the drooping fronds and branches to keep from slipping. Finally, though, it happened—a tree's leafy tendril was so slick with water that it escaped her grasp as soon as she put her weight on it. Then she was tumbling, tumbling down the hill in rolls and bumps, thrashing through short plants with burrs and fine feathery leaves.

At the end of it, she spilled into a shallow puddle of mud. Coated head to toe in muck, her head spinning, she spit out dirt and leaves. Although in pain and still a bit dizzy, she felt lucky not to have collided with one of the many protruding boulders or spiny trees. Naia patted around for Neech, unable to find him. Then a chirp and a squeak came from above as he glided down, unharmed—probably having let go of her as soon as she'd tripped. Plucking him from the air, she hugged him tightly, more for herself than for him.

"*Yesmit!*" she swore, but even the curse offered little relief. Alone in the mud, surrounded by the looming black tower-trees, back and shoulders aching, she let out a scream of frustration. As it echoed back to her, she put her face in her hands and wept. She didn't even know exactly why. Maybe it was for no one thing in particular, but nevertheless, the tears came out faster and harder than even the rain overhead. Naia didn't know why it had come to this, or had to be this way. If Gurjin was a traitor after all, her entire journey until now had been a waste! If they'd captured him, surely they would force him to stand his own trial—so what was she doing out here in the cold and wet, alone and miserable?

I'll hear the truth at the Castle of the Crystal, she told herself. She imagined the warmth within the castle's sturdy walls—and food, there ought to be hot food and maybe *ta* like urVa had served. *One way or another.*

She jumped when something cold and rubbery nudged her elbow. Out of the mud came a bulbous-eyed wide face, followed by a grub-shaped body. The mud made a sucking noise as the Nebrie surfaced, the fresh rain washing grime from its oily head and back. Unlike the Nebrie of Sog, this one was a youngling, maybe even a baby—no longer than twice Naia's height and as big around as a village drum. It nuzzled Naia's arm again, burbling and cooing, and Naia found the ache of a smile on her lips as she reached out and petted the thing's round nubby forehead.

"This mud and rain suits you just fine, doesn't it?" she asked. "Did your mother leave you here while she went to forage? You shouldn't come up out of the muck for just anyone. It could be dangerous."

The Nebrie's mouth opened in a toothless smile. It rolled

from left to right, dipping its face back into the mud and blowing bubbles. Naia laughed despite herself, and as she did, the tightness in her chest relaxed. She sneezed, then wiped her nose with the back of her hand. As if it made a difference in all the rain.

"I'm lost," she told the Nebrie as she petted its leathery hide. "I thought I knew the way, but it feels like I'm only running in circles."

Naia's entire body rocked as the Nebrie shoveled its face under her arm, burbling. Opening her mind, just a little, a gentle dreamfast formed. She saw the Nebrie's mother, big and purple, pulling up weeds from the pond bank, chewing them up before spitting them back in a pulp for her pod of children. Though the meal wasn't something Naia was keen to try, the vision was touching all the same. In return, she tried to dream back, thinking of her and Gurjin's shared Name Day. Her sisters had tied bright ribbons and bells to every one of her locs. The Great Sun had been warm that day, and Gurjin had not yet left for his post at the castle. They had stood together before the people of their clan, eager to take on the responsibilities of their blossoming adulthood.

The Nebrie squealed in delight, and Naia let the memory fade. Careful not to send the thought in dreamfast, she remembered the Nebrie in Sog, with its frothing maw and lethal tusks. *This was how Nebrie were supposed to be*: happy, content to play and wallow in the bog for all the day. Not swollen in a rage, mindless in an empty state of pain—not like the ruffnaw in the burrow, nor the tormented Cradle-Tree, whose branches still surrounded her. Thra was in pain, in sadness, and it originated at the Heart of Thra: at the Castle of the Crystal. Though the castle had not been Naia's original destination, after all that had happened, it did not seem a coincidence that it would be where she would seek the truth about Gurjin.

Sighing, she stood and looked down at her mud-stained clothes. If she had brought her pack with her, she was sure its contents would have been strewn all up and down the slanted hillside, but as it was, she still had everything she'd rolled down with, tied safely across her back and to her belt. She had what she needed. She could make do. If no one would shed light on the labyrinth of questions, not even the soldier of the All-Maudra, then she would have to be the one to find the way herself.

Still, as the pouring rain ebbed again, and the Nebrie settled down to sleep in the mud, something felt incomplete in the quiet. Naia looked back up the hill and saw no one, so she turned ahead. She was still alone, and there was nothing to be done about it now.

She said her farewells to the Nebrie, shushing it back to sleep before brushing off the larger clumps of grass-matted mud from her tunic and traveling onward. Though tracking Tavra in the dry daylight might have been possible, the dark and the rain had made the trail invisible. For a moment, she panicked, realizing she really was lost. Even if she had wanted to turn back, find her way south and home, she wasn't sure that she could in the rain. Her footsteps quickened in her worry until she nearly tripped on an upraised root, shaking herself out of her wandering daze with a spark of hope. She was not really alone in the wood—anything but! Kneeling, sighing in relief, she placed her hands upon the root and reached out in dreamfast.

"Are you listening, Olyeka-Staba?" she asked.

She closed her eyes and gave her touch some pressure, focusing on connecting with it, with feeling its presence, roots deep in the earth and branches up in the clouds. It seemed the tree remembered her, for its dreamfast was warm and gentle.

I seek the Castle of the Crystal, Naia said. *Can you show me the way?*

As if she had been lifted by wind, held aloft by the branches of the Cradle-Tree, Naia saw what the tree saw. The Dark Wood was a vast body of green and black, filling the valley formed between two bodies of highlands: the Claw Mountains to the northwest and the Caves of Grot to the northeast. In a clearing to the west, a day's journey from an elbow of the Black River, was the Castle of the Crystal. Its shining black shape jutted from the flesh of the wood like a clawed hand clutching at clouds.

The tree's voice spoke in the language of leaves in the wind, roots in the ground.

There resides the Heart of Thra . . .

When the dreamfast ended, the darkness of the night felt blinding in comparison. Naia closed her eyes and remembered the way, hoping the vision would stay fast in her memory as long as she needed it to guide her.

"Thank you," she said to the Cradle-Tree. Again, if it responded, she couldn't hear it, save for the gentle creaking of branches in the night wind.

Naia turned at the snap of a twig and what sounded like

familiar heavy footsteps, but in the dark she saw little, and the sound did not come again. She remained immobile, hand on the Cradle-Tree's root, holding her breath and straining her eyes and ears. Many things made noises in the night in the wild, of course, and it had been the same in Sog. Yet something seemed different now, closer, familiar . . .

"urVa?"

The presence faded from her awareness, moving back into the shadows in a rumble of thunder from the south. Naia waited only long enough for another crack of lightning to flash overhead before she hurried onward, hoping she might make it to the castle before the second storm front brought its wrath upon the Dark Wood.

CHAPTER 21

Lightning lit the way, once even striking the top of a tree so it burst into sparks and flames that were quickly drowned by the rain now cascading sideways from the clouds. The downpour came with a vengeance, though much of it was intercepted by the broad leaves of the tower-trees that increased in number and frequency the closer Naia came to the castle. Though she couldn't yet see her destination, she could feel it. Omnipresent, like thousands of eyes watching her from above.

Naia stopped in her fleet jog when she heard something—a snarl, perhaps, or just thunder. The memory of the sound echoed, though her ears heard nothing more, no matter which way they swiveled. She longed for the bigger eyes of a night bird, or maybe the flanged nose of a ruffnaw. Anything that might let her senses pierce the thick night in the impenetrable wood.

A warm draft of air brushed off the skin of her cheeks and then was gone . . . then came again, and her stomach nearly turned: it was *breath*, wafting from the darkness, from some creature so hot and close that its exhales settled on her shoulders in silent heavy waves. The scent of it was somehow familiar, yet *wrong*—but she didn't have time to puzzle over it.

Holding her own breath and moving as little as possible, Naia peered through the dark. She both needed desperately to see and yet dreaded to catch sight of whatever was out there. The lyrics from Kylan's song came unbidden and danced through her mind, setting fire to her fears and imagination.

But the cold wind died still and he heard in the dim
Monstrous breath heavy through pointy-toothed grin . . .

Naia clenched her fist and pushed away the idea. The Hunter was a monster of song, recited over campfires to frighten younglings. Whatever was out there, watching her, was probably just a hungry predator who was hoping for a Gelfling feast. That was the way the world worked—in a great circle where the hunters became the prey, and so on.

Yet Kylan had seen *something* the night his parents were taken. The dreamfasted memory was Naia's, now, too, and she didn't know what to believe.

Now the Hunter waits behind him . . .

Something moved in the shadows, and every one of Naia's nerves fired, propelling her in a rapid dash away from the movement and the breath. Amid the thunder and crackling lightning, the sounds of branches and brush snapping under her racing feet, she thought she heard the ragged breath of a monster, but she refused to look back for fear of being snapped up by whatever it was that chased her. She ran and she ran, jumping and ducking, every leap taking her closer to the castle where, she could only hope, the blazing torches and mighty drawbridge would beckon her to safety inside. Tavra would be there, and the Skeksis Lords, and Gurjin—

The sounds of her pursuer abated and then evaporated altogether, and Naia slowed to a cautious, quiet walk in hope of catching her breath. Had she outrun it? Had it given up? Or was it merely waiting to catch her off guard? No, it was still there, just outside her range of sight. She could feel it circling, and in the ultramarine flashes of lightning, she made out shapes—not anything solid, but textures. It was like rustling, gathered cloth or fur, but shiny in spots as well, as if it were scaled, with a long whip-sharp tail that slithered behind it. It moved in and out of the wood as if it were one with the shadows, black and dangerous, wild and ravenous. Naia shuddered with fear when, in a low hissing voice, it spoke.

"Gelfling . . . yes . . . closer . . ."

Naia's heartbeat quickened to a new height. Whatever it was, it was intelligent enough to speak in the Gelfling tongue, to recognize her alone despite all the other quarry in the wood. When it let out a long rasping chuckle, she smelled its breath again.

"Closer . . . come closer . . . so lively . . . so rich . . . come closer . . ."

Out of the dark, a hand-like claw beckoned her. Paralyzed by fear, pressed with her back against one of the tower-trees, she watched the form step half within sight, as if materializing out of the inky black. It was huge, with a long cloaked back spiked in feathers and spines, and on its face was a mask the color of bone, hooked down and carved with two black holes. It loomed closer, but it was not until she could see the glassy burning eyes within that she smelled its breath again and, with a dizzy rush, realized what the familiar scent was. It was *Gelfling* lacing the monster's guttural, spit-bubbled words—the scent of Gelfling, her people, saturated the masked hunter's entire being, from its thick cloak and toothed mantle to the scaly hooked hand that was outstretched, ready to snare her around the neck.

A rush of fur and spines exploded from Naia's shoulder, shooting toward the monster's claws and latching on in a plume of barbs and teeth. The Hunter screeched in surprise, wheeling backward and thrashing, trying to dislodge the tiny muski that was locked on with spiny poisonous teeth. Jolted into motion by Neech's attack, Naia pulled a *bola* from her belt and swung it, holding the counterweight as a handle and smashing the other end into the monster's head. It landed with a CRACK against the grotesque bone mask, and the thing's shrieks escalated to wild screams. It finally flung Neech from its claw, clutching its cracked faceplate and heaving enraged, strong pants. It fixed Naia with a glare so fearsome, it took all her strength to remain standing . . . But then, without another word, the Hunter slithered backward, enveloped again into the night from whence it had come.

Naia stood in the rain, shaking, clutching Neech to her breast and doing everything she could to remain standing. The rain was pouring in sheets now, and the cover from the canopy was patchy at best. A cough came from her throat, and she realized she had been holding her breath tight in her lungs; another cough and a heavy shudder came out as she slowly remembered how to breathe. The Hunter was gone, at least for now.

Neech squeaked and squirmed, nipping her fingers and

startling her to life. He whined, and she nodded, lurching into motion. They had to make it to the castle, to safety. At this rate, she feared she might collapse from the cold that was driving straight through her skin to the bone. Urging her legs to move, she stumbled onward, hoping it was the direction the Cradle-Tree had shown her. Then again, everything looked the same in the dark, and she half expected to find herself back where she had started.

She looked down when her foot landed on something hard and flat. Half-buried in the soil and brush was a stone slab, as wide and long as she was tall. It was engraved with three arcs converging in the center where they formed a triangle, and spiraling out from the center of the shape was writing. What was the tablet doing here, and what did it mean? Searching the ground for clues, Naia was surprised to find another slab—and then another, all trailing end to end. They weren't tablets, she realized. It was a path. Hoping against the complaining of her body and her blistered feet, she followed the stones, one by one, as they became gradually more pronounced, each with a different engraving. With a gasp of relief, she saw light ahead—and then, suddenly, the wood cleared and she was standing at the foot of a humped drawbridge spanning a thick murky moat.

Towering on the other side of the bridge, magnificent black against the backdrop of the electric storm, was the spire-capped Castle of the Crystal.

CHAPTER 22

Naia gave the Dark Wood a last glance before gladly escaping it. Her shoes echoed on the drawbridge as she crossed it, the thick planks and heavy draw-chains lending a well-missed sense of safety to the night. Any moment, she half expected the masked monster—she dare not call it by the name she *wanted* to, lest her imagination run wild with fear again—to lunge from the shadows and drag her back into the wood, where she might be lost forever. But it didn't. If it had followed her to the castle, it stayed away, and soon she felt the warm heat of the blazing torches that were lighting her way across the wide cobbled path that met her feet on the far end of the bridge. The path was made of more carved stones, some with writing and others simply with pictures, many bearing a strange similarity to the inscriptions in urVa's den. Over and over, she saw the circles within the triangle, though it took different shapes and characters. The path of engravings snaked around the warped castle base, below the extended leg-like buttresses until it finally arched in again, leading to an enormous set of thorny doors that made Naia feel like nothing but a fly at the mouth of a gate made for giants.

"Oh—"

Tavra stood in front of the closed gate, in her silver cloak. Naia's

heart dropped into her gut. But her presence here confirmed what Naia had guessed—that her destination was the castle—and that Gurjin must be there, too. . . although she had not expected to find the Vapra soldier waiting at the gate. Naia wasn't sure, after her trek through the wood alone, that she was prepared for a confrontation so soon, but there seemed to be no getting around it. The only explanation that wouldn't sound completely ridiculous would be the truth, but Naia withheld even that, determined to make her stand no matter what Tavra thought. She was here for the truth, and if that meant facing Tavra—or even the All-Maudra—over punishment, then so be it.

Instead of getting angry, though, Tavra only paled in the bright gold torchlight. Her eyes widened, and she gripped Naia's shoulders.

"Naia, in Thra's name, what have you done?"

The urgency and fear in Tavra's voice took Naia by surprise. Then came a thunderous groaning sound as the gates drew open, pulled slow and wide like the wings of a giant beetle. The two Gelfling were showered in light from the hundred-flame chandeliers that hung within the main entrance hall. From inside, Naia heard cacophonous music and crowing, laughing, cackling voices, and saw a looming, lumbering shadow that danced along the lit side of the massive doors. Lips pressed thin, Tavra put her hands against Naia's cheeks, holding her face firmly and locking eyes. Naia knew it was for a dreamfast, for Tavra to tell her the truth, so instead of accepting the fasting, she simply said, "I want to hear it from Gurjin myself."

"They're coming," Tavra whispered. "You need to go. Now."

"But the Skeksis Lords—"

With a gasp of desperation, Tavra made to dreamfast once more, but they were interrupted as the bearer of the enormous ornamented shadow appeared at the gate. Seeing the creature sucked the breath from Naia's lungs. Although she had seen Lord skekLach and Lord skekOk in Sami Thicket, it had been from a distance. Now, tall and decorated, here was another standing before her, so close she could smell the musty sweet perfume that saturated his robes and oily skin. His cloak and mantle were propped high above his head with a complex structure of ribbed boning, adorned with jewels and shining metals. The cloak itself was crimson red with beaded patterns in black, studded here and there with furry black kiznet tails. Protruding from the mass of shining fabrics and extravagent ruffles, the Skeksis Lord's pale-eyed face dangled off a long muscled neck, sinewy lips pulled back in a wide smile as he took in the Gelfling standing before the gate. Whatever Tavra had been trying to say was lost in the moment as they stared up at him. The silence was broken when Tavra fell into a kneel before the lord, yanking Naia down with her as she bowed her head.

"Chamberlain Lord skekSil," Tavra said. Bowed, her face was hidden from the lord's gaze, but from the side, Naia saw her furrowed brow and pensive frown. "I have come from Ha'rar on behalf of the Gelfling All-Maudra for your council. This is Nadia, my . . . retainer."

Naia watched the pleats at the hem of Lord skekSil's cloak as he rustled it around, leaning far down and inhaling deeply over the both of them. When he spoke, his voice was high and bleating, almost in singsong as it resonated through his hornlike face.

"Katavra!" he cried. "Daughter of Mayrin! Come, come! Retainer, yes! Bring, bring! Everyone in!"

Daughter of Mayrin?

Tavra passed Naia a last urgent glance before Lord skekSil grasped the back of Naia's tunic and lifted, barely giving her time to pull her feet under her before moving briskly inside, half pushing, half dragging with his clawed hand. On his other side, he jostled Tavra forward with playful, rough shoves. Was the soldier really the All-Maudra's daughter? Maybe she had only told the Skeksis so—no, now that Naia looked closer, she saw it: the silver hair and fair cheeks and, now that the Vapra was standing within the halls of the Castle of the Crystal, there was even a fine silver circlet on her brow, finished with a single pearl drop above the bridge of her nose. There was no doubt—all along, Tavra had been no mere soldier of the All-Maudra.

Naia swallowed the realization and her surprise, falling in line behind Tavra—Katavra, one of the many Daughters of Mayrin— as a retainer might do. Ahead, Lord skekSil weaved back and forth in eccentric zigzags, as if his two feet had differing minds of their own, in a constant battle to dominate his trajectory.

"Always, Vapra from Ha'rar, oh yes, yes, come! Tasty! Feast! Food! Welcome!"

Naia's eyes couldn't widen enough to take in all that lay within the castle gate. The entrance hall was vaulted, carved in arches and curved beams, winding and lit by torches and chandeliers covered in melted, dripping wax. Every wall was adorned with some kind of carving or relief, astronomical shapes connected by lines and dotted paths pigmented with dyes or round gems. Chamberlain Lord skekSil bustled between them, his shuffling steps kicking his skirts and robe hems out in frantic waves as he hurried down the hall and sharply to the left. As soon as he disappeared from sight, Tavra reached for Naia's hand—but caught only her sleeve before the Chamberlain was back, clutching their shoulders with a loud shrieking sigh and walking them swiftly through a set of double gabled doors. Whatever Tavra was trying to tell Naia was lost again, and then Naia's senses were overwhelmed with the scene that lay before her.

Two long tables were arranged in a cross formation, draped in gathered silk sheets and dozens of runners and linens. Metal platters overflowing with squirming savory-smelling delicacies were lined up, one on top of the other, barely leaving room for the goblets of wine and glass decanters that poked out of the banquet settings like saplings. Banners and curtains in gold, red, coral, navy, ivory, and white dropped from the high vaulted ceiling like sails, drawn and bunched in an array of textures and colors with braided, tasseled cords and chains. Seated at the banquet table, in feasting thrones resembling the hands and fingers of the castle itself, were the purple-skinned razor-beaked Skeksis.

None looked up when Lord skekSil and the Gelfling entered. They were too engorged in their feast, most elbow-deep in one dish or another, stuffing their shining scaly beaks full of fatty noodles and scurrying whiskered crawlies. Naia looked from one lord to the next—each was garbed in an elaborate mantle, each structured in a different shape and decorated with a different ornament. One had feathers, thick and glossy, and another wore armor, his cloak more of a cape and the plates of his shoulder pieces clanging together as he wrestled with a piece of his dinner that had not been fully cooked. Yet another wore bronze and leather, and a headpiece barbed with half a dozen viewing lenses held by tiny metallic arms.

No music played within the hall, so it was filled only with the gurgling and grunting of their feast, punctuated by the clanging of their knives and skewers as they attacked their food as if it were prey still on the run. Two Gelfling soldiers stood at the door, silent. Had Naia not been looking for them, wanting to see those that shared her brother's duties, she doubted she would have noticed them at all.

"Gelfling! Gelfling! Silverling and Sogling!" cried Chamberlain skekSil. He held their shoulders and shook them slightly, as if giving them motion would attract the attention of his brethren. "Daughter of the Silverling!"

"Daughter?" shouted one of the lords, finally taking notice. His face was blunter than the others, with long black whiskers sticking out of his muzzle like spines. "Here?"

"Now?" asked another, fourth from the left, with a needle-narrow beak and squinting eyes. With a start, Naia recognized Lord skekOk, his claws and arms nearly covered inch to inch in jeweled bands, a tattered stained napkin shoved down the front of his ruffled collar. "Why?!"

"Shut up!"

All went quiet at the voice of the last, which came from the lord seated at the center of the table arrangement. He was not the largest of the Skeksis by size, but the immediate response his sharp voice garnered carried more weight than any of the others were willing to contest. Atop his head was a spiked crown, its metal nearly hidden beneath the faceted gems inset into the band. Hanging from his neck were more jewels, clustered in tripart configurations and dangling from his neck to the table, where they currently were half submerged in a gourd of thick chunky stew. When he rose, the broth from the stew dripped from the amulets onto his robes, where the color was lost in the dark crimsons and burgundies.

Tavra bent at the waist in a stiff bow, and Naia followed her lead. Her cheeks burned under the gaze of the lords, now that there was only silence and all eyes were on them. She had expected to speak to attendants or servants—even Gelfling guards, perhaps, or a retainer to tell her that Gurjin had been proven guilty, that she might see him, but she had never expected to be standing before the sixteen Skeksis Lords so soon after stepping foot within the Castle of the Crystal. And now here she was, coated head to toe in mud, bruised and battered from her race through the wood, with Tavra desperately trying to impart some message to her.

Skeksis Emperor skekSo—for that was the only person the lord at the center could be—cleared his throat and leaned with both claws on the table in front of him. His neck craned forward, drilling down on them with a leveling gaze that had surely brought even the proudest Gelfling to their knees. Yet when he spoke, his voice sounded almost cultured, his accent in the Gelfling tongue much more perfected than the stilted broken phrases of the Chamberlain.

"Katavra," Emperor skekSo said, his voice now the only sound echoing in the hall. "What might the All-Maudra's daughter-soldier be doing here at the Castle of the Crystal, yes? And so late? What's this green thing, a Sogling? Ahhh!" The Emperor shot a look at the Chamberlain. "Is this the one, here, at last?"

Naia looked at the floor, clenching her fists at the accusation, but she knew better than to speak back to one of the lords, especially at a time like this. Did the Skeksis know their guards so little they mistook her for her brother? He'd hardly acknowledged her, much less looked at her long enough to realize she was a girl. The Chamberlain made a humming noise, but Tavra answered first.

"No, Emperor," she said. "This is not one of the guards you asked my mother to find. We have still not been able to confirm his whereabouts."

"The guards? . . . Oh. Yes, of course—the guards. Then what are you doing, wasting time here? Gelfling need to find them. Gelfling need to punish them. Get out, get looking!"

"I wished to directly report to you, Your Greatness, the status of the assignment with which you have so honorably endowed us."

"Waste of time!" Emperor skekSo repeated, so harshly the spines along the sides of his head jutted out like quills on a muski. "*Gelfling* are the ones causing problems, so *Gelfling* the ones that do the fixing! However long it takes, search Skarith, search all of Thra—we care not, just make it clear that Gelfling causing problems for us, Lord Skeksis. Now, get out! Leave! Back to work!"

It didn't seem right to Naia, how focused the Emperor was on finding and punishing Rian and Gurjin. If they *were* traitors, then the rumors they were spreading were just lies—certainly nothing worth being so defensive about! Yet it seemed the Emperor wanted nothing more than for Tavra and Naia to leave the Castle of the Crystal, leading the Gelfling on a vicious hunt for their own people.

Judging from the heavy reservation in Tavra's next words, it seemed the Vapra was of the same mind.

"We will resume our search, of course, my lord. But there's a storm tonight, making travel difficult. I'm sure the All-Maudra would be willing to extend our search efforts if she knew we had the support of the lords of the Castle of the Crystal."

While Tavra spoke, Emperor skekSo watched her intently, at one point with such directed intensity, Naia wasn't sure he was even listening to her words. The tip of his tongue, a pink and gray thing twitching between his upper beak and lower jaw, ran along the edge of his teeth and then disappeared with a soft *clack*.

"We see," the Emperor said. "Well then! We hope you plan to leave in the morning, post-haste. To Ha'rar, to the Silver Sea. To wherever, and for however long it takes to find the traitors. Let *all* Gelfling know they are nothing but lies. We love Gelfling, we do, we loves them, of course, but traitors . . . No one loves traitors, Silverling . . . No one."

The hall fell quiet again, this time with a backdrop of ambient murmuring among the Skeksis, one of them even letting out a quiet little snicker. The Chamberlain, still standing behind Naia, steepled his claws and shifted from foot to foot. She could hear his skirts rustling against the dry stone floor.

Tavra held her chin up. She really did look like the All-Maudra's daughter then, and Naia felt stupid for never having guessed.

"Indeed," Tavra said. Then, with a weighty glance, she said to Naia, "Find me a chamber and have it prepared for me by the time I arrive. I would like to enjoy our lords' hospitality for a spell—alone."

Tavra cleared her throat forcefully, and Naia realized it was not out of contempt that she was being dismissed. She met Tavra's eyes again, and as their gaze lingered, she felt someone else watching her. A familiar watching, like holes burning into her back. At the far end of the room, one of the lords was poised with his claws laced together, chin resting on his thick bony knuckles, red eyes fixed on her. His cloak and garb were all in black, giving him a countenance that seemed too wicked to befit a lord, or perhaps it was just the way he watched her.

"Guards! One! Show the Sogling to the All-Maudra's guest chambers!"

One of the guards stepped forward, standing at attention near the door. Though her stomach ached and she didn't fully understand Tavra's reasons, in that moment Naia would do anything to escape the black-clad lord's awful gaze, and she nodded, bowing first to the soldier and then again to the Emperor. Then, with all the restraint she could muster, she fled, feeling the weight of the Skeksis' stares on her shoulders even after the doors to the banquet hall had closed.

CHAPTER 23

Naia stood with the Gelfling guard, wringing her hands. The tall hallway was curved and empty, with only the faint sounds of footsteps coming from some far-off floors. Gurjin had often described the castle as bustling, busy with guards and servants going about their duties of cleaning, preparing for the Skeksis' daily rituals, cooking, and the like, but Naia saw no evidence of any such activity. Even the single guard she now stood with was quiet, gesturing sharply with one gloved hand before walking down the hall. Neech, quiet and tense, wound tightly around her arm beneath her sleeve. Naia followed, feet still aching. Though she wanted nothing but to sit, rest, and quench her thirst, it was obvious Tavra had been trying to get her out of the chamber as quickly as possible.

Was it because she was here to incriminate Gurjin on behalf of the All-Maudra, or was it something else? If only she knew what had Tavra been trying to say!

"Does the All-Maudra's daughter visit frequently?" Naia asked the guard, who walked a couple of steps ahead of her. He was a little older than she, with thick reddish hair pulled back in a braid. He made no sign of recognition at the sound of her voice. At first she thought maybe he hadn't heard her, but when she asked again and he made no response, she realized it was intentional. Neither of them said a word until he finally stopped before a new set of doors, pushing them open to reveal a guest chamber more elaborate than Naia's mother's own hearing chamber.

She stepped inside when the guard indicated. Turning around and standing across the threshold from him, she finally got a look at him, and what she saw turned her hands cold and clammy. His face held no expression, no life. There was no spark of animation in his wan features. When he spoke, the single word that came out was no more than a further creaking of the chamber doors.

"Stay," he croaked.

Then he pulled the doors shut in front of her, and she was alone again.

What was wrong with the guard? She had never met a Gelfling so reluctant to speak—and his eyes! Anxious, Naia paused only to wipe the dirt and mud from the wood off her shoes—leaving a stain on the textured woven rug that sprawled across the main area of the chamber floor—before pressing her ear to the door. She waited until the guard's footsteps faded then gently pushed it open. The hallway beyond was bare and silent. She knew the answers to her questions lay ahead. Counting first to eight, then straightening her tunic and calming her nerves, Naia slipped out of the chamber and headed deeper into the castle. When a distant scent of food reached her nose, she followed it. Hot food meant cooks. Cooks meant Gelfling attendants, she hoped, and someone who might point her toward wherever her brother was being held captive.

She had not made it very far when a set of doors nearby

opened, letting out a plume of steam that smelled of boiling food, broth, and stew, along with the clanging and chopping orchestra of a large kitchen. Out came a small group of Podlings, dressed in burlap shifts, pushing a tray-topped cart on squeaky wooden wheels. Naia stood aside as they passed, bare feet plodding one in front of the other, headed for the banquet hall. Their numb shuffling steps had none of the animation or energy of the Podlings she had met in Sami Thicket, and when she offered a polite "Hello," none turned to acknowledge her. In fact, their eyes were milky, not even trained ahead but gazing aimlessly at the ground. One in particular looked exceptionally inanimate, mouth hanging open and a gob of thick drool dangling from his gray lower lip. When the slow-moving procession had finally passed, Naia saw wood shackles clasped around their ankles, which, while horrible, hardly seemed necessary given the sluggish state of the little Pod people. What was going on here?

Naia trotted along the corridor more quickly, keeping her footfalls as light as she could even on the veined shining marble that seemed to amplify every sound that fell upon it. She wanted to find a room—anywhere she could stop and think without worrying that some soldier or guard or lord might come along and ask who she was and what she was doing. In such an expansive castle, it was hard to believe it might be nothing but hallway, but that's how it seemed as Naia continued on and on, up and down twisting stairs and along bridge-like throughways that passed over larger chambers. The entire way, she met no one but little scurrying crawlies and skittering bugs—not a single guard was to be seen.

She didn't even see any more of the strange Podling servants.

She stopped when something glinted in the corner of her eye. Deep in the maze of the castle's tangle of passageways came a fuchsia light, trickling through the dimmer shadows lit only by the occasional torch. Naia followed it, passing through a darker narrow tunnel that spilled onto a high balcony in a huge open-roofed chamber. Though no torch lit the walls and there was no ceiling beam to hang a chandelier, the chamber below was radiant with a violet ambience streaming from a source just out of sight. Naia paused. An old metal gate barred the threshold where the tunnel met the balcony. She *recognized* that light. Her insides clenched and her heart pounded, both terrified of what she would see and, at the same time, drawn by an instinct she didn't quite understand.

She shook gently on the gate; it was chained shut. Under normal circumstances, she imagined there might be guards posted here, one at either side, holding spears and keeping anyone out. But this stormy night, the guards were scarce and shadows plenty, and Naia took hold of the gate rails and climbed.

She pulled herself over the spear-pointed top and leaped down on the other side, taking the tunnel to the chamber balcony. The strange light crackled once like lightning, setting the air abuzz with its energy. She wanted to look—she wanted to see it, though she knew with every particle of her being that to see it would be to peer into the void. The void that she had only glimpsed in the silt of Sog—the abyssal dark flickering light that had swallowed the soul of the Nebrie. She could hear it turning, an almost grinding sound that she heard more in her bones than in her ears. Above that, in the atmosphere, she made out a higher sound like that of an instrument or a choir. It was singing, no, *calling* to her, and she stepped forward to see its face.

Below, in a great circular hall honeycombed with entrances and exits, was a flat dais marked with hundreds of runes and other etchings—words and symbols, some of which Naia recognized from Kylan's writing and some which were completely foreign. At the center of the dais was an opening in the shape of a perfect circle; blinding red flames and waves of heat issued forth from it, as though it were a shaft which led directly to Thra's fiery core.

Floating above the dais, as if held aloft by the hot wind and burning light, was an enormous multifaceted stone in the rough shape of a blade, wide at the top and growing narrower as it pointed down into the lake of fire far below. Its blood-violet faces alternated rough and smooth, some shining like ice and others rippled with the texture of time. There it turned slowly, suspended, and from its dark crystalline body came the song that permeated Thra and that rang through Naia's heart with its beautiful sadness.

This was not the white pure Heart of Thra told of in song. This heart was the color of the crystal veins—the shade of a heart already darkened. In the Crystal's crown was a wound, a hole surrounded by fractures from when it had been struck. Naia shuddered at the sight, the source of the broken song, the crack that had caused the Crystal to bleed violet and red, darkening, its pain flowing through its veins to reach every part of Thra.

Naia felt tears on her cheeks, knowing what she wished was not true.

The Crystal was not in danger of infection by the crystal veins. *It was the source.*

The immense overwhelming sadness of the Crystal's song pulled on Naia like no force she had experienced before—the ribbon she had seen in the swamp of Sog had been but a glimmer compared to the blinding gaze of the Crystal she beheld now. As she stared into its bright darkness, she began to see shapes, figures. Imposed upon the face of the Crystal—or in her mind, she couldn't be sure—she saw Tavra standing before the Skeksis in the banquet hall, far from where she stood before the Crystal.

"I believe he is here, within these very walls."

The soldier's voice came loud and clear, as did those of the Skeksis when they broke into sudden raucous laughter. Did she mean Gurjin? Tavra stood before them, back straight and proud, while the lords pounded their fists on the table and crowed with cackles that were not very lordly at all.

"Treason!" bellowed the short-snouted lord in the armor. "Ahhhh! All Gelfling traitors, after all!"

"After all Skeksis does for you!" cried another. "Gelfling came here just to tell such lies!"

"You're awfully eager to get us out of the castle, after so many trine inviting us in," Tavra called over the din, sternly, although her fingers twitched near the hilt of her sword. "I came to find the truth. If you vow to me that there's been nothing of concern—that the Crystal is in fact intact and well—and the rumors that you're responsible for the vanishing Pod people and the two missing guards are nothing but lies—then, I suppose, I will report nothing of concern to my Lady Mother, and we will scour all of Thra to find the two traitors."

"Then begone and report it!" shouted one lord, and his cry was echoed by his brethren. *Yes, begone! Report it! Tell her whatever she would like to hear! Treasonous Gelfling All-Maudra!*

"Then vow it!" Tavra demanded. "Vow to me it's the truth! Vow to me that should I search this castle, I'll find no sign of the guards you accused of treason, and that should I look in on the Crystal, I'll find it shining white and bright as it did the day it became entrusted to you!"

The Skeksis, as eager as they had been to laugh and scream in Tavra's face, fell to a simmer of murmurs and whispers and chuckles. *She knows*, came the words, *oh ho, she knows*, like smoke rising from a kindling fire. Emperor skekSo, who had been quiet throughout, raised his triangle-headed scepter and waved it back and forth in a nonchalant, careless gesture.

"Silverling is sounding like a traitor herself," he said.

"Where are all the castle guards? The last time I was here, there were two at every door and ten at the gate. Tonight, it's quiet as a crypt. My mother has had me searching the land for two traitors who are as scarce as ghosts, but I pursued them without asking questions. I sent Rian and Gurjin's closest kin to the Court of Ha'rar, as I was ordered. I trusted the All-Maudra and you, the Skeksis. But then I saw darkened creatures roaming the land. I heard the song of Thra singing out of tune. I heard testament to the good hearts of the so-called traitors . . . and I received a message from Rian of Stone-in-the-Wood claiming the Skeksis are murderous liars, that Gurjin is here in the castle, and that my people are in danger."

Emperor skekSo clacked his beak twice and continued dragging his scepter through the air in figure eights, the charms and jewels applied to its tip glinting hypnotically. Tavra held her ground, a thin piece of paper in her hand. She tossed the message to the stone-tiled floor.

"I am merely in search of truth," she said. "Rian is an alleged traitor, so I came to find out for myself. If I am wrong, I invite you to prove it . . . because if I am right, it is the Skeksis who have betrayed us. Betrayed the castle, and the Heart of Thra. And I do not want to be right."

The Vapra's words echoed in the hall, and Naia could hear nothing else except for the beating of her own heart. She held her breath, trying to quiet it. The Skeksis Lords were rustling, fidgeting, the feathers and scales on their heads and necks rising in anticipation. Again, the castle itself reacted, creaking as the tension in the room thickened, tightening, soon to snap. The Chamberlain, still standing near Tavra's back, rubbed his claws together.

Emperor skekSo snorted, casually picking at his teeth with a claw. He sighed, stretching his head forward on his sinewy neck.

"I'm very sorry, Silverling. I'm afraid . . . you are correct."

Tavra's voice was unsurprised, slow, and grave when she responded. She asked her next question with the delivery of a regal command:

"Where are Gurjin and the missing Gelfling guards?"

"You can see for yourself. Chamberlain!"

Tavra's hand went to the hilt of her sword as the Chamberlain lunged forward. He caught her by the hair, knocking the sword from her hand. As he grabbed her arm with his other claw, the room exploded into shrieks and laughter, and the Skeksis Lords launched from their dining thrones, clambering over the banquet tables and converging on the Chamberlain and Tavra, sending platters and goblets clanging and shattering to the floor and against the walls. Tavra did not cry out as they amassed around her, clutching her by the arms and legs and hair, and lifting her, crowing with laughter and jeers.

"She wants to see!"

"Show her in person! See the Crystal herself!"

"To the chamber!"

"To the Chamber of Life!"

"No!" Naia cried, but her voice did not reach through the Crystal. In a parade of hysterical celebration and uncontrolled, garrulous fanfare, the Skeksis Lords tossed Tavra back and forth among them, finally dragging her with frantic waves of their berobed arms toward the exit. Even after they were out of sight, their deafening laughter and stomping feet beat through the body of the Crystal. Naia tried to make sense of it all in her fear and incredulousness, but one fact surfaced against the sea of questions.

The Skeksis Lords, protectors of the Castle of the Crystal, had betrayed them.

Heart pounding, Naia turned away from the Crystal, drawing Gurjin's dagger. Tavra had known—she had known even before they had entered. She had been trying to save Naia, and for a moment, Naia thought about finding a window, descending the castle wall outside, and escaping. But even then, the masked monster lurked in the wood, and it would still be night for hours more. In her frantic state, she wouldn't be able to escape a second time. Guarded by the shadowy beast, armored in heavy gates and walls, the castle she had sought for shelter had become the most dangerous place in the Dark Wood.

What was she to do? Tavra was a seasoned soldier and the All-Maudra's daughter, and the Skeksis had treated her no better than an insect. If the lords thought that much of one of Mayrin's daughters, what might they think of Naia? How could she do anything to save Tavra, let alone Gurjin? Even now that she knew he was in the castle, somewhere, it was possible he wasn't alive, and she had no idea exactly where he was. Despite being so close, he might as well have been on the other side of Thra.

Why are they doing this?

Naia felt a desperate tear escape and wiped it away. She thought of the broken light of the Crystal—the milky eyes of the Podling slaves—the hungry look in the Emperor's eyes. There was a connection between it all—she could feel it. It all came back to the Crystal and the Skeksis Lords who had been charged with its protection, but how, and what exactly, she still couldn't divine. The frustration was maddening, and she put her face in her hands in anguish.

Naia sucked in a deep hard breath. She didn't have time for misery, and she didn't have time to wait for answers. The fact was,

Tavra was in danger, and Gurjin, if he was still alive, was likely in danger as well. Either way, they were both captive now, and if Naia didn't act quickly, she knew she would be caught and face the same end. It was death in the wood at the hands of the Hunter, or the possibility of rescuing her brother and her friend if she remained here.

Is that what Gurjin had been trying to do?

Her heart lurched at the thought, nearly toppling out of her chest, caught only by the web of intense guilt that surrounded it like a net. The rumors and the lies he'd been accused of telling—it wasn't that he hadn't told them, it was that they weren't lies.

But guilt would not solve the problem. Gurjin's knife firmly in her grip, she faced the Crystal once more.

"My brother," she pleaded. "Show me where he is? Please, I must save him!"

The Crystal moaned with its ghostly song, turning once again. In the walls of its body she saw a dark figure slumped near a window, and through the window she saw stars and the tops of trees. It was somewhere high in the turrets of the castle, and so without another moment's hesitation, she dashed back into the maze of corridors, searching for a way up.

CHAPTER 24

The Skeksis' voices faded in and out as Naia scurried from hall to hall, searching for a passage that would take her upward. The castle's hard walls seemed made for echoes, amplifying and distorting the lords' crowing so that it seemed everywhere at once. At every corner, Naia braced herself for a confrontation, heart hammering with relief every time there was none.

At one such junction, Neech let out a chirp and launched from her shoulder, gliding quickly up an inclining corridor and disappearing into the dim staircase.

"Neech!" she hissed after him. If she called too loudly, her voice would surely echo—but Neech didn't respond, chirping to himself as he glided farther and farther away upward. Naia gritted her teeth and followed before she lost track of him, hoping he had caught something she had missed and wasn't just chasing some tasty-looking critter that scurried through the shadows. Neech's black body made him hard to spot in the poorly lit ascending spiral passageways, but he gave intermittent chirps that let her track him even in the dark. The higher they climbed, the tighter the spiral stairway wound, and the louder the storm outside became. Glancing out windows as she passed, Naia could see they were climbing one of the turrets of the castle, and the view overlooked the storm raging across the Dark Wood.

Neech finally settled on a big iron bar set across a set of heavy doors, eyes wide and entire body vibrating with anticipation. Did he think this was where the Skeksis were headed? Listening, she didn't hear them approaching. No, Neech was waiting here for a different reason, gnawing at the heavy wood in a vain attempt to gain entrance.

Naia braced her hands below the iron bar and pulled, sliding it horizontally out of the latch with a groaning *creeeak* that she hoped would be drowned out by the many other grumbling noises that lurked throughout the dark halls. Lock disengaged, Naia carefully pressed her weight on the heavy door, pushing it open wide enough to see a dim cell inside. From the warm sour scent that met her nostrils, she knew she didn't want to see what lay within, but she had no choice. Neech chirruped and darted inside, and so she followed, knowing with a rotten gnawing expectation what she was going to find.

Iron cages holding Gelfling lined every wall within the cell. Most captives huddled in the cramped space with their arms wrapped about their knees, while others leaned against the rusty bars. Some were alive—she heard shallow, labored breathing and quiet little whimpers. Some lay so still they were certainly unconscious, if not gone altogether. She saw a palette of skin tones, from the dark umber of the Spriton to the pale, almost white of the Vapra. One of the Gelfling had no hair upon her head, only inky black tattoos along her scalp and neck. Another had matted auburn curls that had long since lost their luster. None moved but a twitch when she entered, and she thought perhaps they were sleeping, but when the faint light from the hallway touched the face of one prisoner nearby, she saw his eyes were milky and vacant, like the Podling slaves . . . like the Nebrie.

"Naia?"

The croaking voice was almost lost in its fragility, but the timbre in it brought tears to Naia's eyes. Crouched in a wood crate in the far corner, nearly hidden by shadows, was a haggard Gelfling with gray-tinged Drenchen skin and thick locs pulled into a bun at the back of his head. So much of his natural bulk was gone, leaving him thin and bony like a child. He twisted, holding on to the thick wood and pressing his face between the slats to get a better look at her. His voice was muffled and weak, but it was definitely Gurjin.

"Naia? Is that really you?"

"Gurjin," she breathed. "You're all right. You're all right!"

"All right?" he repeated with a little cough. "I've been tossed in a bin like a noggie husk."

Naia wasted no time, finding the clasp that held the top of the crate shut and hacking at it with her dagger. The wood was thick but old; the knife's blade took steady bites out of the plank, slowly loosening the metal plate to which the latch was bolted.

"We have to leave," she said in between strikes. "The Skeksis . . . they have my friend—Gurjin, what's happening here?"

When the latch-plate had separated enough, Naia jammed the dagger between the plate and wood, and leaned with all her weight. With a creaking whine, the wood splintered and the plate popped off. Naia threw the top of the crate open and grabbed her brother to help him up. The breadth of his shoulders hadn't shrunk with his weight, and she threw her arms around them and hugged him tightly.

"I'm not sure I can walk," he said. "I've been in there for days—no food, and they've put moonberry in my water—"

"I'll carry you if I have to."

Gurjin wiped her cheeks with his fingertips. His face—the face she shared with him—was changed, sallow and hollow, his eyes unfocused. The moonberry was to blame for the latter, Naia guessed. The effects of the sleep-flower would wear off eventually, but she worried there was no remedy for the other nightmares her brother had endured.

"They'll be coming soon," Gurjin said.

"I know. That's why we have to leave. Can any of the others walk?"

Naia hoisted Gurjin up, bearing most of his weight against her side when his legs nearly failed to support his body. She felt overwhelmed with a wave of hopelessness when she looked around them. She could barely support her brother's weight. There was no way she would be able to carry out all the Gelfling in the cell—even if she had the time to free them. A wood crate was one thing, but the metal bars and chains . . .

"What should we do?"

Gurjin shook his head. His voice was so soft, it was hardly recognizable.

"They're already drained. It's too late."

Naia didn't know what he meant by *drained*, and she wasn't sure she wanted to. The awful fact was, they didn't have time. If she wanted to help the silent dull-eyed Gelfling, she would have to save herself first.

"We'll just have to come back for them," she said, determined. "We'll come back."

Swallowing her guilt, Naia hobbled out of the cell with her brother's feet stumbling along. Together, they made a slow escape into the outer hall. Naia pondered the long stairway down and tried not to think about the distance back to the exit and how long it would take them at this pace. She tried not to think about how easy it would be to find them, if the Skeksis had not been preoccupied with whatever they were doing to Tavra.

I'll have to come back for her, too, Naia thought miserably.

"The Skeksis have betrayed us," Gurjin breathed.

"I know," she said. "What's happened—what have they done? You said the others were drained—did they drain you, too?"

Before Gurjin could answer, a cold wind billowed around her ankles as something moved in the stairway below. With the way the stairs spiraled, she couldn't see far, but she could feel it . . . hear it rustling and creeping and breathing . . . and then she smelled it, that terrible blue scent of Gelfling—of Gelfling *essence*, she realized, with a horrible shudder. She backed up the stairs, one at a time, but she knew she was only putting off the inevitable. There was nowhere to run in the narrow corridor, and nowhere to hide but in the dank cell that would become a prison as soon as the heavy door was shut once again.

"Some *scampabouts* in Skeksis tower," came the lisping, reedy voice. Footsteps followed, one after the other, and the cloaked figure that emerged from the shadows seemed to bring the darkness with him. It was the Skeksis with the burning eyes, the one that had watched her from the banquet. Across his shoulders was a mantle of liquid night, boiling about his feet like black smoke, bulging under one side where he carried something. Though Naia had now seen all the lords, as dark and towering as they were, on this night she knew that this one was to be most feared.

"One and one," he purred. He jabbed a finger first at Naia and then at her brother. "Two, but one. Two, one . . . twin. Had the one and been waiting for the second. Now we have her! Oh, have been waiting for this wonderful night!"

"skekMal," Gurjin whispered. "No . . ."

"Now, come. Closer. End this now, skekMal will do. Time for special draining of twin Gelfling. Waited so long! skekTek the Scientist says may make a special *essence* for Emperor. Ha! Not if skekMal make and take it for *himself*."

The idea that they had been saving Gurjin like some rare holiday treat was bad enough, but knowing the Skeksis had known he'd had a twin—that they'd been *waiting for her*—was dizzying and revolting. Cornered, betrayed, Naia felt her fear ignite into anger, and she planted her feet and raised her voice.

"What have you done with Tavra?" she demanded. She wanted to know, but more than that, she needed to buy time. Gurjin was bearing more of his own weight, beginning to shake off the haze of being trapped in the cell, but he was by no means ready to flee on his own two feet. Lightning crackled outside, illuminating the interior of the whorled stairway through one of the windows that opened into thick stormy air high above the Dark Wood.

"Silverling wanted to know what we does with Gelfling. Wanted to see for itself. Stinking Silverling. Got what it deserves. Just a little drain tonight. . . the rest tomorrow."

Skeksis Lord skekMal held one arm out, spreading his cloak, and Naia's mouth went dry. Clasped within was Tavra, limp and unconscious, eyes wide and misty like fog on a summer morning. She fell from where she was held, suddenly, dropping to the stairway with a broken *thump*, and Naia spied what had held the soldier's body while skekMal's talons had been occupied. Folded tightly against the sides of the Skeksis's torso was a second pair of clawed black arms.

Four arms . . .

"He's no lord," Naia said. "He's the Hunter."

skekMal chuckled and gave an extravagant, patronizing bow with all four arms as he reached within the endless bulk of his cloak. He withdrew a mask of bone, though it had a crack in the temple from a rock the size of a *bola* stone. With a toothy, fanged grin of smugness, skekMal the Hunter placed his mask upon his hooked face.

"Even stupid Gelfling figures it out," he cooed. "So stupid, Gelfling."

"Naia. I'm sorry."

Tavra's voice was little more than a breath, but seeing the Vapra reminded Naia of how determined she had been to bring

Naia out of Sog. How much she had already seemed to know about Naia and her twin brother. Even skekMal paused when the Vapra spoke, steepling the fingers of his two larger hands and watching, as if for sport. Tavra pushed herself up enough to meet Naia's eyes.

"You knew?" Naia whispered.

"I knew they wanted you. I didn't know why. When I found out, I tried to make it right. I tried to stop you, in the wood, but you followed me here anyway. I'm so sorry."

Despite the distant sense of betrayal, Naia felt the pain in the soldier's confession, and then the urgency in the three words that followed:

"Warn the others."

The fog cleared from Tavra's eyes for a moment, and Naia understood. They knew the Skeksis' secret, now, and it would all be for nothing if they couldn't reach the other Gelfling, the other clans, Naia's parents, the All-Maudra.

"No one warns anyone!" skekMal screeched, swiping a claw down and snatching Tavra from the steps. He held her by the neck and shook her like a beast worrying its prey, daring her to defy him again. Tavra withstood the abuse in silence, only looking at Naia and, with a stern and selfless clarity, said the words again, though her voice was strangled by skekMal's grip.

Warn the others . . .

Then skekMal dropped her, and she did not rise again. Stepping over her with all his skirts and cloak, the Hunter growled a refrain:

"No one warns anyone."

Tears on her cheeks, Naia backed away, taking Gurjin with her, pleading a silent apology to the fallen Vapra. A cold storm wind blew rain in from the window, and she looked out, seeing the long drop into pitch blackness below, knowing behind her was only the top of the turret, a dead-end path leading straight to the dungeon cell she wanted with all her life to avoid.

Satisfied with his disposal of Tavra, skekMal climbed the stairs, four arms spread wide, clawed black hands ready to slash, and fanged beak ready to bite. Naia looked to the dagger in her hand, its solid blade heavy in her palm.

"Hard to fight while carrying stone," skekMal cackled.

It was the grim truth: There was no way she could carry Gurjin and fight at the same time. Letting go of the knife would leave her defenseless, but she would not let go of her brother. But perhaps . . .

Now the Hunter waits behind him . . .

He knows not what lies below him . . .

Glancing out the window, a bolt of hope charged her body. She gave the dagger's hilt a last squeeze for luck, saying good-bye before she flung it out the window. The move startled skekMal into silence long enough for Naia to listen, hard, through the howling storm beyond the window.

Splash.

Naia pulled Gurjin onto the windowsill and, giving skekMal a last look of defiance, turned toward the open sky beyond, and leaped. With a shriek of dismay, skekMal dived forward, his claws brushing her ankle as she cleared the sill, holding Gurjin in her arms and taking him with her.

She felt a rush of wind and a blossom of pain in her back and shoulders as the updraft hit them. Naia closed her eyes and prayed, bracing herself for the impact of the water, hoping it could cushion their fall enough to save their lives. Expecting freefall, she clung to Gurjin and prepared for the fast drop to the castle moat. Its thick waters were quiet—save for the single wet splash it had offered when Gurjin's knife had struck from above.

But they weren't falling. Instead, their descent was light and airy, like a plumed seedpod drifting on the wind. Looking over her shoulder, Naia saw skekMal hunched in the window of the castle, screeching madly after them, and then she saw them—*felt* them.

Black and iridescent, reflecting the light of the storm in vibrant blues and fuchsias, Naia's wings held them afloat, high above the wood and away from the terrors within the Castle of the Crystal.

"Naia," Gurjin said. "They're beautiful . . ."

Naia did not have time to enjoy the moment—the wind broke abruptly, and they faltered, dropping from the heights before another updraft came and buffeted their fall once more. Above, in the tower, skekMal's shadow had disappeared from the window. Naia tightened her grip on Gurjin. The Hunter would be coming after them, no doubt. They were not safe yet.

Far below, hidden by the shadow clusters of the wood, she heard the whistling call of a hollerbat, and a smile broke her features before she could think to stop it. The ground was fast approaching, and she gathered her wits, attempting for the first time in her life to maneuver in the air. It was rather like throwing a *bola* with her off hand, familiar but uncoordinated, and they veered suddenly, careening toward the earth. It was all she could do to aim for the water of the moat, and they splashed into it, Naia holding tightly to her brother despite the temporary shock that came from the cold water. Her gills opened, and she took a breath, orienting herself in the murky black water before swimming to the bank. The water was thick with algae and weeds, and almost as cold as ice. Her limbs were numb and aching by the time she broke the surface, sticky black algae stuck to her face . . . and then warm hands grasped her by the arm and hauled her up. When her knees were on the bank, she twisted and, in turn, hauled Gurjin from the deep moat. Cold as the water was, it seemed to have done him good, his body moving with greater control and rising confidence. Naia turned to the one who had pulled her from the water—had whistled the signal from below—throwing her arms around him and hugging him tightly.

"You shouldn't have," she whispered. "It's dangerous—they're coming. The Skeksis—"

Kylan the Song Teller of Sami Thicket nodded, rising and helping her to her feet.

"Then we'd better move, hadn't we?"

Gurjin stood on his own when she and Kylan tugged on him and, though his movements were still sluggish, he was able to run beside them as they made their escape into the wood. The storm had eased, finally, thunder receding into the distance and replaced with only a steady cold rain that Naia hoped would dampen their scent. The Dark Wood was the domain of the Hunter, and now his pursuit of them was personal. Her heart ached when she thought of him, the cruel way he had disposed of Tavra—but she had no time for tears, not even to worry for the soldier, if she was still alive—or mourn if she was otherwise.

"The Skeksis betrayed us," Naia told Kylan, in case they should be separated. "We have to escape. We have to tell the All-Maudra!"

"I left the Landstrider at the river," Kylan said. "A shortcut, I hope, if we can make it in time!"

Something else had to be said, and Naia made sure it was, before it was too late.

"I'm sorry about before," she said. Kylan met her eyes and nodded back.

"I know. Me too."

A crash behind them brought them to a brief halt. Naia knew, in her mind, that stopping to look back was the worst way to flee, but the reaction was reflexive. Through the wood, a monster was coming, and from its loathsome enraged breathing and then the bone-chilling cry it loosed, she knew it could only be skekMal. Gurjin suddenly snagged Naia by the elbow, yanking her to the side and into the hollow of a fallen tree stump. Kylan skidded to a halt and followed. There in the dark, they listened to the sounds of the monster hunting for them.

"Sorry," Gurjin said, panting. "They've taken so much out of me. I don't think I can run."

"Then we'll wait," Naia said. "I'll call the Cradle-Tree. Maybe it can hide us, help us escape."

Gurjin shook his head. "skekMal is relentless and master of the Dark Wood. Unless he is stopped, he will find us. He will kill us."

Tears sprouted in Naia's eyes.

"What . . . what are you saying?" she asked, though she knew the answer.

"We don't have time. Dreamfast with me, now!"

Naia numbly took her brother's hands when he reached out to her, and then all at once, every memory that lived within his mind crashed upon her.

CHAPTER 25

"Rian! Are you in here?"

Rian? I know that name . . .

Naia—no, this was her brother's memory, she was Gurjin, now—shouldered open the door to the room he shared with Rian. Looking upon the little space, it was clear which half belonged to the Drenchen and which to the Stonewood Gelfling. Where Gurjin's posessions were strewn in practical piles of clothing, rope, and experiments in metal-molding *vliyaya*, Rian's were in orderly stacks: books, papers, and a few finely crafted wood sculptures. The only thing amiss on Rian's side at the moment was Rian, pacing, wringing his hands. He was Gurjin's age, with thick brown hair and olive skin, a few stone beads hanging from a cord around his neck. He was still in his uniform from the previous night, and looked up with exhausted, worried eyes when his friend entered.

"There you are!" Gurjin exclaimed. "What's gotten into you? Everyone's looking for you since you and Mira missed your shift this morning. Doesn't seem fair I'm the one who's being held accountable. But I guess it's usually the other way around . . . Come on."

Gurjin grabbed his friend by the arm, but Rian pulled away so suddenly, Gurjin jumped back.

"Mira's gone," Rian said, the first thing he'd had to say since Gurjin had found him. Gurjin frowned in response.

"You two didn't run out last night and get into some trouble, did you? Aughra's Eye! I'll never hear the end of it if you did . . ." Gurjin trailed off at the blank, troubled stare he was getting. Rian was usually full of life, talkative and forthcoming. It did not bode well, and Gurjin's heart sank when Rian's next words confirmed the worst:

"Mira's dead."

It was hardly imaginable. In shock, Gurjin could only ask, "What?"

"The Skeksis," Rian breathed, eyes widening, warmth finally coming to them, though it was a heat of fear. "They took her—last night, when she returned from watch—Lord skekTek called her to his chambers. I wanted to see her when she was done speaking to him, so I waited . . . but she never came back. When I went to the chamber to see where they had gone, I saw . . . I saw . . ."

Rian's voice went empty, at a loss for words. Feeling light-headed, Gurjin closed the door to their barracks before returning and gently shaking his friend by the shoulders.

"What did you see?"

"Lord skekTek bound her to a chair," Rian said. "He opened a window in the chamber wall . . . it opened into the shaft below the Crystal. It was burning bright. I had to shield my eyes. They made her look into it, and . . . it drained her. I don't know how. Her face—her eyes—the life was drained out of her. Withering like a dying flower in the sun."

Gurjin didn't want to hear the rest, covering his mouth and feeling his heart pounding, but Rian went on, unable to stop now that he had started.

"They drained all her life by making her stare into the Crystal's light," he said. "And they pulled her life force into a glass vial. Drop by drop. They stole her *vliya* and she died, Gurjin!"

"You lie," he said, though he didn't believe it. Rian had no reason to lie, and certainly not about something like this. Gurjin shook his head, boxing his own ears gently, trying to make sense of it all. "The Skeksis Lords . . . They wouldn't—why Mira? Why anyone?"

"I don't know," Rian said. "But we're in danger. Our people are in danger. We have to tell the All-Maudra."

Gurjin agreed; that much was obvious. His mind was still spinning from Rian's telling, but they didn't have time to spin in confused circles, doing nothing.

"You know, no one's going to believe us," he said. "I hardly believe you! How are you going to convince the All-Maudra that the lords—the *Skeksis Lords*—have done this? All they'll need to do is call us liars and then it'll be our word against theirs . . . Rian, unless we have proof, we're doomed."

"Then we'll get proof," Rian said. "The bottle of her life's essence. Lord skekTek took it with him. If we could get the bottle, maybe we could save Mira—maybe we could use it as proof to bring to the All-Maudra."

"Rian. Rian, Rian, *Rian*. Do you hear what you're saying? This is death!"

"Isn't it death if we let them continue?" Rian insisted. "Whatever it is they're doing?"

Gurjin paced, tugging on his locs, thinking. They had made Mira look upon the Crystal . . . but why would looking upon the Heart of Thra cause such a terrible thing to happen? The Skeksis were the sworn keepers of the Heart of Thra, the Crystal of Truth—not even the castle guards were allowed in the Crystal Chamber where it resided. Only the Skeksis, but once in daily ritual, were permitted to enter the chamber and look directly upon the Crystal. It gave them life, in return for their protection.

The Crystal is cracked, Naia said within the dreamfast, answering the question in her brother's memory. *I saw it in the chamber. It is no longer the Crystal of Truth, the Heart of Thra. It's broken.*

Yes, Gurjin replied. *But we didn't know that then.*

The dreamfast changed, time passing, memories condensed and flying by in flickers that Naia's mind could not separate. Rian and Gurjin kept their secret from the other guards, waiting for an opportunity. Slowly, their ranks diminished, guards disappearing here and there from different wings of the castle. Once they were gone, they were never seen again. Darkened creatures began appearing in the wood that surrounded the castle; even the forest itself seemed bespelled by whatever it was the Skeksis had done to the Heart of Thra.

The crystal veins have always spread through the earth, Gurjin's voice said from within the dreamfast. *Bringing life. Bringing light. But the Skeksis realized they could use its power. Once that happened . . . once they turned the Heart of Thra against its own creatures . . . that was when the Crystal began to darken. That was when the shadows grew. They are perverting the power of the Crystal and turning it black.*

Once more she took Gurjin's place within the dream. It was twilight, and she was running through the Dark Wood. Someone was running alongside her—Rian. In his hand was a glass vial, a tight cork the only thing preventing the precious blue liquid within from splashing out, evaporating their only chance of convincing the All-Maudra of the Skeksis betrayal.

The vliya? Naia asked. *In the vial?*

Yes. They drink it, like nectar. It gives them life . . . our life. Now that they have tasted it, they are mad for it . . .

Behind them, screams of the Skeksis shrieked like a murder of crow-bats, their enraged echoes making it seem as though they numbered in the hundreds.

"Traitor!" they screamed. "Traitor to the castle! Traitor to the Crystal!"

"They're gaining!" Rian shouted. "How can something so old and big be so *fast?*"

Gurjin's heart labored in his chest, and then his boots sank into wet dirt—they had reached the Black River. Here it cut through the Dark Wood in a sunken miniature valley, and for the moment they were hidden behind the higher land on either bank.

"We need to split up," Gurjin said. "It's the only way. If we're found together, we'll be caught together. You go ahead and take the river. I'll distract them here as long as I can and then meet you in Stone-in-the-Wood."

"I know what you're doing, Gurjin, and I won't accept it!" Rian retorted.

"Come on! We only have one bottle of that *vliya*, and you have allies in Stone-in-the-Wood. You think your people are more likely to hide a stranger from the Swamp of Sog, or one of their own? Now get out of here, they're coming!"

Gurjin made to shove his friend into the steady current of the river, but Rian took hold of his jerkin first.

"If you're caught, I'll come back for you," he said. "I'll save you."

"Should it come to that, you cannot save me," Gurjin said, and listening within the dreamfast, Naia recognized the words. "If you do, you'll meet with the All-Maudra empty-handed—you'll stand before her alone. Our clans will be marked as traitors, and it will only be a matter of time before the Skeksis come for retribution. You're a better leader than I am, and you saw what they did with your own eyes. It's more important that you escape. Now go!"

Reluctantly, but knowing time was precious, Rian nodded and waded out into the river. It was then that the clambering claws and bays of the Skeksis in pursuit mounted the bank—over the hill they came in their black hunting cloaks, six of them with eyes burning in rage, skekMal the Hunter at the lead. Gurjin drew his sword, and they converged upon him, so quickly and ravenously, he didn't even have time to run away from the river, to lead them from his friend. As skekUng the General seized him in his crushing claws, hoisting him into the air with a guttural cry,

Gurjin saw skekMal lunge into the river, raising froth in the black waves as he pursued Rian and the tiny bottle of blue *vliya*.

"It's me, I'm the traitor!" Gurjin cried, grasping for any words that might keep them from the Gelfling in the river. "I'll tell everyone the Skeksis are the villains—I'll turn them against you, the castle—"

"Quiet, Gelfling!" roared skekUng, shaking Gurjin so hard, his teeth rattled.

"Even the All-Maudra," Gurjin gasped. "Your power will end! *Just you wait and see!*"

In a fit of rage, skekUng howled again and brought his big clawed hand across Gurjin's head like a club, and everything went black.

When Gurjin awoke, his head pounded with pain that seemed to pulse through every part of his battered body. Even the tips of his ears and nose ached, and when he opened his eyes, his vision was blurry. He tried to move, but he could not—his wrists and ankles were clamped to a cold metal chair. He was bound to the throne-like contraption in a drafty chamber that groaned with the sounds of the earth, as if he were many miles underground.

"Awake," said a Skeksis voice behind him. "Just in time."

Lord skekTek the Scientist took his time crossing the room, pulling his sleeve back from his artificial arm so he might reach the lever appendage jutting from the wall. The metal claw was the only thing more terrifying than his biological one. It gleamed in the dim light of the chamber like silver-black bone. When he pulled down the lever, a clanking and mechanical moan shuddered

through the chamber. The panel in the wall Gurjin faced began to rise, and a draft of burning, dry air spewed forth. Though the panel was raised only a crack, the red light blazing from the furnace-like shaft beyond was blinding, burning all other images from Gurjin's already failing sight. He could only hear Lord skekTek grunt, pulling another lever to release a control arm from beyond the panel, within the shaft. Gurjin knew what was coming next and struggled, trying to pull his arms and legs free from the metal clutches of the chair.

"Gelfling always cry about not seeing the Crystal," skekTek said, ignoring Gurjin's fruitless attempts to escape. The chair had been engineered to hold a Gelfling, of course, and Gurjin knew that—still, he couldn't bear to remain passive knowing what was coming. If he didn't escape . . . A surge of panic renewed his efforts as a loud CLANG resounded from within the shaft of light. The reflector, a mirror mounted on a long metal arm, was coming into view. Though Gurjin did all he could to look away, the mirror began to shine, then hum, as it caught the light from the darkened Heart of Thra high above it. Its rays found him and its song consumed him and he could not look away.

The Scientist gave a delighted coughing cackle as his captive's struggles died.

"Don't cry, Gelfling," he sneered. "Gets to see the Crystal *now*."

"Wait!"

skekTek let out a loud hiss, throwing back the lever so the mirror drifted just out of view. As the reflection of the light wavered, Gurjin broke out of the gaze, though his body was still strapped to the awful chair. He couldn't see behind him, but the Chamberlain's voice was unmistakable.

"Wait!" he cried. "Wait, wait. Emperor skekSo orders wait. Not this one. Save this one."

"Save? Why?" skekTek hadn't removed his claw from the lever, ready to shove it back into action at any moment. The Chamberlain sighed his melodious sigh.

"This one. Has a sister . . . *hmmm*, a twin. One and one. Two halves, same soul, yes? The Emperor thinks it is worth saving until we have the sister. Special Gelfling. *Rare* Gelfling. Like us. Two halves, yes? Worth waiting for, yes? Maybe special essence. Maybe powerful essence."

skekTek's grip on the lever hadn't wavered at first, but now his eyes narrowed in thought, and he hobbled toward the Chamberlain, leaving the lever where it was. Gurjin's heart hammered against the strap that was buckled across his chest so hard, he felt it might even break him free. He twisted his ears to listen, in case he might survive. He couldn't let them bring Naia into this—but how would he stop them?

"I see what you mean, Chamberlain," skekTek was saying. "Yes, now I see . . . Perhaps the essence of one-and-one Gelfling can revive . . . what we've lost since the separation . . . But how to get the other one here? The twin?"

The Chamberlain let out a giddy hum of anticipation.

"skekSo has plan, and skekSil puts it in action. skekTek just has to wait. Twin will come, yes."

"Then we drain them both. Drink them up. Oh yes, yes."

skekTek chortled, his footsteps echoing as he approached the back of Gurjin's chair. Roughly, he plucked Gurjin from the chair. Gurjin struggled once he was free, but there was no use fighting the unforgiving metal of skekTek's arm. The Scientist held the Drenchen soldier aloft as if he were a wild animal, casting about the crowded room until he gave a sharp chortle of success when he spotted a wood crate with a metal latch.

"Let go of me!" Gurjin shouted, kicking when skekTek's beak was almost in range. His heel bounced off the lord's snout, winning an annoyed hiss. skekTek threw his captive into the crate and as the darkness crowded in, violent panic struck Gurjin, and he fought with what life he had left in him, grabbing the mouth of the crate and screaming. The Chamberlain screamed, too, and together the two Skeksis shoved Gurjin in, slamming the top of the crate shut.

The last thing Naia heard within the dreamfast was the clink of the heavy latch, locking her brother in darkness.

CHAPTER 26

When the dreamfast ended, Naia felt her cheeks wet with tears. She didn't know how much time had passed, but at that moment, she didn't care. Miserably, she grabbed Gurjin's tunic front.

"I'm sorry," she said. "I'm so sorry."

He hugged her and kissed her cheek, though she could feel in his embrace that he was shaking, barely able to stay standing.

"Then this is the best I can do for you," he said. "Find Rian and go to the All-Maudra. I will only slow you down. If it's my fate to fall in these woods, then I'd rather do it as a hero than a burden."

"No," Naia said. She shook him, then ducked within the walls of their hiding place when a huge crash exploded very near, so near that dirt and bugs fell from the ceiling of the old rotting tree trunk. They scattered when another blow destroyed the tree, all three separated in the dark of the wood and clouds of dirt and bark. Then it was quiet. skekMal had vanished.

Naia scrambled on all fours until her back was to the trunk of a tree. She searched for Gurjin, for Kylan, but she couldn't find them in the chaos of the wood. Heart racing, she inched around the tree, eyes darting back and forth, trying to find the beast that hunted them. If she could find him, if she could stop him—or if she could at least find Gurjin and Kylan, maybe they could escape.

Naia turned, fear snuffed with numbness, when she smelled familiar breath. Behind her, close enough that she could see the pink and red veins in the whites of his eyes, was skekMal the Hunter, eyes alight from within his terrible mask of bone.

Closer than ever before, now brimming with excitement from the chase, skekMal spread his arms and gaped with his toothy maw. For an instant, the rain subsided, and as if for the first time in many days, the clouds thinned enough that two of the Sisters were nearly visible in the sky. Their light fell upon skekMal in a blanket of eerie blue, and he turned his head so the eyeholes of his mask were filled with shadows.

"Gelfling twins, all mine!" skekMal cried, and lunged, but his claws only scraped chunks of bark from the tree behind which Naia had been hiding. Naia rolled, dragging her hands through the wet muddy brush in the hopes of finding a rock or a stick—anything she could use as a weapon.

"Hey, you!"

Kylan, on the other side of skekMal, waved his arms before bolting in the other direction. His motion caught skekMal's attention, but Naia's fingers had finally found a hefty stone and she threw it, cracking it against the side of skekMal's temple. Quick as a whip, he turned his hollow mask on her, and she found another rock. She held it ready as skekMal lumbered toward her in his terrible black cloak.

"All Gelfling brought to castle supposed to be saved for

Emperor skekSo," skekMal said. "But skekMal found ways. So gets *vliya* from Gelfling that come to castle . . . But maybe not all Gelfling *get* to castle. Hmm! *Ha!* One for Emperor? One for skekMal . . . and tonight, *one and one.*"

He grinned, sharp uneven teeth glinting in the moonlight, as if he expected Naia to commend him for his cleverness. He took a step forward and she backed away, keeping distance between them, but also leading him farther from Kylan. If only one of them escaped alive, it would be enough. Naia didn't want to die, not here in this awful forest, but she had to think beyond her own life right now. If she could buy Kylan time—and where was Gurjin?

"How many of us have you . . . have you taken?" she asked. "How long have the Skeksis been betraying us? How long have they been feeding us lies, and then . . . then feeding *on* our people?"

skekMal tilted his head, then followed the motion with a dizzying sidle as he began to circle her, rolling his neck at the shoulders and fixing her with those awful ravenous eyes.

"Crystal cracked," he said. He shrugged, as if they were having nothing but a casual conversation. Soft-talk over dinner, more like, but one of them was intent on eating the other. "An accident. Skeksis taking care of it, taking care of Gelfling. How's Skeksis to protect little Gelfling when Crystal cracked? When growing old? Growing weak? Little sacrifices. Is payment. Is Gelfling *purpose.*"

It was a remorseless sentiment. The thought of skekMal slurping down her life essence like a goblet of banquet wine made Naia sick.

No, she thought. *I refuse.*

Summoning her courage, she let out a battle cry and charged. When he reached to snag her in a claw, she leaped, landing nimbly on his wrist and running up his outstretched arm. He shrieked and clawed at her with his three other hands, but she was already to his shoulder, and then his back, and she brought her stone down on the prickly dome of his skull with both hands. The blow transformed his piercing cries into a sudden ribbed wail, and he clutched after her as she brought the stone down a second time. The mask on his face cracked further, splintering into three jagged pieces, and she caught one shard before it fell, flipping it in her free hand like a knife. skekMal tore the remaining pieces from his face before they cut him, sharp edges slicing into the skin around his cheek—and that was the opening where Naia aimed, preparing to drive enough force through her attack that it might pierce straight through the Skeksis's hand and into his vulnerable eye.

As she brought the bone shard back and drew in a breath, a gust of wind blew the last of the thinning clouds from the sky. Vivid moonlight dawned upon them, and her eyes locked on a fresh scar that had been etched into the Hunter's tough, scaled hand. There was no mistaking it, even in the dark, even with her heart beating her blood in a feverish race to survival. In the distinct shape of an X was a mark that exactly resembled the wound urVa had suffered in breaking free of the Cradle-Tree's curse.

The sight of it confounded Naia, and it was her undoing. She had counted three arms when she'd calculated the opening, but she'd lost track of the fourth until he snagged her from behind, little pinching fingers almost Gelfling-size as they wrapped around her neck. She pounded at the little black hand with the stone, and skekMal roared, snatching her up with one of his larger claws, this one big enough to clutch her neck as well as her shoulders and the tops of her wings. She dropped the rock and made to cut him with the shard, but he caught her wrist and held her arm immobile where she'd raised it.

"Why do you have that scar?" she asked.

"Halfies, halfsies, half and half and halfsies," skekMal chanted, cracking his beak with a wicked *SNAP* between each word, spraying droplets of hungry saliva. She struggled against his grip, but it was like iron. She didn't know where Kylan was and could only hope he had escaped. skekMal craned his head up toward her and let out a long eager wheeze, the scent of Gelfling on his breath threatening to send her unconscious in repulsion. "When single shines the triple sun. Halfsies, halfsies, halfsies—"

"*One.*"

The word was so small, yet when it came through Naia's lips, it brought skekMal to a shuddering silence. Even Naia felt chills, though she didn't completely understand it—all she could think of were urVa's words:

For every one there is another . . .

"Not one," skekMal said, angling his head away and eyeing her suspiciously. His grip tightened and he shook her. "*Not* one. skekMal, my own. Just this. Not one!"

"You're connected," she gasped. "For every one there is another—you're connected to urVa . . . You are one . . . with *him?*"

The world heaved as skekMal screamed, throwing his hands in the air and taking Naia with them. He held her above, craning his head back, terrible jaws spread so wide in hysterical wailing that she could see down his pink and purple throat. She gripped the bone shard in her hand, trying not to lose her fight despite knowing in seconds she would be plunged into that toothy maw— she would fight until the end, she would, cutting him open from the inside if she had to.

"NOT ONE WITH NOTHING!"

A spray of spittle and a gnash of teeth exploded as something crashed into skekMal's face. He dropped Naia, and she rolled to her feet, stunned, trying to regain her balance. Before her, skekMal thrashed, clutching his face with two of his hands as his screams became frenetic gurgles. Behind him was Kylan, still frozen in post-throw position after loosing the *bola* that had struck skekMal straight between the eyes.

For a moment, Naia's body charged with fire, and she readied to attack while she had a chance—but then she thought of the scar on the Skeksis's hand, the scar he shared with urVa by whatever mysterious link connected them. What would happen to urVa if she drove the bone shard into skekMal's exposed torso? What if it reached his ugly heart and killed him? She couldn't bear the thought, and so, when she finally found Gurjin pulling himself to his feet nearby, she ran to him and helped him up.

"Run," she said, and Kylan joined them. "Let's run. Let's get out of here."

So they ran, Naia helping her brother, and Kylan dashing

ahead, leading the way. Naia could only hope his sense of direction was true enough to guide them to the river; after being chased by the Hunter and with the storm clouds still thick above, she had no idea where they were or which way the Black River lay. The only thing she knew was that skekMal was behind them, and they were fleeing as quickly as they were able.

skekMal's distant screams stopped, leaving a swell of silence.

"He's coming," Gurjin said. "I told you . . . we can't outrun him. If he has prey, he will chase it."

Naia wanted to resist the idea. She wanted to believe the Black River was just ahead, that any moment they would reach the Landstrider and ride it to safety. skekMal was fast, but surely the Landstrider's long legs were faster. But the heavy crashes of raging footsteps came from behind, growing nearer. skekMal was on their trail, and though he was disoriented and wounded, Naia had neglected the opportunity she'd had to finish him off. Now they were paying the price. She hoped it was worth it.

"If only we could distract him somehow," Kylan panted. "It's still a ways. I don't know if we can make it!"

"We have to," Naia said. "If we don't, there'll be no one to tell the All-Maudra—no one to warn the others!"

She nearly lost her footing when Gurjin suddenly pushed away from her. The haze that had been heavy upon him was nearly lifted, though she knew it would be many days before he was back to his old self—if ever. Even so, when he fixed her with a steady gaze, she knew what he was going to say.

"Gurjin, no—"

"I can't run. I'm slowing you down. Even if I survived, I'd never be cured. The Skeksis—they won't be able to find you, if you can just reach Stone-in-the-Wood."

Naia grabbed her brother's hand and tugged, but he would advance no farther. Kylan stopped ahead, waiting, though she could see every muscle in his body wound tight. skekMal's labored grunts and screeches were drawing closer—even with his injury, he would find them soon enough.

"Gurjin, stop it. We're getting out of here together. Together or not at all!"

"I'll be with you," he said. "When we dreamfasted—I showed you everything I know. More than what you saw . . . you'll see it, someday. When you need me. I'll be with you. Find Rian. He has the vial—he has the proof."

Naia shook her head, grasped his hand and then his sleeve when he turned away, heading toward the oncoming sounds of skekMal's rampage.

"Run and live," he said. He gave a last glance back. "For both of us now."

The shadow that was skekMal erupted from the wood, sending a flurry of smaller trees crackling and flying every which way. Kylan grabbed Naia, and they leaped into the brush, rolling and tumbling out of sight.

"GELFLING!" skekMal cried. "WHERE THE ONE WITH WINGS?"

Naia felt tears streaming down her cheeks as Kylan pressed his hand over her mouth to keep her cries from being heard.

He apologized to her, over and over, silently and in dreamfast. She heard Gurjin's voice—he coughed, then chuckled wryly. Controlling herself despite her panic and grief at what Gurjin was about to do, she peered through the nettles. Gurjin stood before skekMal, back straight, moving slowly away from where she and Kylan were hidden.

"Gone," he said. "Gone far from here, and you'll never catch her."

"Lies," skekMal growled. He crouched down, following the Drenchen, leaning on his front two arms, spiny hackles on the mantle of his cloak rising like quills. "It lies. skekMal smells 'em, closer. Closer. What says Gelfling if skekMal snatches it up and eats it here? Gelfling wings comes fluttering out to save it!"

"Better not," Gurjin muttered, shifting his stance. "Rather, Gelfling wings fly her to Ha'rar and tell the All-Maudra about all of this. See how many Gelfling skekMal smells then, eh? Without Gelfling essence? How quickly will skekMal shrivel up and die?"

skekMal let out a bloodcurdling cry and swung a claw, striking Gurjin with the force of a falling tree and knocking him into the air. He struck the hard trunk of a tower-tree and then fell, face forward into the leaves and dirt, and did not move. skekMal admired his handiwork only a moment longer before snarling an uneven laugh. Just as Naia thought Gurjin had met his end, he stirred. Climbing to his feet, he gave another laugh.

"skekMal kills this one, then it kills the others," skekMal snarled.

"She is already gone. You can't stop her now."

The words were loving, resolved. As much as Naia couldn't stand to leave him, she knew that if she stayed, his sacrifice would mean nothing. No one would know of the Skeksis' betrayal if their journey ended here. No one would know that the Crystal was broken, bleeding its despair into the veins that reached every part of the realm of Thra. Her heart broke with the knowing of what she had to do.

To save her people, she had to let go of her brother.

"No," she said, but the truth had already taken root.

She felt other words on her lips, though they were silent— *thank you, I'm sorry*—and then Kylan's hands on her arms, taking her away, and she went without protest. Leaves and branches scratched her cheeks and shoulders, still wet like everything else—the ground half mud, the plants slick with blooming algae, and Naia's cheeks with tears that left a trail of vanishing saltwater behind them on their escape.

The underbrush broke and gave way to a familiar sight—the Black River, as peaceful as ever, winding through the Dark Wood on its way north. Waiting beside a tree was a Landstrider. Tavra's Landstrider, it seemed, as it was still saddled and bridled with gear. The sight of the beast shot Naia full of fresh remorse for its rider, still within the Skeksis' grasp at the Castle of the Crystal, if she was even alive. Naia let out a cry of anguish, feeling pain take hold of her heart as she thought of the Gelfling in the tower, withered and weak and drained of their essence, their whereabouts unknown to anyone.

And Gurjin . . .

"Up," Kylan said. He was standing on the reins to the Landstrider, climbing high up to its back. "Up! We have to go!"

"Gurjin," she said, but that was all she could say, the rest of her sentence lost in grief. Unable to climb as the feeling overwhelmed her, all she could do was cling to the reins as Kylan pulled her up behind him. She couldn't stop the oncoming tears, pressing her face against Kylan's back as he shook the reins, and muffling her sobs in the thick hood of his cloak. With an escalating lope, the Landstrider headed off along the riverbank under a sky slowly brightening with the rise of the Three Brothers.

CHAPTER 27

Naia dreamed of a blue and open sky suddenly split by a shock of blinding fire. It cut through the heavens like a flaming sword, and it was only because she was dreaming that the heat of its light did not burn her eyes from her head. Above, in the zenith of the sky, the white, rose, purple light of the Three Brothers pulsed as they fell in line, one in front of the other, merged—one—and then they fell, quickly, as if knocked from the sky by one another. They split in their descent, each sinking below its own horizon with a green flash. Then the sky grew darker and darker still, and instead of thousands of stars within its arms, Naia counted only seven, laid out in the hoop of Yesmit, Aughra's Eye.

It was a memory, she felt instinctively; but she wasn't sure whose. Was this a dreamfast with Kylan, a glimpse into one of the many colorful songs he had stored in him? Maybe this was what a song was to a song teller, this sublime, awesome spectacle . . . Or maybe it was a dreamfast with Thra itself, the living earth below and all around them, a memory imprinted into the life force of all that came of it. These questions went unanswered, but the meaning was clear: Night was coming, the inevitable, and darkness would soon be upon them.

When she woke, she saw thick branches supporting a thatched

roof overgrown with woody vines and flat three-pointed leaves. Spiraling tendrils and clusters of berries dangled from the green foliage, reminding her, foggily, of home. Her head was half-sunk in a soft pillow, and a quilt hand-stitched in forest greens and reds was folded carefully around her shoulders. It was morning—or day, perhaps. How long had she been sleeping? Trying to think back, all she remembered was the cold ride on the back of the Landstrider, and her throat and chest ached from the hundreds of apologies she had whispered and hundreds more tears she had shed. After, that she remembered nothing.

She heard voices and sat up, holding her forehead when her vision swam from the movement. She had bandages here and there, and her body throbbed from dozens of bruises and little cuts, but for the most part, she was in one piece . . . or more so. Folded gently against her back, her wings rested like a mantle, tender in their new state but already more developed than when they had first appeared. She stretched them, feeling the foreign sensation.

A wood crate took up most of the cozy room, upon which the remains of her belongings were laid out with care. She had left Sog with her father's pack, full of supplies for the long journey to Ha'rar. Now, here she was, nowhere near the northern home of the Gelfling All-Maudra, with only a pair of Spriton shoes and the bone shard she'd broken off the Hunter's—*Lord skekMal's*—mask. That was all—not even the tunic she'd left in was to be found, probably discarded after all the stains and tearing it had taken. Naia felt tears coming again, and she put her face in her hands when she realized Gurjin's knife was gone as well, lost somewhere deep at the bottom of the castle moat, and with it, the last of her brother she would be likely to see. But, like Gurjin, she had lost the dagger so that she might survive, as much as she wished it could have been otherwise.

She pulled open the heavy window curtains and gasped. Outside, she saw dozens—maybe hundreds—of gray stone dwellings with pocketed windows, arranged in a crescent around a clear indigo lake. Naia had never seen so many homes in one place, nor seen Gelfling dwellings of this type. Many bloomed at the roof with flowers as big as two hands together, red and pink and orange; some even jutted from the lake itself, all grown over with dense forest foliage. Between, beside, and even growing out of the center of some, huge trees wove in and out of the dwellings and narrow streets. Their upper canopies cast safe shade from above, decorated with lanterns and climbing ropes and ancient engravings within the bark. The homes were one with the trees, the village one with the forest. There was only one place they could be.

There was a light knock at the entrance, and she straightened the pale shift she had been clothed in before calling for the visitor to enter.

"Kylan!"

Naia embraced him as soon as he entered, holding tight to let him know how much his safety meant to her. Her tears began anew when she saw the furry slippery form perched on his shoulder. Neech, quivering with joy, wound up and down her arms and showered her with a mix of chirps and friendly nose- and whisker-kisses. She held him and kissed his ears, falling back to the bed in relief.

"I was so worried I'd lost you, too, little eel. Rotten spithead! Making me worry."

"He caught up with us after we crossed the river," Kylan said. He dipped his hand into his sleeve and withdrew a small cloth-wrapped parcel. "With this."

Naia knew what was within, but the sight of Gurjin's dagger brought a last tear to her eye regardless when she revealed it. It seemed like such a stupid thing to care about, especially after she had been resigned to having lost it. She had carried it so long in resentment—or in faith?—that she hardly remembered whether it had been more lucky than not in the end.

"Kylan," she said. "You brought us all the way to Stone-in-the-Wood?"

Her friend folded his arms and looked at his toes.

"I wouldn't be much of a song teller if I couldn't find the way to the home of Jarra-Jen, would I?"

They sat in silence, and Naia looked at her reflection in the freshly polished blade of Gurjin's knife. She missed him. That was all she could think in the dull aftermath. She had just managed to save him, and now he was gone. It was a pain she couldn't really comprehend, something bigger than she was, too big to hold on to in a way that she could control. The most she could do now was hope it wouldn't grow so big, it would overwhelm her. Gurjin had given his life for her, willingly, and that was all that kept her from dissolving into tears of remorse. She would not regret his sacrifice.

"Thank you . . . Where are we? I mean, I know this must be Stone-in-the-Wood, but whose house is this? Do they know who we are? Are we safe from the Skeksis?"

Kylan answered her question with a smile and a nod. He was excited about something, but he was holding back. It was almost as if he didn't want to tell her.

"Yes," he finally said. "This house . . . is Rian's."

"Rian? You already found him?"

Kylan held up his hands to calm her. "No, no! It's his family's house. I found them when we arrived last night. He's not living in Stone-in-the-Wood, but he's made contact with his family. He told them everything, and they believe him. He told them to wait for Gurjin. When we got here and I told them you were Gurjin's sister, they helped. They told me where Rian is. I was going to meet him later today."

Naia crossed her arms and felt her wings flick with suspicion.

"If you know where Rian is and we're going to see him *today*, then why do you sound sad?"

Her friend looked out the window and tugged on a braid. He wasn't sad, she realized. It was reluctance. He confirmed it when he spoke.

"You lost your brother," he said. "And you lost your friend Tavra. You've been through so much. I don't think it's fair that you have to do all that one night and keep moving the next afternoon. You deserve time to mourn . . . I was thinking you might want to go home, to Sog."

Naia thought of her hammock and her parents and sisters, the warmth of Great Smerth. The secluded, isolated safety of the heart of Sog. She wanted it all, to be surrounded in it, to close her eyes and be taken away from what she had seen in the Dark Wood, the Castle of the Crystal—in her dream. She wanted to pull her own blankets above her head and hold on to the memories of before Gurjin had left, before Tavra had appeared. Before she had known what was going on in the world outside the swamp. Before she had seen the tall black shadows cast by the Skeksis Lords of Thra.

She opened her fingers and placed her hands in her lap, palms up. As much as she wanted to go back, to hold tightly to the days of the past, it would not stop the seasons, nor the Brothers or Sisters. And it would not stop the Skeksis from their plot. The only way to be sure she could return home again, the place that had sheltered her for so long, was to let go of what had been and take sight of what could be.

"I do want to go home," she said, straightening her back. She felt her wings flutter with her determination and knew she was making the right decision. "But I left Sog to meet with the All-Maudra. Tavra charged me with relaying a message—and she was captured protecting me and the rest of our people. I don't want her sacrifice, or Gurjin's, to go to waste. Our people are still in danger."

Naia took Gurjin's knife and slid away from the warm comfort of the bed to stand beside her friend. Her feet were sore, but she would bear it. She had good Spriton shoes, after all. There was no way she could have made it this far in her sandals made of tree bark. She suffered to think how miserable and impossible it would have been.

"I want to go home, and I will . . . but not yet. So, let's get packed and meet Rian, and figure out what we're going to do."

Naia held out her hand to Kylan. He was still reluctant, but something about his smile was relieved, too. He took her hand and squeezed.

Over Kylan's shoulder, Naia glanced at her shoes atop the crate, satisfied with the wear they had admirably endured. They had seen fields and highlands, tripped through bramble in the Dark Wood, and muffled her footsteps within the Castle of the Crystal. All that and still in one piece, and for that Naia was glad. It would be many more leagues before they could retire.

GLOSSARY

bola: A Y-shaped length of knotted rope with stones tied to each of the three ends. Used as a weapon, the *bola* can be swung or thrown, enabling the wielder to ensnare prey.

daeydoim: Six-legged desert-dwelling creatures with large dorsal scales and broad hooves. Frequently domesticated by desert nomads.

fizzgig: A small furry carnivore native to the Dark Wood. Sometimes kept as a pet.

hooyim: One of the many colorful leaping fish species that migrate in large schools along the northern Sifan coasts. Often called the jewels of the sea.

Landstrider: Long-legged hooved beasts common to the Spriton plains.

maudra: Literally "mother." The matriarch and wise woman of a Gelfling clan.

maudren: Literally "those of the mother." The family of a Gelfling *maudra*.

muski: Flying quilled eels endemic to the Swamp of Sog. Babies are very small, but adults never stop growing. The oldest known muski was said to be as wide as the Black River.

ninet: One of nine orbital seasons caused by the configuration of the three suns. Arcs in which Thra is farthest from the suns are winter ninets; arcs in which Thra is nearest are summer ninets. Each ninet lasts approximately one hundred trine.

swoothu: Flying beetlefur creatures with strange sleeping patterns. Many act as couriers for the Gelfling clans in exchange for food and shelter.

ta: A hot beverage made by mixing boiling water and spices.

Three Brothers: Thra's three suns: the Great Sun, the Rose Sun, and the Dying Sun.

Three Sisters: Thra's three moons: the Blue Moon, the Pearl Moon, and the Hidden Moon.

trine: The orbital period of Thra moving around the Great Sun, roughly equivalent to an Earth year.

unamoth: A large-winged pearly white insect that sheds its skin once every unum.

unum: The time for Thra's largest moon to circle Thra once, roughly equivalent to an Earth month.

vliya: Literally "blue fire." Gelfling life essence.

vliyaya: Literally "flame of the blue fire." Gelfling mystic arts.

APPENDIX

THE GELFLING CLANS

VAPRA

Sigil animal: Unamoth

Maudra: Mayrin, the All-Maudra

The Vapra clan was an industrious race with white hair, fair skin, and gossamer-winged women. Considered the oldest of the Gelfling clans, the Vapra resided in cliffside villages along the northern coasts, making their capital in Ha'rar. The Vapra's *maudra*, Mayrin, doubled as All-Maudra, matriarch leader of all the Gelfling clans. Vapra were skilled at camouflage; their *vliyaya* focused on light-changing magic, allowing them to become nearly invisible.

STONEWOOD

Sigil animal: Fizzgig

Maudra: Fara, the Rock Singer

This clan was a proud and ancient people who dwelled on the fertile lands near and within the Dark Wood. They made their main home in Stone-in-the-Wood, the historical home of Jarra-Jen. Many Stonewood Gelfling were valuable guards at the Castle of the Crystal. They were farmers and cobblers and makers of tools. They were inventive, but pastoral; like their sigil animal, they were peaceful but fierce when threatened.

SPRITON

Sigil animal: Landstrider

Maudra: Mera, the Dream Stitcher

Age-old rivals of the Stonewood clan, the Spriton were a warrior race inhabiting the rolling fields south of the Dark Wood. With such bountiful land to raise crops and family, this clan's territory spread to cover the valley in several villages. Counted among the most fierce fighters of the Gelfling race, the Spriton were often called upon to serve as soldiers for the Skeksis Lords and guards at the Castle of the Crystal.

SIFA

Sigil animal: Hooyim

Maudra: Gem-Eyed Ethri

Found in coastal villages along the Silver Sea, the Sifa were skilled fishermen and sailors, but very superstitious. Explorers by nature, the Sifa were competent in battle—but they truly excelled at survival. Sifan *vliyaya* focused Gelfling luck magic into inanimate objects; Sifan charms enchanted with different spells were highly desired by travelers, craftsmen, and warriors of all clans.

DOUSAN

Sigil animal: Daeydoim

Maudra: Seethi, the Skin Painter

This clan made their settlements on sandships—amazing constructs of bone and crystal that navigated the Crystal Sea like ocean vessels. Resilient even within the arid climate of the desert, the Dousan thrived. Their culture was shrouded and unsettlingly quiet, their language made of whispers and gestures, their life stories told in the intricate magic tattoos painting their bodies.

DRENCHEN

Sigil animal: Muski

Maudra: Laesid, the Blue Stone Healer

The Drenchen clan was a race of amphibious Gelfling who lived in the overgrown Swamp of Sog, deep in the southernmost reaches of the Skarith region. Sturdier and taller than the rest of their race, the Drenchen were powerful in combat, but generally preferred to keep to themselves. Though one of the smallest Gelfling clans, the Drenchen had the largest sense of clan pride; they were loyal to one another, but remained as distant from other clans as possible.

GROTTAN

Sigil animal: Hollerbat

Maudra: Argot, the Shadow Bender

A mysterious, secretive breed who dwelled in perpetual darkness in the Caves of Grot. Generations in the shadows left them with an extreme sensitivity to light—and solid black eyes that could see in the dark and large ears to make out even the faintest of echoes. The Grottan clan was said to number less than three dozen Gelfling, and their life span was said to be unheard of, lasting three to four times as long as other Gelfling.

Here's an exciting sneak peek at
the next chapter of Naia and Kylan's journey
in *Song of the Dark Crystal*.

CHAPTER 1

"This way. Almost there."

Kylan pointed to where the path forked. One way led back to the village behind them while the other twisted down and away, under arched branches and beyond. He followed the latter, trusting Naia to keep up. All around them, the air was full of morning song.

The Stonewood girl was waiting for them at the very edge of the village, where the trail changed from a row of flat stones to dirt and moss. She was young, still without her wings, and perched atop one of the many gray rocks that populated the wood. Hopping down when they arrived, she grabbed Naia's hand.

"Naia, you're awake! I'm Mythra. We met when you were asleep. Did you rest well? Is it true you fought skekMal? Kylan told me you did. And escaped from the Castle of the Crystal! That's so amazing and brave!"

Naia rubbed her cheek. She said nothing, but Kylan could tell that they shared thought. Their flight from the Skeksis in the Dark Wood had hardly felt amazing or brave. Really, they were just lucky to be alive, but there was no point in frightening the youngling.

"We nearly trampled Mythra on the Landstrider when we

found Stone-in-the-Wood last night," Kylan explained. "She brought us to her home for you to recover."

"So . . . you know about the Skeksis?" Naia asked. "And you believe Rian's stories, even though the Skeksis have told everyone he's a lying traitor?"

Mythra was already skipping down the path, disappearing into the curtains of hanging foliage. Her voice echoed back as they followed her.

"Of course I believe Rian. He's my brother!"

Kylan followed the girl through the Dark Wood, losing track of the path after one too many twists. Was this where they had come through on their flight from the castle? He probably wouldn't even know the place if he saw it. Mythra stopped when they reached a small clearing overgrown with shrubs.

"Rian!" she called. "It's me—I've brought the others I told you about. Gurjin's sister, and her friend!"

There was no one in sight, and Mythra tried Rian's name again. Naia stepped forward when no one answered, ears twisting about and eyes sharp. When Mythra went to call a third time, Naia covered the younger girl's mouth.

"Shh," she hissed. "Listen."

Kylan perked up his ears. Naia's instincts in the wild were strong, crafted and honed from growing up in the Swamp of Sog, where everything from the trees to the mud could be a danger. Sure enough, when he held his breath and listened, he heard a far-off *snap* and *crash!* followed by curses in a Gelfling tongue.

"Rian," Mythra gasped.

"This way!"

Kylan and Mythra followed Naia as she darted into the wood, hand on the hilt of the knife that was sheathed on her belt. Kylan lost track of the clearing as they hurried through the trees, bounding over rocks and thorned shrubs.

Another loud crash sent birds into flight as they mounted an outcrop of rocks. Below them, a green-furred beast with whorled horns and a clubbed tail grappled with something much smaller. When the horned creature reared and let out a broken roar, Kylan saw massive flat teeth—and under its hooved front legs, a Gelfling boy armed with a stick. Lying uselessly on the other side of the glade sat a spear, likely his usual weapon.

"Rian!" Mythra cried.

The boy rolled away, out from under the beast, looking for the one who had called him.

"Mythra! Stay back! This horner has seen the Crystal!"

"A darkened creature?" Kylan asked, heart still pounding from their flight. "Like the ruffnaw?"

"And the Nebrie," Naia agreed. "But . . ."

The last time they had come across darkened creatures, Naia had been able to heal them with dreamfasting, pushing the darkness from their hearts. It was something Kylan had never seen before. But despite her remarkable ability, dreamfasting with beasts still meant connecting with the mind and the heart. After all she'd suffered through so recently, Kylan worried. It might be dangerous for Naia to try healing a darkened creature if she was not yet healed herself.

The horner bucked, uprooting a sapling in warning. It would not be long before it tried to do the same to Rian. Kylan caught Naia's sleeve as she readied for a fight.

"Don't push yourself," he said. "Please. I know you want to fix it, but you shouldn't hurt yourself in the process."

She grimaced and hopped up onto a rock and drew her dagger.

"At least I can help get him out of there."

Before Kylan could stop her, she leaped, wings unfolding just enough to slow her fall as she landed between Rian and the green horner. The creature plowed its hooves into the earth again, swinging its head and narrowly missing the two Gelfling that stood before it.

"I don't need your help!" Rian shouted. Then he saw her clothing, her green skin and dark locs. "Wait, are you—"

"Introductions later!"

Naia and Rian dove to either side when the horner charged. Unlike the thrashing, maddened beasts Kylan had seen before, it did not seem wholly out of control. When the creature saw Naia, it paused before lowering its horns, almost as though it recognized her. It snorted, pawing the ground and unearthing rocks and roots.

"Get out of here," Naia ordered. "While I have its attention!"

"I said I don't need your help!" Rian spat back, though he took the opportunity to move closer to his spear. "This one's different than the others—I don't know how, but it's different!"

Kylan's fingertips hurt where he gripped the stone in front of him. Naia stepped steadily, drawing the horner's red gaze away from Rian. If he went down to try to help, he would only get in the way. His fingers found the rope of his *bola*, and he pulled it from his belt.

"I know you're full of darkness now," Naia said to the beast, holding out her empty hand. "But please, remember! Remember what you were before!"

Rian reached his spear and with only a moment's pause to aim, he threw it toward the beast. It sank into the horner's exposed flank, but the beast barely reacted. It was fixed on Naia, and with thundering hooves, it charged. The breadth of its horns was so wide, there was no way she could escape in time and at such close range. Rian shouted after the horner in dismay, and Kylan let his *bola* loose. It nearly missed, bouncing off the horner's back like a pebble.

Naia didn't need saving. As the horner neared, she sprang, grabbing one of the beast's horns as it swung toward her. There she clung, stubborn eyes bright with determination while the horner wailed in anger. Kylan's breath rushed out in relief just in time to be caught again. The horner was clever, even in its rage, and instead of being lost in confusion, it changed its attack. It sighted a tree and headed for it, angling its head to strike as soon as it was in range. If Naia dropped to the ground, she would be trampled, but if she didn't get out of the way, she would soon be crushed between the horn and bark.

"Naia," Kylan shouted, because it was the only thing left he could do. "Naia, hurry!"

She scrambled along the beast's horn as the others watched. She had almost made it along the horn to the beast's head when she slipped, her shoes sliding against the rough bone. She nearly lost her grip, dangling from the spiraled horn as it swung through the air and brambles toward the tree that would be the end of her.

Something dark and serpentine shot out from under Naia's hair, diving into the thick green mane at the nape of the horner's neck. Startled, the horner jerked. Instead of striking the tree full-on, only the tip of its horn glanced off the trunk, throwing the beast off balance. Naia yelped and let go, flying through the air and tumbling into the brush. Kylan watched with her as the horner stumbled, nearly toppling, then screeched and thrashed.

"A muski?" Mythra asked, eyes wide.

The black eel that had come to Naia's rescue darted in and out of the horner's fur like a water serpent leaping through ocean waves. The horner threw itself against the tree, trying to squash the little flying eel, but Neech was too agile. Naia and Rian regrouped, readying their weapons, knowing it was only a matter of time before Neech's distraction wore off. There was no way the little eel's teeth, as sharp as they might be, could penetrate the horner's thick hide.

Just as Naia and Rian were about to renew their attack, the horner's thrashing stopped. Its cries and bellowing ceased, and the glade was quiet as the great creature's knees buckled and bowed. Then it fell, bloodshot eyes closing. At first Kylan thought it had passed on, but as Neech surfaced from its mane, he saw the beast's side rise and fall. It was unconscious. He and Mythra climbed the rocky hill to meet the other two below.

"What happened?" Kylan asked.

Naia wiped her forehead and tossed her locs behind her shoulder.

"I don't know. Maybe it heard my plea without dreamfasting and let go of the darkness . . . I can only hope. Oh, Neech. To the rescue again. Did you find a snack in there?"

The flying eel drifted through the air and alighted on Naia's shoulder. A black, arthropodic leg stuck out of the eel's weasel-like mouth, still twitching. Kylan didn't want to know how many other bugs lived within the horner's dense coat. With a last few crunches, Neech finished his victory treat with an audible gulp.

"You're Naia. Gurjin's twin."

The hardened voice was Rian's. He was tall for a Gelfling, with olive skin and dark eyes. His thick dark brown hair was tousled and wild, broken by a single streak of blue above his right eye. His face was young and kind, though his eyes were weary and his lips were pressed in a tired line.

"And you're Rian," Naia said.

They had heard his name so often since they had begun their journey. In fact, at many times, his name was almost all they'd had for guidance. To finally meet him in person had seemed impossible, yet here they were.

"Another darkened horner!" he said. "They dig where the Crystal's veins are buried, and they're too dim-witted to look away when they uncover it."

"It was certainly darkened, but something felt different," Kylan said.

Naia agreed.

"It was focused. Like it recognized Rian and me . . ."

Rian watched the sleeping horner, brow drawn tight.

"If you've seen the darkened creatures, then the darkness is spreading. Maybe it's changing, too. Just last season we saw our first glimpse of it in the wood. At this rate it won't be long before all of Thra is gazing into the shadows and turning on itself."

Rian shook the thought off and pulled his spear from the poor horner's hide. Mythra climbed up with a bundle of forest moss and pressed it against the bleeding wound as Rian hopped down.

"You look just like Gurjin . . . Is he with you?"

"He didn't make it," Naia said flatly, as if to deliver the sad news as quickly as possible and be done with it. Maybe it was for the best. Kylan had no idea what to say to her about it, and he imagined Rian would feel even more at a loss if they dwelled on it too long. "This is Kylan, a song teller of the Spriton clan. We're here to . . ."

No one wanted to say what needed to be said next, though it was the reason they were meeting here so secretly. The reason neither Gurjin nor the Vapran princess who had also helped them was here with them. Kylan chewed on his lip, pushing back the feelings of remorse over their friends who hadn't escaped.

"We're here to figure out what to do about the Skeksis!"

The bright voice came from above. Mythra finished dressing the horner's wound and climbed down. She pushed Rian and Naia together, close enough that they could clasp hands.

"You two should dreamfast. Then we can make a plan."

Rian's ears flattened a little, though he wiped his palm off on his tunic in preparation. He held it out in offer, neither eager nor reluctant.

"She's right. It is the fastest way."

Kylan watched Naia, feeling a pinch of protectiveness. If she had not felt well enough to dreamfast with the horner, was she really in a safe place to open her heart to another Gelfling, to share what had broken it? They had heard Rian's name many times, and sought him for days, but he was still a stranger. An ally, but not a friend.

When Naia glanced at Kylan in hesitation, that was all he needed to know. He stepped forward and offered his own hand.

"Naia's heart is broken now," he said. "But I was there, and she told me what she saw. I can't give you her memories, but I can give you mine and my memory of her tale."

"Very well," Rian said.

He didn't seem to care either way, all action and little emotion. Kylan reminded himself that Rian had gone through his own trials since his escape from the Skeksis—trials Kylan was likely about to be witness to himself.

He braced himself. They grasped hands, and the dreamfast began.

CHAPTER 2

Dreamfasting was like diving into a pool of water without knowing its depth or what might wait below. Kylan remained at the surface at first, sensing Rian's memories and knowing at the same time Rian could peek into his. It was often disorienting in the beginning, to dreamfast with someone for the first time. Even when they had agreed to dreamfast, there were still so many thoughts and visions, protective barriers and waves of wariness.

After a moment the waves calmed, and Rian began. His mental voice sounded far away and inside Kylan's mind all at once.

I was a soldier, like my father . . .

The vivid image that came first was of the Castle of the Crystal, obsidian and magnificent, towering over the Dark Wood like a claw and crown. Rian's memory of the castle was powerful and detailed. He knew every spacious hall and stately room, had traveled and patrolled every spiraling passageway. The only chamber he had not seen was the center pavilion, forbidden to the Gelfling guards and servants. Only the Skeksis Lords, the raptorial velvet-cloaked keepers of the castle, were allowed to enter that place. There, they and they alone communed with the Heart of Thra—the heart of the world. After they heard Thra's song, they entered its words in tomes and sent out orders to the *maudra* of each of the Gelfling clans. So the will of Thra was passed on.

Or so it seemed. Kylan already knew the terrible secret the Skeksis kept. He had seen its evidence himself and in dreamfast with Naia after the nightmare they had survived. Now he waited to see it as Rian had.

Our friends went missing, one by one. When we asked the Skeksis, they paid no heed. Then they called for Mira . . .

Kylan saw a flash of a Gelfling girl, all winks and tall tales. Rian walked with her, back to the castle after an evening patrolling the wood that bordered the grounds. In Rian's hand, hidden in his uniform cloak, was a glowing bellflower. He would give it to Mira when they said good night. He would tell her that even though they had been on duty, he had enjoyed their time together, and perhaps they could enjoy time together some other evening . . .

Two Skeksis were waiting at the castle, the decorated Chamberlain and the Scientist, Lord skekTek, a shrewd, tendony beast with a metal-and-glass eye. They crowded around Mira, the Chamberlain beckoning her for official business.

"Vapra, are you? Oh yes, lovely Silverling . . . come for orders . . ."

The Skeksis with the mechanical eye jabbed a talon-like finger at Rian.

"Retire for the evening, guard."

Kylan felt Rian's memory more than he saw it: anger, fear, anxiety. He knew he should trust the lords, or at least obey them, but his gut was telling him that something was wrong. Then impulsiveness as Rian followed, knowing if he were caught, he might be discharged, but if his instinct was right, Mira could be in danger.

She was. The memory was a rush of disorganized fragments of sounds and images: Rian's path through the castle, the jarring echoes of the Skeksis' harsh laughter. Mira's questions that started calm but escalated into alarm. Over it all, Kylan heard the memory of a grating crank, as if an enormous piece of architecture was in motion on a hundred gears and cogs.

Here the vision was sharp and painful. Rian found his way to where the Skeksis had taken Mira. The Skeksis Scientist's lab, deep in the gut of the castle. The door was open a hair, just a sliver of fiery red in the dark hall. Mira's voice was quiet now, just whimpers, and Rian peered through the crack in the door. He saw her bound to a chair, facing a panel in the stone wall. skekTek, the Scientist, stood near the panel with his claws on a lever. The cranking and shuddering of machinery intensified, and then the panel opened and flooded the room with brilliant red.

"Look into the light, yes, Gelfling," skekTek said. He reached to another lever and maneuvered it, bringing a second piece of the contraption into view—a reflector, suspended in the cavern of fire beyond the wall. Mira began to cry out for help, struggling against the bonds. Rian almost burst in then, but skekTek rotated the reflector, placing a blinding dagger of light on Mira's face. The instant she looked into the light, she went still.

Kylan felt the memory weaken as Rian's focus lapsed.

It's all right, he said. *You don't need to show any more. I understand . . .*

No, Rian replied. *No, it's important. You should see it. You should see just how terrible the Skeksis really are.*

Kylan watched through Rian's eyes as Mira's limbs went limp. Her skin paled and dried, her hair turning withered and brittle, as if her life force was being drained from her body. As she slowly died, her eyes turning milky and unseeing, another machine went into motion. A series of tubes shuddered to life, slowly filling with a glowing liquid. The substance was pristine, blue tinted, almost like liquid crystal, and it passed slowly through the conduits until it finally filled a glass vial, drop by drop.

The worst came next. The Skeksis Scientist plucked the vial once it was full. He sniffed it and gave a pleased sigh, and then, to Kylan's horror, tipped the vial into his mouth for a tiny, sickening sip. As the drops touched his tongue, light flashed in his eyes, clearing them of their aging haze. The wrinkles and distortions in his withered face and beak smoothed, the hairs on his scalp growing thicker and filling with a glimmer of shine. Mira's life force was now his, her youth flowing into his old and deteriorating veins.

Her vliya, Rian said. *As if it's wine.*

Kylan shuddered. Naia had told him as much, but seeing it so clearly in Rian's memory was horribly different. He was relieved when the vision dissipated.

I'm sorry about Mira, he said.

Me too, Rian replied. Yet the grief had given birth to courage

and purpose, it seemed, *Now tell me the tale you and Naia share.*
Tell me how you came to join me in the fight against the Skeksis, who've
sent the rest of our people after me as a traitor and a liar.

Kylan took hold of the dreamfast, remembering what he
knew of Naia's journey. He had to speak for her as well as himself.
Although they had dreamfasted together during their travels,
and she had shared with him the story of how she'd left her home
and traveled north, it was impossible to dreamfast another's
dreamfasted memories. Instead, he had to speak it, so he kept it
short and to the point.

Tavra, one of the All-Maudra's daughters, came to Naia's village
searching for you and Gurjin. When Tavra didn't find Gurjin there,
Naia left for Ha'rar to defend Gurjin's honor. I met her north of Sog,
when she passed through the Spriton plains.

Kylan remembered the day Naia had come to his village,
knowing that as he called up the memory, Rian would see it, too.
He remembered Naia's aloof appeal, and how reluctant she had
been to make friends, but Kylan had liked that about her. He
had seen his own outsiderness reflected in her. It might not have
meant much to her, but for Kylan, it had been the beginning of
the journey that had eventually brought him here, to share in this
dreamfast with Rian, and to fight against the Skeksis.

The lands were filling with darkness, he told Rian. *We saw the*
darkened creatures, mad with a sickness from looking into the earth.
Even the trees in the Dark Wood were ill.

He showed Rian the night they had been lost in the woods.
Kylan stood watch while Naia dreamfasted with the Cradle-Tree,

trying to calm its madness. She had healed the tree, but it hadn't soothed the darkness. Those shadows had been born somewhere else.

In the end, we went to the castle . . .

That was where he'd learned that the Skeksis Lords had betrayed them. That they had captured Tavra, the All-Maudra's noble daughter, and put her in front of the reflector in the Scientist's laboratory. That the Crystal itself was the source of the darkness, and the Skeksis were responsible.

And Gurjin? Rian asked.

The solemn question brought only one memory to mind: the terrifying Lord skekMal hunting them in the wood, chasing them like a shadow storm with glowing, fiery eyes. That was all Kylan had seen, and so that was where the dreamfast ended.

Kylan folded his arms around himself. His senses returned to reality, but it wasn't immediate, just as one couldn't be instantly dry after emerging from a swim. Naia sat on a patch of moss, waiting attentively beside the sleeping horner, while Mythra ate a fat peach-berry plucked from her traveling pouch.

"He sacrificed himself so that we could meet you and warn the rest of our people," Kylan said. "As did Tavra."

Kylan watched Rian's face, trying to guess what was going through the soldier's mind. Seeing Rian's memory had been difficult, and he couldn't imagine what it was like to relive it. Rian shook his head, thick brows eternally furrowed.

"Gurjin died proud as ever," Rian said. "We won't waste his effort. Nor Tavra's, nor Mira's. The Skeksis will pay for what they've done. I'll see to it single-handedly if I have to."

"You won't. Gurjin is—was—*my* brother," Naia said. "If anyone will teach the Skeksis what Gurjin's sacrifice meant, it will be me."

"You? Who haven't seen a day of duty in the castle?"

"I've seen plenty of days in other places."

"The Skeksis would crush you a second time! I will do it alone."

"Stop it!" Mythra scolded, so forcefully that a bit of fruit flew out of her mouth. "Rian always tries to go it alone. Look how that's worked out for you so far, big brother!"

Rian scoffed, blowing his shaggy bangs away from his face.

"I do it for you. And for Timtri, and Mother. I always have, and I'll continue to do things on my own if it saves the Gelfling people. I don't need anyone else's help."

Naia rolled her eyes so hard, her whole head moved. Kylan couldn't decide what to think of the Stonewood soldier. He was certainly brave and willing to act, but he had a streak of nerve that had nearly been the end of him at least once. Following the Skeksis scientist into the depths of the castle could have been the last thing he had ever done, but instead he had escaped and lived to tell the tale. Either his courage was being rewarded or he was just plain lucky.

Mythra finished the peach-berry and threw the pit at her brother, who deftly avoided it.

"Speaking of Mother. She wants to invite you all to supper—like we used to do, before Rian left to serve at the castle."

"I should stay here in the wood," Rian said. "I'm a traitor, remember?"